VOODOO VOWS

BOOK 1 IN THE VOODOO VOWS SERIES

DIANA MARIE DUBOIS

Published by Three Danes Publishing L.L.C.

Cover art by Anya Kelleye | www.anyakelleye.com
Cover photo by Melissa Deanching, RplusM
Model: Tionna Petramalo
Edited by Maxine Horton Bringenberg
Book design by Inkstain Design Studio

VOODOO VOWS

This book is dedicated to my Dad. Russell thank you so much
for your constant persistence for me to write a book.
I love you more then you'll ever know.

NOTE TO READERS

Voodoo…a religion, Marie Laveau perfected while living in New Orleans. Marie was raised as a Catholic, but she also learned the religion of voodoo, the religion her people brought over from Haiti. She combined the two religions of Catholicism and voodoo to become one of the most famous Louisiana Creole practitioners of voodoo.

It's a common misconception voodoo, and specifically a voodoo doll, is used for evil. That isn't necessarily true it depends on how you use it. Some people use it as an added good luck charm, like a rabbit's foot is used in other common beliefs. Voodoo dolls are also not used in today's standard practice of voodoo they're actually a tourist item. Back in the day Marie Laveau would have worked with and prayed to certain Loa.

Also, not many people realize there were two Marie Laveaus, the original one and her daughter. I have actually merged the two in my story since it is, after all, fiction.

This story will show both sides of the religion of voodoo and the voodoo doll, good and evil. Enjoy!

GLOSSARY OF TERMS

Bourre: A trick-taking gambling card game primarily played in the Acadiana region of Louisiana.

Bread Pudding (New Orleans Style): Lightly spiced bread pudding, flavored with bourbon, bourbon sauce, and bourbon-soaked raisins.

Cabildo: A Spanish seat of government, and has now been made into a museum.

Café Dumonde: A famous landmark established in 1862 before the Civil War. Well known for its beignets and café au lait.

Cajun: Descendants of the people of Nova Scotia who settled in Louisiana.

Carnival: Carnival is the season prior to Lent, where Mardi Gras is celebrated with parades and revelry.

Cher: Cajun word for "dear." Mostly used in Cajun Country as a term of affection.

Creole: Several definitions exist: in Louisiana, a Creole is a white person descended from French or Spanish settlers or a person of mixed European and African blood. It's also a style of cooking and architecture.

Creole Cream Cheese – A farmer style cheese similar in fashion to a combination of cottage cheese and sour cream.

Doubloon: Pronounced "da-BLOON." A coin, approximately the size of a silver dollar, minted on a yearly basis by the various Mardi Gras krewes. The standard type is made of aluminum and they're thrown from Mardi Gras floats by the parade riders.

Flambeau Carriers: Started out as a tradition of slaves and free men of color to earn extra money. They carry huge torches lighting the way for certain parades.

French Market: Founded in 1791, it began as a meat market but has expanded to what it is now known for, selling fruits, vegetables, local delicacies, and the usual tourist trinkets and souvenirs.

Gris-gris: Is a voodoo amulet originating in Africa which is believed to protect the wearer from evil or can be considered a good luck charm. It can also be the physical objects that are used in spells (such as gris-gris bags, which are either made of material or leather, Voodoo dolls, and other items used in a spell) and the verbal supplications that are made to invoke the magical properties of voodoo.

Gumbo: Thick, spicy soup prepared with ingredients such as rice, sausage, chicken, and okra.

Holy Trinity: Onions, celery, and bell pepper.

Indians (Mardi Gras Indians): African-American Carnival revelers who dress up for Mardi Gras in suits influenced by Native American ceremonial apparel.

Jackson Square: A historic park in the French Quarter that houses the famous equestrian statue of Andrew Jackson.

Jambalaya: Spicy dish always made with rice and combinations of seafood, chicken, turkey, sausage, peppers, and onions.

Jazz: Swinging Louisiana music made popular by Louis "Satchmo" Armstrong and others.

King Cake: A New Orleans cake served during Mardi Gras season. A small plastic doll is hidden inside of the cake, and whoever "gets the baby" has to buy the next King Cake.

Krewe: A krewe (pronounced in the same way as "crew") is an organization that puts on a parade and or a ball for the Carnival season.

La Petite Theater: A community theater in the French Quarter, also rumored to be one of the many haunted buildings in the Quarter.

Lagniappe: A little something extra.

Laissez les bons temps rouler – Let the good times roll.

Levee: An embankment built to keep a river from overflowing; a landing place on the river.

Loup garou: Also known as Roux-ga-roux or Rou garou, is French for werewolf. Many versions of this folktale are still told to this day around the bayou areas of south Louisiana.

Mais: the word 'but' in Cajun French.

Mardi Gras: The grand pre-Lenten celebration for which New Orleans is famous.

Muffaletta: A round Italian sandwich as big as your head, made with a variety of meats and olive salad.

Neutral Ground: Median.

Pass a good time: Have a good time.

Pass by: To stop by.

Pat O's: Is a bar located in New Orleans, Louisiana that began operation as a legal liquor establishment on December 3, 1933. Known for its Hurricane cocktails.

Parish: County.

Pecan: A nut indigenous to the South, and beloved in New Orleans as an ingredient in pies and pralines. Pronounced "puh-KAWN," not "PEE-can."

Piti: Creole French for the word child.

Praline: A sugary Creole candy, invented in New Orleans (not the same as the French culinary/confectionery term "praline" or "praliné") The classic version is made with sugar, brown sugar, butter, vanilla, and pecans, and is a flat sugary pecan-filled disk. There are also creamy pralines, chocolate pralines, maple pralines, etc.

Preservation Hall: Established in 1961 to preserve, perpetuate, and protect one of America's truest art forms—traditional New Orleans Jazz. Operating as a music venue, a touring band, a record label, and a non-profit organization, Preservation Hall continues their mission today as a cornerstone of New Orleans music and culture.

Roux: Flour and oil mixture used to start almost all Louisiana dishes.

St. Louis Cathedral: The oldest continuously operating Catholic

Church in the United States.

Throw me something mister: This is what New Orleanians yell to Krewe members of parades during Mardi Gras.

Ya Mamma: Your mother. Used in a variety of ways, usually endearing. Also usable as an insult, specifically as a simple retort when one is insulted first; simply say, "Ya mamma." Y-a mama'en'em – New Orleans slang for "your mom and them."

Vieux Carre: Also known as the French quarter, one of the oldest neighborhoods in New Orleans.

Voodoo: Mysterious religion involving charms and spells that came to Louisiana via the Caribbean.

"There's magic all around you, if I do say so myself…"

STEVIE NICKS

PROLOGUE

arkness clouded the night sky as I tugged the curtains closed. A deep sigh escaped from my mouth as my busy day had ended, but before I climbed into my bed, Momma knocked on the door.

"Come in."

"Rosie, are you ready for bed? Would you like me to brush your hair?"

Her questions caught me off guard, like the way she had acted so oddly earlier in the evening. It seemed as if she were trying to tell me something she wished she didn't have to. But I nodded. Even though I was twenty six, the ritual of her brushing my hair was as ingrained in me as listening to her sing "Chantilly Lace." With every brushstroke, my mother's hands moved in sync with the song until my hair was silky smooth.

Finished, her hand shook as she placed the brush on the nightstand. She stood from her perch on my bed, where I glimpsed a stray tear on her face, which she quickly wiped away. As she closed my door to retire to her own room, a sense of foreboding crept over me settling in my chest, sending my heart plummeting.

Thoughts spun in my head for a while; nonetheless, I finally dismissed her behavior as fatigue. Sleep wreaked havoc on my eyes as I slipped under the beautiful pink lined with white, handmade wedding ring patterned quilt, my head buried deep in the comfortable bliss of my feather pillow. Before long, I had succumbed to a dream state, becoming unsettled in my bed, wading through the web of all that was evil…

Three cloaked figures stood in a semi-circle partially concealed within the darkness of the bayou. My eyes grew wide as they chanted and swayed like the Spanish moss dripping from the oak trees. Hidden behind a tree nestled in the shadows, I gasped when I saw a large concrete slab appear and disappear between their bodies. I held my breath as I watched them raise their arms high above their heads in unison, their sleeves revealing hairy arms followed by clawed hands. The clouds swirled in a magical formation, followed by the pitter patter of rain. Their chants increased, keeping time with the rain. Another gasp escaped my mouth when one of the figures removed their cloak revealing their naked body.

The skies opened wide sending the rain pelting down around me. As the water stung my bare arms, it fell to the ground creating little mud puddles. I looked up through the trees to see the storm brew, and blinked as the water clung to my eyelashes.

My focus returned to the scene before me. The two cloaked figures stood still, their backs to me, while the naked one danced in the rain. I wiped at my eyes, trying to get a better look. I didn't know if I stared at a male or a female figure until it turned to face my direction. I was stunned when I saw the figure of a woman.

Thunder roared in the distance. When the lightning crackled and cascaded in bright lights across the sky, it illuminated a tattoo on the woman's arm. I strained my eyes then blinked, but couldn't make out the design. The two remaining cloaked figures glided backward deep into the shadows, away from the altar, their cloaks drenched and dragging the ground with every movement. The naked woman still twirled in the rain, and abruptly stopped. My eyes danced in fascination until I saw someone lying in the middle of the...

I choked back a scream, as tears streamed down my face at the sight of my mother. Her ringlets of auburn hair now were plastered around her form, her limp hand hanging over the side of the stone slab.

I pulled myself from my hiding spot and ran toward her, but I tripped and fell. As I stood my hands were coated in mud. Before I could reach her, a cold hand grasped me from behind. In an instant, I found myself staring into the dark abyss of one of the hooded entities that had retreated earlier. Red eyes penetrated deep into my soul as it whispered, "Tell no one or you and your friends will meet the same fate." My body shook uncontrollably with deep-rooted fear, the maniacal laughter echoed in my head, and in a flash, the creature vanished.

I woke in a mass of tangled sheets. My frenzied heart hammered in my chest as if it were about to burst free. Once it slowed its incessant pounding, I unfurled my body from the jumble of material and sat up. Like a burst of confetti from a carnival popper, I jumped off the bed with a quick thud. My feet carried me, without any hesitation, toward my mother's room, where the light from within the bedroom shone through the crack under the door. I hurled myself into her room, but found it empty.

With her nowhere in sight, I stumbled down the steps to the closed store below our apartment. "Momma!" My voice became hoarse the more I screamed. There was still no sign of her, and as panic erupted, my body trembled in terror.

A white slip of paper on the counter drew my attention. Trying to control my fear, I slowly, unsteadily walked over and saw the familiar wax seal. My hand shook, and as my fingertips touched it, the paper fluttered off the counter, floating like a feather to land on the cold floor. Tears threatened to escape, but I held my eyes closed tight as I slid down and scooped the paper up with an unsteady hand. I couldn't read it. Not yet. I just couldn't....

CHAPTER I

A cross the street from Jackson Square, I stood and gazed up at the sculpture of Andrew Jackson, shading my eyes from the blinding sun with my hand. The figure of Jackson, elegant in all his glory, surveyed the area from atop his bronzed horse. With an elated sigh, the realization I had returned home smashed into me. Being back in my city thrilled me.

Making my way toward Cafe Du Monde, I heard the clip clop of the mule drawn carriages as they carried tourists down the street for their daily tours of the city. On the street corners, musicians blew into their instruments and moved people to dance to the city's heartbeat. Artists who lined the cast iron fence around the Square were overjoyed to sell their work to the tourists.

Out of nowhere, the joyful, high pitched squeal of my best friend,

Jahane Olivier, boomed around me. I turned in time to see her headed straight for me with arms outstretched.

"Rosie, I didn't know you had come home," she squealed with delight, as I braced myself for her hug. "Why didn't you tell me you were back in town?"

"Oh I got in yesterday." As she hugged me tight I fell into her embrace, then took a step back to get a better look at my friend.

Jahane hadn't changed one iota while I had been on a six month hiatus from home.

A beautiful girl, my best friend's light toffee colored skin offset her deep set brown eyes and showed off her Spanish mixed with African heritage. As she bounced with excitement, so did her ebony curls.

"Oh my gawd, it has been forever since I've seen you. Why Jahane you haven't changed a bit." My lips tugged at the corners.

She took a long look at me and laughed. "You, Rosaleigh Delacroix, haven't changed a bit, either. Well, you look a little shorter," she laughed as I rolled my eyes at her.

Arms linked together, we made our way down the street. "Let's get some café au lait and beignets," said Jahane, with a cheeky smile spread across her face. "And dish over some gossip." At the sound of her laughter, I knew she would regale me with a marathon session of juicy gossip.

There was no line outside the café, but all the tables were jam packed with people. While we waited for a table, the chicory coffee aroma swirled around me like a steamy hot day on the bayou. Soon I saw a well-dressed couple leave, so I nudged Jahane in the direction of the empty, round, metal table. "Come on, hurry let's go sit over there."

We scooted between the other patrons and made our way to the vacant spot. My chair scraped against the floor as I claimed it. Reaching over to the napkin holder, I pulled a few of them out and wiped as much of the thick coating of powdered sugar from the table as I could. We sat down on the "comfy" green padding of the metal chairs. Her persistent chatter about the goings on since my departure washed over me.

Before I could ask her the question burning in my heart, a waiter in his crisp white uniform and little paper cap approached us. "What can I get for you ladies?"

"Two orders of beignets and two café au laits, please."

While we waited, a trumpet's melody of soulful jazz music emanated from down the street. Finally, our order arrived, and my mouth watered at the scent of the powdered beignet. I bit into one hot, sugary donut, causing white, dusty powdered sugar to spray into the air like dust motes caught in sunlight. The steam swirled upward from my tiny ceramic cup, which was filled to the brim with delicious chicory coffee and hot milk, and I savored a small sip.

"So Rosie…" When Jahane leaned across the table to grab a napkin and sat back in her chair, powdered sugar clung to her shirt. "Why did you leave?"

In mid bite of my beignet, I shook my head. "I can't discuss it, Jahane. It's still too painful." She never pushed me, even though I knew she wanted to. I decided to change the subject from me to her. "So, how have you been?" I cracked a smile and my eyebrows hitched upward. "Do you have any new love interests?" I cocked my head expectantly. Her grin held a hint of secrecy, so waving my hands in the air, I relented. "All right, I promise I won't pressure you on this. But, you know, girl, you can't hold out on me forever ... you will have to concede sooner or later."

"Oh, I know, and I will, then I will tell you who he is," she promised.

Jahane and I laughed as we sipped our café au lait while she caught me up on all the juicy gossip I had missed since I had been gone. Once we were done with our food, we dusted as much powdered sugar off as possible. An impossible feat, because no matter how careful you were, the sugar somehow managed to coat you from head to toe.

Familiarity hit me as we strolled down the street as I took in all the sights and sounds I had missed. A sudden swarm of memories of Julian Quibadeaux surfaced. Thoughts of us with our fingers laced together as we meandered down this very street invaded my brain. With these thoughts resurfacing, I knew I still loved this man with all my heart, and it broke at the mere thought of having left him without a word. In Addition, he had also lost a parent, so I knew he would probably be angry with me when he saw me for not leaning on him for support.

When I couldn't take it anymore, I placed my hand on Jahane's arm to stop her.

Biting my lip I looked at her and asked the inevitable. "Jahane, how is Julian? Have you seen him? How does he look? Has he mentioned me?"

Her head spun in my direction curiously, and she stopped in the middle of the sidewalk, her face sad. "Well, he moped around every day like a lost puppy after you left. I know he missed you very much. He hoped you would return one day. He like me, wanted to help you when your momma disappeared."

My gut stopped its sudden urge to let go of my food when Jahane settled my fears. Julian may not hate me. Hope flourished at the possibility he still loved me, even after I'd run off and left him without an explanation. "So you think he may still want to see me?"

"Oh bestie, now come on, you know he will; and before long, all will be back to normal." She nudged me to keep going down the sidewalk.

I felt a mischievous grin etch across my face, and I grabbed her pulling her into a run. "Jahane, let's pass by the French Market."

"Uh, yeah, what for?" she asked as she dug in and stopped any further movement in the direction I was pulling her.

"I need a new voodoo doll."

With her hands on her hips, her spiral curls bounced as she shook her head. The incredulous look on her face only caused me to giggle. "Uh, hell to the no; and besides, um yeah, Rosie, what in the world do you need a voodoo doll for?"

I waved my hand in the air. "Oh, you know." I pasted a wicked smile on my face. My laughter almost bubbled to the surface at the quizzical look on her face. "Come on Jahane...you remember what we did when we were little."

"Oh, no, no, Rosie, you are not going to." Her voice was full of disbelief.

Hysterical laughter exploded from me as I doubled over and held my sides. "No, Jahane, I wanted some fresh fruit. Satsumas to be exact. I missed its sweet, citrusy taste." My mouth watered at the thought of peeling the green skin off and biting into the sweetness. I heard her sigh in relief. I asked with a sincere tone. "Do you seriously think I would have done that to you?"

"Well, let's see it was you who broke open your piggy bank to exact revenge on the bullies at school."

Jahane's response brought long-lost memories to the forefront of my mind. I'd been thrust back in time to days of long ago, and a nervous laugh escaped. "Jahane, you do remember it was your idea to go to the voodoo shop, right?" I cocked my head at her. "And do you remember the look on your mom's face when she caught us with all the voodoo paraphernalia?"

"Hell, I sure do. My mom was so pissed I thought I would be punished forever." Then she cackled and imitated her mother. "'Girls, if you play with voodoo, the spirits will call Marie Laveau herself to reign terror down on y'all." She laughed so hard at the memory she had to wipe tears from her face.

A low sigh escaped as the memory of the kind words her mother had spoken to me flooded my head. "Rosie, you are a beautiful girl; don't let bullies drag you down. Those scars are your battle scars. One day they will make you stronger in more than one way. Those kids are not worth your time. Do not think twice about them." I smiled at the memory and looked at Jahane. I watched her shudder knowing she'd actually taken her mother's threats to heart.

"Come on, let's get to the Market before it closes."

We continued down the street until I saw the archway of the French Market, I sighed and sniffed the air. The aromas of onion mixed with garlic floated around us and hung in the air like a warm cloud, solely for the purpose of enticing us inside. Other spicy seasonings permeated the air and tickled my nose.

We sifted through the crates containing numerous fruits and vegetables. Afterward we loaded up our bags, and I paid for our purchases, then we headed toward Central Grocery, which was well known for its muffaletta...an Italian sandwich piled high with a variety of meats, cheeses, and topped off with a signature olive salad. The smell greeting us inside was like manna from heaven. The aroma of the spices, mingled with deli meats, cheese, and fresh bread, was intoxicating.

We ordered our sandwiches, and after paying stepped outside to head for our last stop for the evening. The sun had begun to set sending the shadows of the passersby disappearing into the alleys. As we walked down the uneven cobblestone sidewalk the air was thick with silence. Turning right down Pirate's Alley I finally spoke. "Jahane I am very sorry I left without any word. I know I hurt you both. I hope y'all can forgive me."

She stopped, turned to me and hugged me with such force it almost knocked me down. "You're my best friend, so I understand and I do forgive you." She pulled back and smiled at me as a tear slid down my cheek. "I also have it on good authority Julian will forgive you as well. Now come on we have plenty of catching up to do as well as drinks to buy."

We continued our trek to our destination, which was Pat O'Brian's, a local bar well-known for its Hurricanes. When we arrived Jahane turned to me with a smile. "Wait here Rosie, I'll only be a few minutes. Jahane ran inside the bar and came out a few minutes later with a smile plastered on her face holding two Styrofoam cups in her hand. The red liquid of the alcohol called out to me like a bad habit. We giggled as we headed to my place to have one of our infamous sleepovers.

We returned to the studio apartment I had shared with my momma above the shop she'd owned. Our arms laden with the famous Italian sandwiches and Hurricanes from Pat O's, we settled into our familiar routine.

My mother had come from a long line of witches, or so she'd claimed. She'd owned a store where she sold all sorts of herbs and trinkets, but I always thought it to be just a ruse to make a sale. I laughed at the memory of her claiming to be a witch. Thoughts of my mother brought on a trickle from in my eyes, and I unsuccessfully blinked back the wetness threatening to ruin our evening. I choked back a sob, but the pain of her absence was intense. My mind wandered back to the exact reason I'd been forced to flee my home six months ago. I tried not to think about the horrible experience, willing myself not to let the waterfall loose.

Jahane looked at me with sympathy, "Are you all right, Rosie?"

My fingertips wiped away the last remnants of tears from the corners of my eyes. "I'm doing fine now. I'm back with the people I care about."

The previous day, my first real day back home, I had taken care of the legal matters in order for me to take over my momma's shop. The police believed she'd maybe left town with someone voluntarily, but I knew deep down she'd been murdered and we hadn't found her body yet. Just because they didn't have a body or a crime scene didn't mean it hadn't happened. A reminder of the vision in my dreams sent a cold tingle down my spine, like someone had walked over my grave. I knew beyond a shadow of a doubt everything I'd seen in my dream was real, as was the message I'd received. And the one person I could've confided in, but didn't, sat at my kitchen table. I knew the decision to not reveal my dreams to anyone would be the wisest one. I would never say a word to anyone; my friends who were like my family were too important to put them in danger. I'd decided to return because the thought of continued dread angered me more, besides I vowed to find out the truth about my momma.

I shook the thoughts of the past from my head as I sat down at the table, and we both peeled back the white paper wrapped around our sandwiches. Excitement overtook me when I saw the variety of meats and cheeses peeking from under the bread. The cheeses melted in my mouth, and I savored the tartness of the olive salad with each bite.

"Mmmm," I exclaimed. The explosion of flavors hit my taste buds, and I licked my lips for more. I washed it all down with a huge sip of my Hurricane. "Damn, I missed this."

Jahane looked over at me smiling. "I'm sure you did. You could always drink me under the table." I slapped at her arm playfully, as we devoured the remainder of our dinner in silence.

My chair rocked a little as I scooted back letting out an elated sigh.

When we'd finished our scrumptious dinner, I stood, balled up the wrappers, and tossed them in the garbage. I jumped when Jahane touched my arm. "Rosie, when you're ready to tell me what happened, I'm here for you."

I released a sharp breath and nodded in agreement. "I know, Jahane, I know." My head bowed low so she couldn't see the tears emerging at her compassion. I composed myself, and with a slight grin, I looked up at my best friend. "All right, what do we want to watch on TV?"

Jahane didn't reply, seeming to wait for my opinion. After a few minutes, deep in thought, I tapped my lip with my fingertip, giggled, and blurted out, "I call *Supernatural*."

"It's settled," she quipped.

Erupting in laughter, we stumbled into the living room arm in arm. I stood in front of the DVD player, pulled out the first season of *Supernatural*, placed it inside the player, then pushed the button to close it.

"Hold on, Jahane! Press pause for a second. We forgot the most important thing. I'll be back." I hurried into the kitchen and returned with our cups full of alcohol. I offered Jahane a cup and plopped down on the sofa next to her. For the next hour our attention was fixated on the TV, and of course, the swoony Dean and Sam Winchester.

At the end of the episode, I looked over at my friend. "Hey, bestie, do you need a towel for the drool?" I joked with her.

She tapped me lightly and I held my arm in faux pain.

"Oww!" I exclaimed, and our hysterical laughter flowed through the room once more.

She moved closer to me wrapping her arms around me in an unexpected tight embrace. I returned the hug, "What was that for?"

"Oh, you know, for … well … you … I just missed you is all." She dismissed my question. But, the sadness remained in her voice for a moment.

"I missed you as well. All right, enough mushy stuff. We must finish our swoon session with the sexy hunter of things that go bump in the night." My head on her shoulder, I curled up on the sofa. I nudged her, looked up and batted my eyelashes, and in my best breathy voice I said, "Isn't he divine? Look at those lips, they're like kissable pillows. It makes me want to just fall into them."

Her laughter exploded, as she swatted me with a pillow, then shrugged nonchalantly and shook her head. "Hmm…no, I think I will be Team Sam from now on." Her impish smile gleamed under the light of the lamp.

"Hmmm, really?" My eyebrows rose sharply.

"Yup."

"That, my dear friend, is blasphemy, and I won't heed to your trickery." She nudged me. "What about Julian?" she scoffed.

The comfortable sofa swallowed me as I leaned back and sighed. "Oh, you know I'll always love Julian. I mean, who wouldn't? He's tall, gorgeous, and I could run my hands though his long brown hair for an eternity. His dark green eyes can penetrate your soul. It melts every fiber of my body the moment his eyes graze over me." My lust for Julian blew through me like an active volcano. In an instant I wanted his hands on me; after all, it had been awhile since his touch had lit me on fire. *That might have to change sooner rather than later*, I thought. When I pulled myself from my daydream, I stared over at Jahane.

A Cheshire Cat grin was plastered across her face. "Why, Rosie, I do think you blush at the mere mention of his name."

"Oh, shush it." I returned her grin.

Later, when I woke, the silence of my apartment soothed me. The credits were on a continuous loop on the TV, so I shuffled over to it, popped the DVD out, and turned it off. Before I retired to my room, I glanced over my shoulder and saw Jahane still passed out on the other end of the sofa, her arm thrown over her head. I backtracked, threw a blanket over her, and headed to my bedroom. After one final look into the living room, I whispered, "One day … one day I will tell you and Julian why I left."

Sleep took over as I slipped under the covers, and soon I was ensconced in a dreamlike state…

I looked over my shoulder as I ran through the dew filled grass. The tall, sharp blades whipped my legs as I ran faster and faster, emerging into an open area cleared of all trees. Before me I saw a figure lying atop an altar,

but I couldn't stop to see who it was. As my weary legs continued to move me past, I glanced over my shoulder and saw the figure of a man-like creature. I shook my head and tried to quicken my pace, but my legs felt like jelly. I doubted they would carry my body any further. I knew, though, if I didn't try, at any moment it would catch me. Behind me, the sounds of heavy feet pounded through the grass, getting closer to me with every moment that ticked away. The thunderous footsteps made the ground shake, and I didn't dare look back. A cold sensation sifted through my veins and radiated through me as I felt its warm breath on my neck, and because I moved in slow motion, it grabbed me. When I faced it, its deep sunken red eyes stared coldly at me. The creature poked one hairy finger out to touch me, and I screamed in terror as it leaned into my face as its putrid breath permeated my nostrils.

With a jerk, I woke and my heart began a rapid double time beat. I rolled over, and through my half shut eyes, I blinked until I made out the time on the alarm clock. Damn, I must have forgotten to set the alarm. When my breath had steadied, I climbed out of bed and shuffled into the living room. On top of the folded blanket which lay neatly on the empty sofa, I found a note with Jahane's familiar scribble.

Sorry, I had to leave, but I will check back on you later. Would you be up to meeting at our favorite club tonight to listen to some jazz?

Love,
Jahane

Dressed in a flowing skirt and a blue camisole, I swung my purse over my arm and descended the curvy stairs to the courtyard. When my foot hit the last step, I froze. Flowers bloomed in an array of different colors, and the sun sparkled down on them, creating a kaleidoscope. My lips curved slowly across my face as I wondered why I hadn't noticed this earlier.

With a shake of my head, I continued until a flash appeared off to the side of the brick wall by the fountain. A nervous laugh escaped while my mind played tricks on me. I shook my head knowing I had to be seeing things. I knew séances used to be held here, in this courtyard in particular. Since I had played here when I was a child, I had heard the rumors of the rituals performed here by so called famous witches.

Out of the corner of my eye I once again saw a hazy blur flitting around.

"Oh, hell no … I need more sleep. I'm going crazy now I'm seeing things. This is not happening."

I rubbed my eyes, hoping it was my imagination, because according to my mom, the usual ghost was said to haunt here, but in all the years I'd lived above the store with my momma, I had never been privy to such a sighting.

I brushed the thoughts from my head and stood at the back door of my momma's shop, stuck the brass key in the knob, and turned my wrist. The moment the door swung open the sweet musty smell of dust gripped me tight as it hit my nostrils.

I waited while it swirled in the air and finally settled, then sucked in a breath. "Oh, wow, this will take the rest of the day to clean," I muttered as I traipsed inside and wiped my hand along the grimy counter. "Ewww." Frustration overcame me as I considered how in the world I would ever revamp this place.

My mother's familiar voice invaded my thoughts. "You can do this, Petal." I stood, gaping at the dirt and cobwebs. My scream bounced off the walls when a tiny mouse squeaked as it skittered across the floor. Mentally, I jotted down mousetraps on a shopping list as the first items to buy. With a new found courage, I jotted down a few more supplies. After my list was completed, I grabbed my purse and keys and walked out, locking the door behind me.

CHAPTER 2

As I returned home from the store, my arms were burdened with numerous bags full of supplies. I hoisted the bags up and balanced them on my hips. After three tries, the key managed to end up in the lock and it clicked open. One of my bags caught on the door frame and I lunged forward. Before my face met the floor, strong arms righted me to a standing position.

"Thank you, sir."

"My pleasure, Rosie."

My breath caught in my throat at the Cajun accent I recognized so well. *Oh, please no, please no,* I pleaded, not wanting to turn around for fear my suspicions were correct.

Slowly I turned and faced him. From under my lashes I peeked up, to see his sultry green eyes dance as he grinned back at me. Brute strength emanated from him. It took all my self-control to keep from running my fingers through his dark brown hair cascading down and ended at his shoulder blades. He took the bags from me and placed them on the floor. Before I could stop him he pulled me closer to him. In mere seconds, he'd wrapped his arms around my petite frame. "I...uh... My breathing felt like it stopped for at least ten minutes.

"Julian, what are you doing?" I asked, fearing the inevitable but wanting it more than I would admit.

"Shhh, Rosie. I missed you, and the one thing I need is my lips on yours." His fingertip brushed along my cheekbone to rest on my supple lips and caused a firestorm to spread throughout my body. Even though I willed myself to breathe, I couldn't as his finger brushed back a tendril of my dark chocolate hair. Our souls entangled as he pierced my hazel, almond shaped eyes with his. When our mouths met, it was as if a dozen electrical pulses vibrated through my body. My legs turned to jelly, and I grasped onto him more firmly.

Once the kiss was broken, I pulled away slightly. When I was able to stand without falling, I tucked a fallen strand of hair behind my ear, wiped a hand down my skirt, and stepped backwards a few steps. He looked scrumptious enough to devour in his tight jeans hugging him in all the right spots, and his shirt clung to his well-defined muscles.

"Um...yeah..." My face was burning hot, and I was sure it was bright red as I stuttered, trying to remember what I had been doing before the kiss.

His mischievous smile crinkled along his face, as he leaned in, he nipped my lip. "You, Rosie, are the only woman I can make stutter."

"Ahem...Julian, what are you doing here? How did you know? Oh wait, Jahane told you I had returned, didn't she?" My gaze stayed focused on him as desire consumed me.

"Yes, Rosie, Jahane called me first thing this morning; I'm so glad you're back," he smirked.

Under my breath I mumbled, "I'll have to thank her sometime."

"Come on, Rosie; did you really think Jahane wouldn't call me the minute she found out you were home?"

I rolled my eyes, picked up my bags, and sashayed to the counter. The growl of pleasure I heard escaping his mouth sent goose bumps prickling along my skin. After I placed the supplies on the counter, I turned to him, hands on my hips. "Julian…" Before the words left my mouth, he stood before me, his body pressed against mine like a comfortable soft blanket. The sincerity of his look brought on a flood of tears from my eyes.

"Don't cry, Cher." With his thumb, he brushed away a stray tear as it trickled down my cheek. He leaned down, and his hot breath tickled my ear as he whispered, in his thick Cajun accent, "Ce qui est erroné dans mon amour? What's wrong, my love?"

"It's just…well…I hiccupped, but soon a swirl of calmness went through my body as he traced rhythmic circles on my back and pulled me closer to his hard chest.

"Rosie, what's wrong? Please talk to me," he begged as I breathed in his unfamiliar scent of fresh cut wood and ferns and clung to him, not wanting to let go.

"Is this a new cologne you're wearing?" I asked, and wiped my nose on his shirt. When he realized what I had done, his laughter made my head shake. Embarrassed, I grinned up at him. He returned the grin as his six foot three frame towered over my five feet of height.

"It is, yes." He continued to smile down at me.

Surprised at his kindness, my voice was soft when I spoke. "Julian, I'm surprised you still care about me, especially after my abrupt departure."

He was silent for a moment, and then his muscular arms comforted me as he pulled me in tight against his warm body. He pulled back a smidge, tilted my chin up with his thumb, and his green gaze melted all hesitation from me, like ice on a humid summer afternoon. "Rosie, why wouldn't I? I'll admit I was hurt you left me, thinking maybe I could have been there for you. After all, you knew I'd lost my father. But, I know it must have been something big to make you leave."

His kind, heartfelt words consumed me. "I can't discuss it, Julian. I'm so sorry." Neither he nor Jahane pushed me on the matter, even though I knew both wanted to be there for me. They knew I would talk when I was ready. But, my dream still scared me; the memory of it was vivid and played over and over in my head like a broken record. *Don't tell anyone.* Since my momma's disappearance, I got little sleep whenever the dream came to me.

The immediate need to change the subject made me ask, "So, Julian...how, umm...are... you?" With my thoughts and words still discombobulated, I had no idea why I had become a giant ball of nerves around him.

"Rosie, I've missed you." He licked his lips, and the seductive movement sent my body into overdrive again. When he pulled me even closer to him, I relished his warm embrace.

Out of nowhere, an eerie vibe circled around us both, a strange sensation with an evil tone I couldn't put my finger on. The sinister shadow had wrapped itself around him and pushed me away. Determined, I brought his body closer to mine and a weird instinct overtook me as I pushed at the evil to leave. Once it had dissipated, warmth wrapped around both of us, and I sighed at being in his arms again.

Julian smirked at me, apparently unaware of the danger. "Come on, Rosie, let me help you get this place ready." He cocked a brow at me, and in an instant those green eyes turned my stomach to mush.

"Sure thing, Julian. I could use some help."

Even though we remained busy the rest of the day, I stole glances at him when I could. Off in my own little world, I wiped down the counter with a soft white cloth, and turned around just in time to see him slip his shirt off over his head. As I craned my head and moved closer to see more, I knocked over the bucket of water by the edge of the counter.

He tossed his shirt and it landed on the floor. "Wow, you aren't becoming a klutz, are you?" He laughed as I tried to feign ignorance.

Nonchalantly, I turned back to my own task, but took a chance to sneak a few more peeks at his god-like body. The sinewy muscles of his arms moved and stretched while he scrubbed. When I turned back to my task, I knew he stared at me, and the sudden heat on my cheeks spread like a wildfire. Before he had a chance to question me, I grabbed the broom and swept the nonexistent dirt in front of me.

After about an hour of scrubbing, I walked over to the little fridge in the corner of the store and grabbed two bottles of water.

"Hey Julian, would you like some water?"

He nodded. "Sure thing, cher."

When I tossed it, he caught the bottle in midair, twisted off the cap, and took a long swig. Mesmerized by the movement of his Adam's apple, I couldn't pry my eyes from it as it bobbed up and down with every swallow. I stood there in awe as he pitched the empty plastic container to a nearby trash can. Then he leaned down, grabbed his shirt, and with seductive movements, wiped it down his chiseled chest, straight down to his abs. The sweat glistened on every ridge of his six pack.

For a moment, I stood there and got my emotions in check. If it hadn't been for my tight hold on the counter, I would have crumbled to the floor. His gaze rested on me in all my glory, my mouth all agog, as he smirked at me. Bashfully, I turned away and began to dust off the counter some more. All of a sudden, I felt a slight breeze and turned to see his shirt slide then hit the ground in a heap. The grin on his face made me roll my eyes.

"Come on, Julian, quit it. We have work to do." I reached down, picked up the shirt, and tossed it back at him. He caught it and pulled it back over his head, smoothing it down to mold to his abs.

"Mais, Rosie, you were the one ogling me," he joked.

"Uh, I just noticed how quickly you drank that bottle of water." Exasperation reigned in my tone.

"Uh huh, so you say." He wiggled his brows at me and turned back to his task.

We worked in silence until the store glistened. Exhausted, I leaned against the counter. I tugged a stray piece of hair from my sweaty brow and tucked it behind my ear. Julian came up and stood in front of me, placed his hands on my shoulders, bent down, and touched his lips to mine. He slipped his tongue into my mouth, parting my lips, the sensation sent shivers down my spine as he deepened the kiss. He pulled back and winked at me. "Rosie, I'll see ya later, cher."

"Uh huh." Breathless, I watched him walk out of my shop. After he left I let out a sigh. Damn, I had missed him. Immediately, I picked up my phone and texted Jahane to set up a time to meet.

Jahane knocked on the door, and when I opened it she stood there in boots up to her thighs and an off the shoulder shirt, covered by her black jacket. Her ample breasts tried to peek out at me, and I stifled a laugh.

"Are you ready to go?" she asked.

"Yes, let me grab my coat, and we can head out."

Outside the chill in the air made me button my coat all the way up. Stopping at a tourist shop down the street, we stepped inside the brightly lit shop and smiled at the array of different colored masks plus boas hanging from the walls.

"Rosie, how about this one?" Jahane twirled with a multicolored boa wrapped around her neck.

I shook my head "no" and she moved on, pulling off a couple more boas and checking herself out in the mirror. My hands passed along a few different colorful ones with an array of bright feathers. I wrapped a pink tinted with white, feathered boa around my neck, and I saw Jahane looking at me with a mischievous grin on her face as she laced her fingers around the string of a mask and gently pulled it off the wall. We nodded to each other and both pretended to search for other items as every step brought us closer to the exit. When we were mere inches from the door, we quickened our pace and made a run for it with our treasures in hand. The manager yelled at our retreating figures as feathers floated behind us and blew in the wind.

"Oh my gawd, I thought we were going to be caught this time," we both said at the same time. Amid a fit of giggles and hand-in-hand, we traipsed to our next destination.

The door to our favorite club opened the moment my hand touched the handle. We stepped into darkness, and when my eyes adjusted, I walked over to the bar. When the bartender noticed us, he sauntered over, wiping his hands on a towel he tucked back into his belt. "What can I get you two?"

"One Sazerac and an absinthe frappe, please." After I'd ordered, I turned to watch Jahane as she danced to her own tune and smiled at the people who gawked at her. I shook my head and turned back to face the bar as I heard the glasses slide in front of me. Jahane, still shaking her ass, reached past my shoulder and handed the guy some bills. "Here ya go, sexy." She clucked her tongue at him.

"Come on, bestie." With two drinks in hand, I followed my gyrating friend to a table to relax until our next stop. After two more drinks each, we decided on our third stop. Jahane led me out of the bar and down the uneven street to the jewelry store. Once inside, we separated to pick out our gifts to each other. The glass cabinet I stared at contained a beautiful silver bracelet.

"How may I help you, miss?" the woman behind the counter asked me.

All I needed was a sideways glance to check out where my bestie was before I continued. In a hushed voice I pointed to an item encased in glass. "Yes, ma'am, I would like the silver bracelet."

"Nice choice."

"Thank you, and I would like it to say 'To my best friend. You are my rock.'

After I paid for my item, Jahane sauntered over to me with a grin as big as the moon. We walked arm in arm out of the store with our slips in our hand to pick up our items in a week or two. Once we stepped outside into the brisk cool air, we headed to our final destination, a haunted history tour.

As my feather boa started to slip, I tugged it back in place and grabbed my best friend's hand as we headed to buy our tickets. "Which tour do we want to do tonight?" A mischievous grin splayed across my face.

We flipped through the brochures and both came to the same conclusion. "The ghost tour it is!" We giggled and made our way to buy our tickets for the eight o'clock tour.

After buying our tickets, Jahane turned to me. "Okay, we have about an hour until we go; so Rosie, let's get a bite to eat."

She pulled me down the street in the direction of our favorite restaurant, and I followed her inside The Brackish Tavern, famous for its oyster bar. The owner, Mr. Jacque Dupre, was an old family friend. The hostess waved us in, and we seated ourselves in our favorite booth. When Mr. Jacque saw us sit down, he ran over to us. "Miss Rosie, Miss Jahane, how have you girls been?" His voice sounded elated at the sight of us.

"We are doing well. I just got back in town," I said.

"It's been too long since I've seen you two here." Mr. Jacque slid into the booth next to me and waved a waiter to our table. The young man promptly walked over. "Billy, could you get two sweet teas, son?" He turned to me and squeezed me in a tight hold. "Miss Rosie, I'm sorry to hear about your momma, but I know the police will find some sort of clues soon," he sputtered out in his French accent.

At Mr. Jacque's kind words, I nodded and pushed back the tears threatening to spill. "Thank you, Mr. Jacque."

He stood up from the table, smiled, and asked, "Well, ladies, will it be the usual?" In unison, our heads bobbed up and down. He turned on his heels and walked through the swinging doors to the kitchen to place our order.

While we waited for our food, I gave Jahane the stink eye. "By the way, thanks to you,

Julian paid me a visit."

Satisfaction her plan had worked shone on her smug face. "Well, someone had to let him know you were back in town."

"He...uh...he...uh...," my words stuttered out. She waved her hand, knowing full well my tongue tied in knots at the mention of him. Sighing heavily, I said, "I know, and he is still as sexy as ever. His damn six pack is so..." We erupted into giggles, but were interrupted when the waiter placed two hot steamy bowls of

gumbo, potato salad, and fresh French bread in front of us. Mr. Jacque also brought us a fresh plate of raw oysters as an appetizer.

"Enjoy, girls, and if you need refills or more French bread, please let Billy know." Spoon in hand, I nodded at him as he headed back to the kitchen through the double doors as they swung back and forth.

"Hey, Jahane, can you pass me the Tabasco sauce?"

When she handed it to me, I dashed a little on my gumbo, just enough to add a little kick. My spoon dipped into the gumbo, and with my first bite the spiciness of the flavors exploded over my taste buds. "Mmm, damn, this is

delicious." Jahane nodded in silent agreement.

Billy returned to fill our glasses, and we ate the rest of our meal in silence, with no time to talk as we inhaled the savory dinner. Once we were done, we paid Mr. Jacque.

"Don't be strangers, Miss Rosie and Miss Jahane."

"No sir, we won't. Promise!" I assured him, and hugged him tightly.

Back outside, the cooler air blew around us as we strolled towards Jackson Square. On the way, we passed several tables covered with multicolored cloths. A sign in front of one table read "Tarot Cards read by…"

"Come on, Rosie, let's do it." Jahane interrupted my thoughts and pushed me towards the table covered in a deep purple.

An unknown feeling circled around me as I approached the metal chair. Even though I didn't believe in futures being told by the cards, something was stirring in the air, which did not sit well with me. This didn't feel right, and a creepy feeling inched its way through me. I shook my head no, but my BFF shoved me towards the table as if she knew the thoughts flowing through my head. I sat in the chair begrudgingly.

"Rosie, come on, it's not so bad… for fun."

Every synapse in my brain fired off in sequence and screamed at me to run, but I ignored them. My teeth tugged at my bottom lip, and a shy smile tugged at the corner of my mouth as the woman sat across from me and waited for me to get hold of my apprehension.

"It will be ten dollars." The ginger-haired woman held out her hand, palm up.

Jahane passed her a ten dollar bill over my shoulder. The fortune teller took the bill and shoved it between her ample bosoms.

She took my hand and let it rest on the table, and her genuine smile put me at ease. "Easy child, my name is Madame Claudette." She shuffled the deck of cards and splayed them across the table. "Go ahead, pick three cards."

With a wave of her hand she instructed me to pick my cards. Hesitance flowed through me as I looked up at Jahane, who stood behind me.

"Rosie, come on, it will be fun." She nodded to reassure me. My hand trembled as it passed over the cards. But I chose my three cards, the last one taking the longest to pick.

Once I had picked all the cards, I wiped my sweaty hands on my skirt. Madame Claudette's bony fingers turned over the cards one at a time and studied them, her expression hard to read. The beautiful designs disturbed me, and I itched to find out the meanings they held.

Her hands waved over the cards from left to right, and she looked up at me. "My child, these first two cards," she pointed to The Wheel of Fortune and Lovers, "are not bad, but the Death card, my dear...well, it one can mean a vast array of trials and tribulations."

Her concerned expression sent my mind into overdrive. She pointed to the Wheel of Fortune card. "This one, my dear, represents your past, and it shows external factors that may have influenced what you have dealt with in your life and were completely out of your control."

A loud gasp escaped when a vision of my mother popped into my head. I felt the comfortable touch of Jahane's hand on my shoulder.

My fingertip traced over the beautiful card with two nude lovers on either side of the sun. In a thick accent I couldn't place, Madame Claudette spoke. "This symbolizes your present; the card tells me you will have a great love in your life." At the mention of a great love, an electrical current shot through my body. Oh, Julian.

Jahane's hot breath touched my shoulder as she eagerly waited for what would be divulged next. I shrugged my shoulders to get her out of my personal space. She mumbled something incoherent and I turned my attention back to Madame Claudette. My focus on the fortune teller, I leaned in close, my curiosity getting the best of me.

Her head bowed, her full attention was on the last and final card, the Death card. "This, my child, is your future card." For a second her face darkened, but returned to a smile as she looked over the card. "You, child, have had bad luck and death in your family." All of a sudden her eyes rolled back in her head, and she grabbed my hand, which rested on the table. Her stare was vacant as she looked through me. "And it...is...coming for you next."

Fear and bile rose to the surface of my stomach. When I stood up to bolt, she gripped my hand tighter. With no luck, I strained to free my hand from her grip. She seemed to come back to herself, but she still held me tight as she reached somewhere underneath the table and pulled out a small, brown burlap bag. Madame Claudette placed the bag in my hand and closed my hand over it. "When you get home, my child, open this and wear it at all times."

Close to tears, I jerked my hand free and ran till I was approaching the Cabildo, with

Jahane close behind me.

"Rosie, Rosie, slow down. What the hell happened back there?"

My pace slowed when I reached the front of the Cabildo. Tears streamed down my face, and my dream of my mother popped back into my head. Out of breath, Jahane reached me as I wiped the tears away with the sleeve of my jacket.

"What's wrong, Rosie?"

"Nothing, it was a reminder my momma is gone." With the bag in my hand, I fiddled with the coarse edges and stuffed it into my pocket. For a second, I contemplated the idea of cancelling tonight but thought better of it. I decided to have fun and deal with this later. "Come on, let's go on the tour…we are almost late." She followed me as I grabbed the cuff of her jacket and dragged her to the steps of the cathedral.

"No, Rosie, you need to tell me what's wrong." She tapped the toe of her black boot on the step with her hands on her hips.

"Later, Jahane, please; let's go on the tour and have fun." The tone in my voice pleaded with her even though I knew she wouldn't let it go. Thoughts swirled of how I had to find a way to delay the inevitable conversation as long as I could.

Before I could stop myself, I began to pace in anticipation of the start of the tour. Down the street we saw a ghostly figure floating towards us. The crowd gasped loudly, and a dozen cameras clicked in a flurry of bright lights. Jahane nudged me, which sent me into a tizzy of giggles.

In a thick fake accent the ghost spoke. "Good evening, my name is Drayton and I'll be your ghostly tour guide tonight." A hush floated through the crowd and everyone but Jahane and I stood with their mouths open wide.

"Follow me now for the first house on our tour." The ghost guide floated down to Royal Street and stopped in front of the scandalous LaLaurie House. His voice low and creaky, he began his story.

"Back in the 1800's, well-known socialites, the LaLaurie's, lived in New Orleans. The parties they threw were the talk of the city. Because Delphine LaLaurie was a creative story teller, the townsfolk gravitated towards her and hung on every word. But the deep set cruel and sadistic actions of the mistress of the house were unknown. And they only came to light because of a fire inside the house."

A hushed silence flowed around the crowd, and he continued his tale.

"Most of the upper-class people had slaves, but this was not what would later appall the people of the Vieux Carre. Everyone knew what it took to maintain a house of this caliber. But that fateful day was not unlike any other day…a slave girl had disrespected Delphine. Infuriated, she beat the girl with a leather whip. With every lash and welt mixed with blood, the slave girl had no other recourse but to run. Her legs carried her through the house until she reached the balcony above us. With no other way out, because she knew her fate, she jumped to her death. As Delphine stood and gazed at the girl's dead body, she knew what must be done. She had the body buried, only to be witnessed by another slave. It is said you can sometimes get a glimpse of the repeated actions of the slave girl jumping from this balcony."

The crowd began to talk in hushed tones, and when they had grown quiet, Drayton continued.

"The slaves were removed from the house, and the people abandoned their old friends. Now, as I told you before, the townspeople did not know what Delphine and her husband had been capable of, but the truth surfaced after a fire in 1834. The fire uncovered what the lady of the house had done to her slaves, and the truth the firemen discovered could never be unseen, and the horrifying sight would never be forgotten. The depravity astounded the people when dozens of bodies, some barely alive, others dead, all tortured, and some dismembered, were found locked in a small room in the attic. Doctors did what they could for the ones who survived this evil. Rumors began to spread and amplify about the LaLaurie, even after they fled in the middle of the night. They were never seen again, but many speculated on what happened to them. You can still hear the screams coming from the house on any given night." The crowd of people murmured about what they had heard.

"All right, on to our next stop."

Drayton glided, and his black cloak flowed in the slight wind. He turned the corner and glided over a crack in the sidewalk toward St. Peter's Street. On the corner of St. Peters and Chartres, we stopped in front of the infamous Le Petit Theater. The air around me went icy, the hairs on my neck stood up, and I looked down the street. My fear was getting the best of me, and I needed to calm down. The tour guide babbled, but my attention was on the air and the darkness of the street. Scanning the crowd, I blinked when I saw a fuzzy form before me. It ducked into the alley, and my fear bubbled to the surface.

Jahane nudged me. "What did you see?"

"Nothing." With all the courage I could muster, my focus went back to Drayton's story. My arm placed around my best friend, I leaned forward in order to hear a little better.

"This is the haunting story of a well-known actress who worked with the theater briefly in the early years. She still haunts the back stage today. The older actress was said to have been involved in a torrid affair with a maintenance employee. Inside, from the catwalks above the main stage, she fell to her ill-timed death, hanging loosely tangled in the wires and curtains. When they found her, her naked body was draped in the curtain she hung from. It was reported she died from a broken neck and related injuries on impact. The maintenance man who had been involved was never located; he had no family to name and had been known to be a drifter. Many have speculated through the years whether the fall was accidental or murder…"

A gasp from the crowd made Jahane and I look at each other. The strange sensation I'd had earlier remained with me, and I could not get it out of my head. Now the entire crowd, even more engulfed by Drayton's story, leaned in closer to hear his words.

"In the otherwise empty theater, you can catch a glimpse of the actress's earthbound spirit on the cat walks above the stage. The change in the air to icy cold, and the heavy theater curtains billowing eerily, as if they had been pressed into motion by cold, unseen hands, precedes the spooky sight of the ghost."

At that precise moment, someone ran past me, and the area left in their wake was wrapped in coldness. Jahane's eyes went wide, and I whispered, "Did you feel it, too?"

Jahane nodded, and my skin prickled with the realization something sinister was in the air. Without a doubt, I knew it had used the cover of the theater's ghost to get close to me. A sense of foreboding overshadowed all thoughts, and I felt a sinister energy wash over me again. This time when I looked over my shoulder, Madame Claudette headed towards me. My arms wrapped tightly around my body to comfort myself, I told myself the tour would end soon, and I could return home and huddle underneath the covers. I turned my head back to the tour and tried my best to ignore the woman who stood across the street. But when our tour ended, the crowd dispersed, and the fortune teller walked across the street in my direction.

The air around her shifted as she pulled me aside. "My child, have you done what was asked of you yet?" she asked.

My hand went to my pocket and the little bag scratched as my fingers touched it, making sure it was still there. "No ma'am, I haven't yet."

Disappointment etched across her face, and she lowered her mouth inches from mine so I could hear her. "Child, it is after you and won't stop until it gets you. Do as I say, child." She turned on her heels, her long red and orange skirt billowing and fluttering in the non-existent wind.

Her figure retreated into the darkness of the night, and deep in thought, I shook my head in disbelief.

"So what did she want?"

"Ahhh!" My scream echoed around us. "Damn it. Don't sneak up on me! You almost gave me a heart attack. I swear, girl, you need a damn bell placed around your neck." I held my hand over my chest. Once my erratic breathing stabilized, I muttered, "Oh you know, the crazy old fortune teller trying to scare who she thinks is a tourist. It's all for show."

She shook her head and laughed. With her arm entwined with mine we huddled close to each other and headed home.

Later, as I was preparing for bed, I remembered the item I'd received from the creepy fortune teller was still stuffed into my pocket. I dug inside my skirt and pulled the little burlap bag out by the string. Hesitant, I let it dangle for a second from my fingers, then sighed, sat on my bed, and opened it. I gasped as I pulled out a beautiful amber tear drop amulet. I knew this was something special, so I shook the bag to see if perhaps it contained a note. A small folded up piece of paper floated out and landed on my lap. I unfolded it and read it.

Love, Mom

I smiled and clasped it around my neck, then snuggled into my bed and fell asleep.

CHAPTER 3

The sun shone through a crack in the curtains and danced in lines across the floor to my bed. The gorgeous sky and warm sun revealed themselves as soon as I shuffled out of bed and spread the drapes open wider. I turned from the window and stretched my body to get the kinks out from last night's sleep. Still groggy, my bare feet slapped along the hardwood floor as I headed into the kitchen. I pushed the button on the coffee maker and in no time, steam rose from the coffee pot spitting a dark brown liquid into my huge mug. The heaven sent liquid warmed me from the inside out as I sipped. A text buzzed and sent the phone scooting across the table.

Hey, do you want to go to our favorite club for some jazz music and get a bite to eat for your birthday?

Quickly, I replied, Sure thing!

A buzz shook my hand as her reply came, and a smile creased my cheeks at the fantastic night we would have. Cup in hand, I walked back to my room to get dressed. I stood and stared back at the mirror and then spun around to check my reflection. I swooped my long hair up, tied it with a band, and headed out the door.

Outside in the courtyard, the bright sun sparkled on the water shooting from the fountain. A few inches from the fountain the aroma of the flowers floated toward me. My body followed the scents and I walked over to the array of colors as a single bud opened. The flowery scents invaded my senses, as I inhaled as I bent down to sniff a single red rose.

Before I continued on my way towards the cast iron gates, my head turned at a rustling noise. The flaps on a cardboard box flipped back and forth, and a little black nose peeked out but popped back under. Soft whimpers muffled by the box grew louder as I tiptoed

closer. My knees touched the ground as I

squatted down and flipped open the lid. Before the flaps had been released, the hairy contents pounced out, and its wet tongue licked my face. I landed backwards sprawling out on the ground as the puppy bounced around as if in a windstorm.

My examination of the puppy was a whirlwind of feet and tail as it wiggled in my arms and licked me every time my face got near its wet tongue.

"Hold still." I laughed, and when she dangled from my grasp I noticed her dark blue mottled coat with gray and white markings. A teardrop stone or something swayed from her collar. The sun bounced off the stone, and the lights and colors danced like a kaleidoscope.

"What's this?" I wondered aloud. My fingertips grazed it and all of a sudden, the stone felt hot. At my touch it turned a myriad of different colors. A slight electric current pulsed through my body, as the teardrop slipped from my hand and swung back and forth from her collar.

"Okay, let's see who left you here." I peered into the box and dug around for some sort of note from whoever had brought this puppy to me. "Eureka!" My voice squealed as I found a crumpled up note. The paper felt familiar to me, but I dismissed it and glanced at the pup

settled in my arms, her soft fur tickling me.

"Let's go see where you came from and why you are in my courtyard."

The puppy sagged in my arms as I walked down the red-bricked path past the cathedral and further down the street to meet Jahane. She stood a few feet away from me. She waved jubilantly when she saw me.

She ran across the street and almost knocked over a stack of hand painted masks. "Rosie," she screeched, "where did you get it?" The puppy jumped from my arms into hers licking her eagerly. When she caught me rolling my eyes, she snorted. "Damn girl, you know you look like you're getting a few new wrinkles." I rolled my eyes even further back in my head at the joke she always told on my birthday. When she grabbed me tight, I chuckled. "You know I love you, Grandma, and happy birthday."

We laughed as we stepped up the concrete steps and through the iron gates leading into the Square. We sat down on a cold black metal bench.

As the puppy licked Jahane, I couldn't control my snicker. With the puppy wiggling in her arms, she turned. "Where did you find her?"

"In a box in my courtyard."

Then, I remembered the crumpled up note and pulled it from my pocket. My hands nervously shook while I peeled the familiar wax seal apart. They continued to shake as the paper unfolded in my hands. "It can't be." At the sight of the words written in my mother's beautiful script, I gasped and covered my mouth. Jahane looked over at me.

"It's from my mom, but...but...she is...dead..." I sputtered. Tears flowed down my cheeks to land on the back of the puppy, who now sat in my lap. The handwritten note brought a flood of emotions to me. Jahane's arm comforted me, as she pulled me closer to her. My newfound friend nestled even closer to me and I petted her, feeling the wetness of my tears on her soft fur. Before I read the note aloud, I choked back a sob and read it to myself. Jahane moved closer, and I let her read the note over my shoulder.

My dearest Rose Petal,

All will be revealed to you in time. I'm sorry I had to leave you, but I had to protect you. Because you are a powerful witch, you have been chosen to receive a Guardian on your twenty-seventh birthday. There is an evil out there, but with this dog y'all together will be able to fight it. This puppy will grow to an alarming size. Do not fret though; she will protect you with every fiber of her being. I know what you are thinking, my little Petal...

Her nickname for me ignited sadness in my soul, but after a moment, I continued to read, and the reassurances from Jahane along with my new companion came in waves. Thoughts popped into my head of the possibilities of her message. Could this mean she wasn't dead?

This is not a regular dog. Yes, her breed is a Great Dane, but she is a Guardian, and it runs in her bloodline. Please keep her by your side at all times. But if for some reason she is not, she is still with you always. I have made sure of this. She is a very powerful entity. Your life is now different from what it used to be, my darling; please stay safe. I love you, my little Petal ... happy birthday, my darling daughter.

Love,

Mom

After I finished, the crumpled note lay in my lap, my fingers tracing the edges of the paper. With tears brimming at the corners of my eyes, I folded the note back up and stuffed it in my pocket. Another thought popped into my head... could she be alive, or was this a trick? Quickly, the thought dissipated as I felt a wet nose brush against my cheek. My pup wiggled in my lap, and her blue eyes stared into mine.

"Hello, little girl." Her tail swished back and forth.

Curiosity settled in, and I wondered if she had been booby trapped. Her eyes changed in an instant to chocolate, and in a flash, they were blue again. Light swirled in many colors behind her, but I blinked and it was gone. This dog was surrounded by magic...it ebbed from every part of her, and I needed answers...answers from someone who knew my mom. Besides, there was also the fact I needed supplies to take care of my

Guardian. Before the words came out, Jahane interrupted me. "Yes, Rosie, I know our plans have changed. So let's go."

"You ready to go, little one?" At my question, the pup jumped off my lap and ran in circles around my feet. "I guess that's a yes." On her haunches, she smiled at me. "Oh shit, Jahane, I'm going crazy now...my Guardian just smiled at me."

"No, you aren't, honey." She shook her head in disbelief.

Inside the most prestigious dog boutique in all of the Quarter, a chime went off above my head as we stepped inside, and Miss Alina looked up from the counter. Her gray hair was in a tight bun, but she didn't look her age. She looked so much younger, almost like she hadn't aged. Her smile grew when she noticed us standing in the doorway.

She came from behind the counter and stood in front of us. Before I could utter one word, she grabbed us both and kissed us on our cheeks, then stepped back as if she was reading us or something.

She still looked the same as ever. She wore a pristine pantsuit in a shade of blue that highlighted her eyes, and her jewelry was still silver and turquoise. "Well, if it isn't Miss Jahane and Miss Rosie. How have you girls been? Please, come sit," she said in her thick New Orleans accent as she hugged us both and whispered in my ear, "It is good to see you back, my dear. The Quarter has not been the quite the same without you here."

When she stepped back, she noticed the now quiet puppy in my arms. The expression on her face was like an *aha* moment. Startled, she ruffled the dog's ears. "Ahhh, a Guardian."

Shocked, I said, "You know about Guardians?"

"Yes, child." She winked at me. "Your mother and I shared quite a bit. So, have you named her yet?"

My head shook like a bobble head doll sitting on the dashboard of a car.

"Oh, no worries, it will come to you, and she will help you. A Guardian knows a lot more than you think." I knew a puzzled look etched over my face at her question. "All your questions will be answered in due time, my child, in due time. But first, we must get you the supplies needed to take care of this puppy; she will not stay little for long."

Miss Alina bustled around the store and picked out a dozen or so items, the whole time humming a tune I could not quite make out. The pup followed us around but stopped every so often to check out remote corners. She bounded back over to me with her nose covered in dust bunnies.

After I paid for my purchases, Miss Alina beckoned us to the back.

"Now, Rosie, a Guardian is a special animal not unlike a familiar, but much more powerful." She grinned at me when a look of disbelief shone on my face. "I know, Rosie, you don't believe your momma was a witch, but in fact she was, which in turn makes you one."

"I don't know what to believe anymore." A deep sigh escaped, and I shook my head at this statement. "But truth be told, in the last couple of days, there has definitely been something to believe in."

"Pish posh, Rosie in fact, both of your parents came from powerful families. Which, my dear, makes you a powerful entity." Miss Alina ruffled the soft fur of my Guardian. "And this is why you have received this precious gift. This is a magical creature infused with the most potent of magic, but most important it is always a Great Dane. These dogs are used for their strength and their loyalty."

My mouth fell open at her blasé use of the word magical. Jahane reached a hand over and popped my mouth closed. Miss Alina smiled at me and continued. "Rosie, you come from a long line of witches who protect the weak and help those less fortunate. You have powers beyond your imagination. She will protect you against those who want to harm you."

I sat stone cold still while I let things sink in. "But...but...how come my momma never told me the truth about my father, or her, or this so called witch business?"

My mother's best friend's expression turned grim. "Your momma should have been the one to tell you when you turned twenty-seven, which is today. But with her untimely death, the task passed to me, her best friend and coven sister. Besides, the protection of her daughter was her main concern."

Encased in the soft cushions of the leather sofa, I sat there, shell shocked. If it hadn't been for Jahane's presence, I would have sworn this to be a dream. Once my shock had worn off, I hoisted myself up from the sofa and grabbed my packages and my pup. Alina's embrace wrapped around me and sheathed me in magic.

"I promise we will be back soon."

"When you do, I'll tell you everything you need to know."

As the door closed behind me, uncertainty hit me at the thought of waiting and the fear of the unknown. An evil lurked around the corner; though I had no idea when it would strike.

CHAPTER 4

Jahane and I stood in front of the cast iron fence leading into my courtyard. With no notice at all, she wrapped me and the pup in a tight embrace. "Get some rest and I'll see y'all tomorrow."

"I'll see ya later, Jahane." My arms sagged at the weight of the puppy and her supplies, and she gently jumped from my arms. "Wow, what did you eat where you came from? Because you sure are heavy." I shook my head. "Never mind, I'm exhausted."

She whimpered, and a dozen butterfly wings fluttered through my head. The railing next to the steps caught me as I rubbed my temples. After the pain dissipated, I shrugged my shoulders and ascended the steps. She padded ahead of me, but slowed to a crawl. A giggle escaped my mouth as I watched her scoot up each wooden step. She tumbled down a couple, but regained her stance and pawed up again. Her nails scratched at the wood, and on the last step her little legs wiggled as her butt swayed back and forth. She scrambled up and over, turned, and sat on her haunches, her tail swishing. When I stopped laughing, I ascended the stairs and got the "it's about time" look.

I stuck the key inside the lock, and the door swung open with a creak. I peered around the door and the puppy bounded in, yipping as she ran from room to room. Before I was all the way inside, the TV blared on and my skin prickled. With caution, I tiptoed in and saw my dog sprawled in front of the TV.

"Wow, I don't think today could get any weirder; I don't know if I'll get used to a magic dog and being a witch." My Guardian's soft wet nose bumped me in the leg.

"What is it, what do you want?"

She barked and nudged at the dog food bag, almost tipping it over.

A laugh bellowed out of me. "Oh okay, you must be starving." I poured some food in her new bowl, which scraped on the hardwood floor as she gobbled up the food. Food flew as the pup scarfed it down. While she ate I petted her, and her soft fur under my fingers was like a downy blanket. She looked up at me with an almost human expression. But, again, two people I trusted had told me she had magic in her. Eventually, I knew I would get all my questions answered, but tonight was not the night.

After she finished eating, we trudged off in the direction of my room. I was exhausted from the day's excitement, but the puppy ran to every nook and cranny with curiosity. In the privacy of my room, I slipped into a pair of striped boy shorts and a comfy cotton t-shirt and crawled under the warm blankets. Before I even closed my eyes, I heard a soft whimper from the floor, so I peered down at her and picked her up. "Come on, little girl. Let's get some sleep. We have lots to do tomorrow."

Her tongue reached out and met my face, then she nestled beside me until she was under the covers, her warm body next to mine. Before long she was snoring, and the soft sounds calmed me and we both found sleep.

Dark red eyes stared out at me through the cypress trees; coarse black hair framed those evil eyes filled with hatred. From behind the ghostly tendrils of moss hanging from the glorious cypress trees, a presence took an interest in me and reached for me. As the creature did so, I tried to scream, but my muffled voice caught in my throat. He cocked his head at me as my fear registered on his face.

The next morning realization, and the dread that evil hunted me, made my heart pound a thunderous beat. From under the quilt, a tail wagged and wagged until one floppy ear and a black nose peaked from under the edge of the blanket. Her head popped out, and her blue eyes flashed to brown, settling on blue as she stared at me. Her head rested on my chest, my hands in her soft fur, and the smell of puppy breath calmed me.

I cupped her little head in my hands as she wagged her butt. "What do you think? Should we come up with a name? I can't keep calling you puppy!"

Before getting out of bed, I sat propped up on the pillows and tapped my chin. "It must be the name of a guardian, one of great stature. I have it!" I exclaimed. "Athena."

A high pitched yip came from the bed as she bounded around and around, pulling the sheets and quilt into a tangled mess with her intensified excitement. Soon she settled next to me, and the warmth that emitted from her brought a smile to my lips.

"Well, it's settled. And it's a fine name indeed." I ruffled her floppy ears then hopped out of bed, and a shiver went through me when my bare feet hit the cold hardwood floors. Under my bed, was an assortment of items. I dug around until I found my slippers, which had been pushed far under the bed. Slipping them on, I padded down the hallway to the kitchen. On our trek, Athena followed and nudged me with her nose. I laughed at the cobwebs draped over her nose after she'd sniffed every single corner and empty spot along the way. With her nose to the ground she found a dust bunny, but it ran from her every time her nose sniffed, so she chased it down the hall. I shook my head and laughed. "Come on, Athena, let's get breakfast."

She looked up at me, cocked her head, and followed me. In the kitchen, I pushed the button and the coffee pot made sputtering noises. The scent of chicory coffee permeated the air. Grabbing the items I'd bought the previous night, I poured a few kibbles into her metal bowl and placed it on the floor. Athena almost knocked me out of the way to get to her food.

"Geez, girl you must be starving." A small laugh escaped as I prepared to make breakfast. At the gas stove, the flame burned orange as I placed a small pot over it. When the tiny bubbles of milk hit the edges of the pot, I poured some into my ceramic mug and topped it off with the coffee and sugar. Steam rose and curled around the top of my mug as I folded my hands around it and took a sip. I placed two slices of bread into the toaster, and when they were ready, I spread a thick layer of creole cream cheese. I bit into my breakfast and took another sip of my coffee. After another bite, I began to read over my list of new items to buy for the store.

All of a sudden a rat-a-tat-tat sounded on my front door. A low growl from beside the table got louder the closer I got to the door. I peeked through the peep hole and turned to the dog. "Shh, Athena, it's only Julian."

When I opened the door, my breath caught in my chest. Julian leaned on the door frame, and my gaze took in all of his lean muscular body, and soaked in all his manliness.

"Come on in, Julian."

He pushed off the doorframe and sauntered into my house, and I shivered. I caught every movement of his relaxed body as it moved like a predator, whose sole purpose was to stalk his prey. The dark jeans he wore wrapped around his long, muscular legs showed off his assets, and my mind danced with ideas of how to rid him of them. Before I followed him, I stood by the door frame for support as he turned to face me.

His sexy smile, played havoc with my emotions. The emerald green cotton t-shirt showed off his well sculpted muscles, every ridge visible to the naked eye. The shade made his eyes even a darker shade of green, similar to lush grass after a rainstorm. Warm heat ran up the length of my neck to end at my cheeks as I noticed he'd caught me with my hand in the proverbial cookie jar. At the expectation of what was to come, I licked my lips.

Steady steps carried him further inside, and he leaned back with his elbows resting on the counter. His face lit up, and his mouth curled into a wicked smile. "You like what you see, mon cher?"

"Oh, yes I do." I sashayed over to him, and as I passed by him I brushed my hand over his tight, chiseled abs. I stopped for a brief moment, smiling as my fingers touched every crevice.

Athena barked and pulled me from my naughty thoughts. "What's up, girl?" Athena stood still as a statue, and my head played tennis as I looked from Julian to the dog. "Umm, sweetheart, would you like to meet Athena?"

"Sure thing." He took a small hesitant step towards the pup.

My dog stood there, and a low growl escalating to a loud one sprang from her chest. "I swear I have no idea what has gotten into her." I pivoted towards the dog and spoke sternly. "No, Athena, we don't growl at Julian." Out of nowhere the same little flutter from before flew through my head. I shook my head and turned to Julian. "I'll be back." For a brief moment, his eyes seemed to change to a dark red. Quickly I blinked, and they had changed back to his normal green. "Oh, wow, my imagination must be playing tricks on me today."

Once Athena was safe in my room, I ignored her constant scratching and pawing at the door to get out. But, the warning in the note from my momma popped back into my head. The thought of Julian harming me seemed ridiculous, so I removed it from my mind and sighed, "It's Julian."

A hot, smoldering, come-hither stare from the world's sexiest man met me the moment I set foot back in the kitchen. The scent of sex now poured from him, and his want and need for me came off in waves and floated around me.

When I was closer to him, he folded me into his arms. His heartbeat reverberated hard against my body. My heart pounded deep in my chest in rhythm to his, and it made me lean closer to him. When his mouth claimed mine, I fell into his embrace and my body molded to his. A muffled moan slipped from my mouth at the large arousal against my stomach.

"Julian," I breathed out as he kept kissing me. "Why are you here?"

His low raspy chuckle warmed me all the way to my toes. "'To see you, Rosie. I told you I wanted to contact you. I texted you, and when you didn't answer, I came to check on you."

My purse lay haphazardly on the sofa, so I grabbed it and shuffled the contents around until I found my phone on the bottom. Pulling it out, my fingers pushed the button to turn it on. "Damn, it's dead; sorry, Julian." I spun around to face him and quickly plugged it in. "So, what did you have in mind to do today?" I smirked up at him.

"How would you like to visit the zoo?" he asked me.

Exuberance overtook me as I clapped my hands like a little girl. "Oh, yes, Julian. I haven't been to the zoo since Jahane and I went when we were young." A joyous feeling encompassed me. "Ooh, ooh, Julian, can we take a pic on the bear statue, puhleeasse?" I begged, and laughed, trying to hide my excitement.

"For you, Rosie, anything you want to do, we'll do." He quirked a smile at me.

"Oh, but Julian, what will I do with Athena?"

"She'll be fine here; we won't be gone long."

My mother's message played over and over in my head, then I remembered she'd said my Guardian would always be with me. *What harm could it do leaving her by herself for one day?* I asked myself.

"Oh, all right, I'll be back. Let me get dressed."

"Do you need any help?"

"No, sir, I don't want to miss the zoo." His laughter followed me to my room.

Once I was dressed, I filled Athena's metal bowl to the brim with the crunchy dog food and left enough water in her other bowl. "Okay, let me text Jahane and ask her to check on my dog." After I sent the text, I ushered Julian out the door and clicked the lock. Hand in hand, we walked down the street to The St. Charles Streetcar. The car started to move as we approached, so we ran the rest of the way to catch it. Out of breath, Julian helped me up the steps. One seat was left, so I scooted in and stared out the window as the streetcar began to move. Julian's fingers intertwined with mine and his sweet, lingering, kisses on my knuckles gave me the chills.

"Rosie, I'm glad you're back." With his confession, he pulled me closer to him. The essence of him as I snuggled closer made the world around me disappear except for the clickety-clack of the streetcar on its journey to the Audubon Zoo.

"I am too, Julian." My lips met his for a small, intimate kiss.

The closer we got to the zoo, the more my excitement flowed, and I got antsy. I sat up in my seat, wishing we would go faster. When we stopped, we jumped off the car and ran the few blocks to our destination. I stood by the gates, tapped my toe on the ground impatiently, and crossed my arms over my chest as I waited for Julian to purchase our tickets.

He turned to me and waved the tickets. "Where to first, Rosie?" He laced his fingers with mine as we entered the grounds.

With a sigh, I looked around and saw the bear statue was no longer there. Disappointed, I thought for a minute. "Oh, Julian, I want to see the white tigers. You know how I love the jungle cats." I pleaded smiling.

"Okay, my Rosie, the big cats it will be." He winked at me and led me down the path to the cat enclosure.

Loud roars, chirping, and other sounds escalated as we headed down the brick path, passing enclosure after enclosure. Around the corner, the birds chirped louder and their wings flapped in a tizzy. My head pivoted around to look up at him. "What do you think has gotten into them?"

"No tellin'." He shrugged.

Throngs of people stood in front of the iron fence enclosing the tigers. Being in such close proximity to Julian sent waves of dizziness through my body, but when he placed kisses on the top of my head, and his strong arms wrapped around my waist, every other person there ceased to exist.

In the enclosure below us, the magnificent jungle cats sprawled lazily in the grass and dirt. One of the giant white cats picked his head up and scanned the crowd, his nose and whiskers twitching in the air. The tiger's pink tongue lolled out of his mouth, showing a hint of his sharp canines. His gaze fell upon Julian and me, and his stare fixated on us for a few moments. The cat stretched his massive body, stood and stalked toward us. Deep rivets in the ground were left as the tiger pursued us, and the people's excitement increased at its calculated movements.

"Look, Mommy," a little girl exclaimed. "The big kitty is walking around." Her squeal became louder as it synced with her excitement. The closer the tiger tracked, the harder she tugged on her mother's arm.

"Yes, Candice, I see, sweetie," her mother replied.

My gaze stayed glued to the tiger, and I watched the intensity with which he paced back and forth. His roars became louder and seemed more agitated with every step he took. My intuition sensed a disturbance in the air, and I wondered if that was the cause for the tiger's anger. Flashes and clicks from a dozen cameras went off as the tiger roared, its canines dripping with saliva.

"Julian, let's go to another exhibit." My voice was tinted with fear.

He looked down at me. "Mais, Rosie, I have never seen the tigers move this much."

"Come on, Julian," I squeaked, trying to hide my worry. The hair on my neck and arms started to prickle along my skin.

The crowd grew as the magnificent jungle animal was joined by his brother. The two tigers perused the habitat around them like well-refined hunters. With each step of their paws, they inched closer and closer to the front of the enclosure. "Oohs" and "ahhs" echoed throughout the crowd as they moved.

"Please, Julian, I want to go see the seals." My panic rose as I clenched his sleeve to pull him away.

I skimmed the crowd for a way to get out. Behind the throngs of people stood a looming figure in dark sunglasses and a hat pulled down to shield his face, staring straight in my direction. In utter shock, my mouth fell open as I tried to figure out why he seemed intrigued by me. My head whipped around to look for Julian, but a loud commotion stole my attention. Out of my peripheral vision, I saw one tiger jump at the fence enclosing the habitat and snarl at the crowd. His huge paws clung tightly to the fence as he tried to climb over. Strings of saliva dripped from his teeth as he snapped at the fence.

"Help, the tigers are trying to get out!"

The screams echoed in my head and I saw three zoo keepers with dart guns run to the back gate behind the enclosure. People scrambled in a blur, and loud screams resonated as the tiger tried to claw his way over the fence.

"Watch where you're going," Julian bellowed, and pulled me closer to him as a group of frightened people almost trampled me.

As the people dispersed, a blood curdling scream rang out, and for a split second I sensed the air around me grow ice cold as it passed straight through me.

"Candice! Oh my gawd! Oh my baby, oh my baby, wake up, Candice." The mother's scream broke my heart.

My gaze followed the screams to the still body of the little girl on the ground. Wrenching myself from Julian's tight hold, I rushed over to the mother and the little girl and knelt beside them as the mother sobbed and held the little girl in her lap, rocking back and forth. Her pain sliced through me.

"Someone call 911!" I screamed at the crowd. "What happened ma'am?" I asked her.

The woman's body shook as she tried to form her words. "She got knocked down, and the air turned cold around us. It was as if…I could feel something around us." She stopped. "You're going to think I'm crazy."

"No ma'am, I won't, trust me."

"It's like an odd sensation. You know the old saying 'it felt like someone walked over your grave.'" She started crying and held on to her daughter.

I couldn't breathe, and then I felt Julian's presence surround me. Feeling his calming effects, I assessed the little girl's breathing. Fear developed when my fingers touched her neck. Her pulse was weak, and it was getting weaker. *Please don't let her die.*

A man's voice pulled me from my thoughts to let me know the ambulance would be there in ten minutes. I smoothed back the little girl's hair, and when she started to stir, I checked her pulse again. The more I touched her, the stronger it seemed to get.

"Sweetie, you'll be just fine," I whispered in her ear.

A hand grasped mine, and I heard a low voice. "Thank you."

My head turned to see the sad face of a mother worried for her child's welfare staring at me. Flashbacks of my mother slammed into my head, but I quickly dislodged them. "Ma'am, she'll be fine."

Finally the paramedics arrived. One of them came up to me and asked, "What happened, ma'am?"

"I'm not sure, sir. She went down after all the commotion," I answered, and headed back over to Julian.

I watched as her mother made sure her daughter was safely strapped onto a stretcher, then ran over to me with tears still in her eyes. "Thank you, young lady. How can I ever repay you?" She asked me as she enclosed me in her motherly embrace.

For a brief moment when I returned her embrace, it felt as if it was my mother's arms wrapped around me. I pulled back slightly. "Please make sure she's not scared to come back to the zoo, ma'am."

"Ma'am, we're ready; we need to get to the hospital." The EMT ushered the woman over to the waiting vehicle. A man standing by the ambulance spoke to the mother, they got inside the vehicle, and the sirens blared.

After the ambulance drove off, I remembered the strange man I'd seen, but when I glanced back to the spot where he'd been, it was vacant. Shrugging my shoulders, I laced my fingers through Julian's. Before we left, we looked over at the enclosure. Over the fence we saw the tigers out cold and stretched out on their sides. Their loud snores resonated through the air.

"When were they tranquilized?" I wondered aloud.

"Not sure. Mais, we were wrapped up in what had happened with the little girl. What do you think happened, Rosie?"

"Julian, I have no idea." I decided not to mention the mysterious man or the cold air which had passed through me before the little girl collapsed.

The tender kisses he placed on my palm instantly soothed me. "Now, where would you like to go next, Rosie?"

"Let's go visit the Louisiana exhibit and see what's new." I nudged him with my hip. "Come on, let's go," I giggled, and ran off ahead of him.

He caught up to me, grabbed me, and threw me over his shoulder. From my view, his ass looked scrumptious. "Put me down, Julian, we are getting stared at by little old ladies." As he laughed, I took the opportunity to slap him on the ass.

Julian stopped, and I slid down his body slowly, letting each body part tease him. "Rosie, my dear, you know it's because they're jealous." I turned around and headed in the opposite direction. He caught up to me, laughed, and popped me on the ass.

"Oh, come on, Julian." I dragged him towards the Louisiana swamp exhibit. After a fun filled day at the zoo, which thankfully included no other strange incidents, we headed home, and I realized the first happiness I'd felt since my mother had disappeared.

Back at my place, I unlocked the door and the sexy man beside me pulled me towards his rock hard body, walking me backwards into the room until I bumped into the wall. With his mouth pressed against mine, my legs became jello, and I gripped the back of his shirt in a fist to stop myself from ending up on the floor. He pushed harder into me and pressed me against the wall. My fingers gripped his shirt tighter as our kiss intensified, sending explosions to consume my body.

Finally able to wrench my hands around, my palms rested on his broad chest. My breathing was heavy as I pushed back.

"Would you like something to eat?" I asked, resting my hands on my hips, hoping he would stay.

A wicked gleam brightened his emerald eyes, and he licked his lips. "Are you on the menu, cher?" His mischievous grin made me want to rip his clothes off and throw them all over the place. Still close to me, he nipped my earlobe, and the sensation of his teeth on me sent me almost over the edge.

Fire scorched my face at his question. "No, Mr. Quibadeaux…maybe later, but first I can whip up a pot of Andouille sausage jambalaya. And for dessert, how does bread pudding with rum sauce sound?" I breathed out.

"Hmmm, it sounds delicious, Rosie." He bent down to place a tender kiss on my shoulder.

I detached myself from his body, but before I started cooking, I walked to the counter and picked my phone up. A text message blinked at me.

I checked on Athena and she is sleeping in your room. Love you, Jahane.

A smile curved on my lips at what a wonderful best friend I had.

Julian followed me, his steps close to mine, and when he reached me, he spun me around. His index finger tilted my chin up, and I gazed into his beautiful deep green eyes, his body mere inches from mine. "Do you also have French bread?" His voice was husky and sexy.

I playfully slapped him in faux shock and hurt. "Duh, of course. What is jambalaya without buttery French bread?"

"Good, because I don't think I would've been able to stay," he grinned.

I rolled my eyes at him. "So, Mr. Quibadeaux, would you like to help me?" I winked at him.

He dipped his head down and brushed his soft lips against mine. "It would be my honor to help you, Miss Delacroix." I giggled as I reached into the fridge and grabbed a few ingredients.

"Julian, can you chop these please?" I handed him a stalk of celery, an onion, and a green bell pepper.

"Of course." He nodded at me, opened a drawer, and removed a knife.

My back to him, I clutched the handle of the Dutch oven. "Wait, Rosie, let me get that for you," he said after he saw me struggle with the heavy cast iron pot.

Once the giant black pot was over the burner, I turned the flame up. It danced underneath, heating the pan as I began to make a roux. Wooden spoon in hand, I stirred the oil and flour together until it had a smooth consistency and a dark coffee color. Julian came over and dropped the vegetables he'd chopped and the sausage into the pot. Before long, the aromas of the dish drifted through the kitchen.

Julian disappeared into the pantry, and I wondered what he was up to. After a few moments, he sauntered back out with a bottle of wine in his hand. I smiled and waved my spoon at him. "If I didn't know better, I would almost think you were going to try and get me drunk," I said in my best Scarlett O'Hara voice, and smiled.

The cork popped, flew into the air, and sputtered to the ground as he winked at me. "Who, me?" He placed a hand over his heart. "I would never do such a thing," he replied in his best Rhett Butler imitation.

Once our dinner was cooked and ready to eat, I scooped the jambalaya into a bowl and placed the warm, buttered French bread on the plates. When I bent down to check the bread pudding in the oven, a strong hand grabbed and cupped my ass. "Julian," I squealed, and jumped.

He laughed. "I couldn't help it, Rosie, it just begged me to grab it." His roguish grin crinkled the corners of his lips as his strong capable hands grabbed both plates and placed them on the table. I filled our glasses with the muscadine wine, grabbed some forks and the Tabasco sauce, and followed him.

As we sat across from each other and ate our dinner in silence, I watched Julian devour his food.

"It must be good."

All he did was put another bite into his mouth and nod. The last of the crunchy French bread on the plate called out to me, so I reached for it. I took a bite, and the butter dripped off and onto my chin.

"Cher, you are so sexy with butter dripping from your chin," he joked as he reached over and wiped it off with his finger, placing it seductively into his mouth.

"Geez, Julian, is sex always on your mind?" My face burned furiously when he smirked at me.

After we'd finished, he stood up and grabbed the dishes and headed into the kitchen. A few minutes later, he returned carrying two small plates with bread pudding soaked in rum sauce and the bottle of wine.

I scooped some of the bread pudding from my plate and slid the spoon into my mouth. "Mmm." My mind reeled and my taste buds went on overload at the taste of the dessert sent from heaven. With slow and methodical movements, I slid the spoon back down my tongue before dipping it back into the orgasmic delicacy. Tiny bits of rum sauce trickled down my lips, so with a flick of my tongue, I licked any remnants. Afterwards, my eyebrows hitched up and my mouth curved into a devilish grin with thoughts of a well-deserved second helping. While I delved into my sensuous dessert, Julian's eyes sparkled and intensified at the sight of me. With his green gaze focused on me, I took a much bigger bite this time.

"Ahem. Rosie, I would like to ask you a question."

I stopped mid bite and smiled at the look on his face. "Uh sary, wad whar do sarvin?" I hurried to swallow the rest of my bite and sipped some of my wine to help wash it down. The muscadine grapes infused with a hint of blueberries electrified the bits of raisins and rum sauce as it rolled around on my tongue.

He shook his head, and a wicked grin curled his succulent lips.

"What?" I asked, pretending to be shocked. "You know how I've an envie for bread pudding." My hazel eyes lowered at my use of his favorite Cajun word when he was in the mood, but I had to smile

"Yes, I do, Rosie." He cocked a brow at me. "Mais, if you don't let me ask you this question, I may be inclined to take you and the rum sauce into the bedroom." He nodded in the direction of my room, and his look of lust had a sudden intensity to it.

A low moan escaped my throat and a deep burning consumed my cheeks at the thought of Julian licking rum sauce off my naked body. The thought triggered something deep inside me and wetness began to pool between my legs. The look on his face was comical as he watched me shift in my chair.

"Anyway, Rosie, want to go to a parade or two with me? It could be like the old days, and I know we'd have fun."

"Damn, I forgot it was almost Mardi Gras, it's around the corner, isn't it?" I did a mental face palm and groaned.

"Yes, Rosie." He sat there, a nervous smile on his face, like at any moment I would crush his dreams.

I smiled back at him. "Of course, Julian, I would love to."

As I smiled at him, we were interrupted as Athena suddenly came bounding into the room. She plopped down in front of me with her tongue lolling out the corner of her mouth. She placed her head on my lap, and I ruffled her ears. "Hey girl, how did you get out of the room?" Her eyes looked up at me, as she lifted her paw and promptly placed it in my lap. "Ow!" I exclaimed. "Why the hell does your paw weigh a ton, and why does it look huge?" I picked up her paw, flipped it over, and inspected it. "Well, girl, it does look like you will be huge. I'm amazed at your size in such a small amount of time. Though, I think a trip to the vet to weigh you is in order."

I struggled until I had removed her paw from my lap, but finally it was on the floor. Dishes in hand, I scooted around the table and stepped into the kitchen. Julian stepped away from the table and headed in the direction of the living room. Off in the distance, the raspy voice of Stevie Nicks engulfed the room with music so alive you could almost touch and taste it. As I put away the dishes in the kitchen, I felt Julian's strong arms wrap around my waist. He brushed my long hair from my neck and nibbled down the back of it and around to my collarbone. Shivers erupted with every seductive nip of his teeth.

"The dishes can wait, cher." He twisted me around and led me into the living room. He ushered me with his hand on my lower back, then wrapped his arms around me and nestled me closer to him as we began to sway to the music.

Our eyes met when I lifted my head and whispered, "I will always love you, Julian." My confession finally out of my mouth, I snuggled even closer to him.

After the song ended, he tilted my head back and gazed into my deep hazel eyes. His brilliant smile lit me up from the inside out, and his green eyes sparkled even deeper the more his gaze penetrated me. My heart exploded with a ton of emotions, one being amazement he would forgive me for leaving without any kind of explanation. He leaned down and his mouth caressed mine, and dozens of reactions rolled through me like a powerful rainstorm. With every movement of his tongue, I sighed and realized with every fiber of my body I would never again want to let him go. His lips trailed their way to my ear and he friskily nipped my earlobe.

With his mouth still next to my ear, his whisper tickled. "I will text you tomorrow and set up a time, and we can get together and go to the

Krewe of Endymion Parade. Maybe Jahane would like to come with us."

Still in close proximity to him, his soft cotton shirt rubbed against my face and I breathed in his woodsy scent. "I would love to go with you."

His calloused hands on either side of my face, he kissed me goodnight one last time, then leaned down and whispered in my ear. "Rosie, save some of the rum sauce for the next time I am over." Julian pulled back with a wicked grin as the heat spread from my cheeks to my neck.

CHAPTER 5

The next few days flew by without any evil dreams, for which I was grateful. But, deep down, I knew the dreams would start again. Deep in thought, the toe of my tennis shoe dug at stray grass in a crack outside the entrance to my courtyard as my Guardian and I waited for Jahane and Julian. Athena pranced around and sniffed everyone who passed, but when Julian and Jahane approached us, she growled at him.

"Stop it," I told her. She whimpered in protest, and the ever present flutter went through my head.

Jahane ran in my direction and began her god-awful gibberish when she saw my dog. "Awww, how's ooh baby puppy? Yous so coote today, aren't wuue?"

The laughter inside me erupted at the incessant baby talk, and my dog's head shifted from side to side until it rested on Jahane and she licked her. I shook my head at the display between the two.

"Jahane, could you please stop talking to my dog like she's an infant? She's a Guardian." Jahane rolled her eyes at me, took the leash from me, and headed towards the parade route.

Julian stood beside me and watched me shake my head at my friend's and my dog's retreating figures. He draped a long arm around me, and for a brief moment, I leaned into his embrace. His hard body felt good as mine melded into his. His muscular arms dropped to wrap around my waist, he pulled me to face him, and his lips met mine for a toe curling kiss. The air around us warmed and swirled as we kissed. I smiled as he pulled back from me and brushed a hand through his long brown hair. His emerald eyes sparkled, his intense gaze penetrating my soul and touching every fiber of it.

"Are you ready to go?" I asked him.

With a wicked grin he said, "Well now, that all depends on you, Miss Rosie. What will you show me for a few of them beads?" he said, his Cajun accent thicker with lust.

Faux shock registered on my face, and a playful slap connected with his shoulder. Before he could react, I ran to catch up to Jahane and my Guardian.

When we arrived at Canal Street, it was littered with throngs of people. A few too many breasts were being brazenly shown, and as I scanned the crowd, two cops headed towards the two females with their shirts raised. They exchanged words with them, and I glanced over to Julian and pulled his face to mine, mouthing the word "no." He looked abashed and mouthed, "Mais, I only have eyes for yours, cher."

"Rosie." Jahane's frantic wave had us scrambling over to join her. We reached her just in time to see the fire trucks roll down the street with their sirens blaring, which signaled the start of the parade. Jahane inclined her head to me and whispered. "Hey, did you hear who will be the grand marshal of the Krewe of Endymion?"

I shook my head. "Who?"

A mischievous smile played across her face.

"Wait and see, my dear friend."

Float after float full of decadence outdid the one before it. With a large shit-eating grin plastered on my face, I yelled, "Throw me something, mista." Every jump up and down brought more beads from the air into my arms.

When the next one rolled into view, my mouth dropped open, and for a split second my body was frozen in place. Ian Somerhalder looked down from his spot on the float, and I swore he looked right at me. His knee-weakening smile threw me off guard, and I was surprised I managed to catch the group of beads he tossed in my direction. My hands held tight to the bundle of beads with a sensation of euphoria.

But my jubilation suddenly faltered and was replaced with an eerie sensation evil lurked in the shadows of the crowds. The hair on the back of my neck rose as I perused the horde of people.

Across the street, a dark figure emerged from a narrow space between two buildings. The figure was cloaked all in black, and two bright red eyes stared out from under his tattered hood. A scream developed in my throat, but was muffled by the throng of Mardi Gras revelers clustered around me. Suddenly, the noise silenced, and I blinked.

When I focused on the shimmering figure once again, it placed its long boney finger to its lips. "Shhh," it said silently, and then disappeared.

Fear threatened to encompass me, and when I reached for Julian, my hand touched only air, absent of him. Before my panic could take over, a head full of fur bumped my hand. One look at my dog and I burst into a nervous fit of laughter. She was covered in beads, and when she turned her head, her ears flopped with the movement. Her expression read, *Yes Mom, I'm the shitz.* I shook my head as I laughed at the dog.

Once the parade was over, I began to panic again as Julian's absence hit me like a ton of bricks.

"Jahane, have you seen Julian?"

"No." She shook her head. "It got crowded."

"Where in the world could he have gone?"

Jahane and I walked back to Bourbon Street as my Guardian tugged on the leash. Finally, on the other side of the street I saw Julian. His quick, measured steps hurried towards us.

"Where did you go?" My voice rose in an exasperated tone.

Athena's leash slipped from my hands as I rushed toward him. He caught me as I bounced off his chest and held me, and with his intent gaze, he searched my worried face. "I had to go to the bathroom, and as you well know, Rosie, there are no bathrooms on the parade route."

A low exhale escaped my mouth. Deep down, I knew Julian hadn't been truthful with me, and the wind once again stirred around us in a sinister manner. But as soon as the air swirled, it settled and I relaxed. He dipped his head down, and his teeth tugged on my bottom lip. When my mouth opened, my body whirled with at least a dozen sensations of emotions and passion. Wicked thoughts of me up against a wall with my legs wrapped around his waist popped into my head, and a grin spread slowly across my face.

"Come on, Julian." We walked together to where Jahane and Athena stood. As we continued down Bourbon Street, decadence spread through the street in full swing. A few people stumbled out of the bars, drunk, and Julian quickly pulled me out of the way before their drinks were spilled on me. As the partiers continued down the street, their drinks sloshed out of their plastic cups without a second thought about us.

After a few moments strolling down and passing bars on either side of the street, my stomach growled.

"Rosie, why don't we go get a bite to eat and catch up?" Julian whispered in my ear, and his hot warm breath tickled my skin. The passion he had for me poured off him in waves. My body heated at his touch as he linked his fingers with mine.

"Yes, baby, let's go."

I turned to Jahane as she spoke to a guy outside of the bars. "Hey, Jahane, we're headed to get some dinner by the river and catch up." I winked at her as she hugged us goodbye.

She patted Julian on the shoulder. "Now, don't you go taking advantage of my bestie. Oh, hell…better yet, y'all may be in need of taking advantage of each other," she said, wiggling her eyebrows.

He shook his head at my best friend and laughed. "Damn, she must be a handful," Julian said as she submersed herself into the crowd.

The wind blew as we walked hand in hand down the street to Jax Brewery. A contented silence fell over us on the walk, and Athena stayed close, almost leaning on me with each step. At our destination, Julian placed a hand on my lower back and guided me up the steps to the little balcony overlooking the river. The night air grew breezier, and when we stepped out onto the balcony, wisps of my hair blew across my face. My hand slipped free from his, and I trailed it along the railing. When I stopped, I observed how the moonlight danced and reflected off the dark river water.

"You know, Julian, I love the city at night: the way the water ripples as the wind blows across it, and the river has a unique smell of fresh water."

"Hmm." His hands rolled over my shoulders; his presence was irresistible, and had me leaning into him. His hunger for me overpowered everything else at the moment. Two strong arms twisted my body around to face him. A slight touch of his finger caressed my cheek, and then he brushed a stray hair from my face and tucked it behind my ear.

"Julian." I breathed out as I arched my head back to reveal my neck, and he bent his head down, his feather light kisses trailing up to my ear. Once again, his kiss on my earlobe ignited full blown embers that burned deep and long. My arms circled around his broad shoulders. When they moved down his solid arms, every muscle tensed under my touch. His kisses lingered first on my cheek and ended at my lips.

"Oh, cher, how I've missed you," he spoke against my lips. His deep voice tantalized my body and made it tingle all over. Our kiss got even more heated as our tongues danced together, and I could feel him smile as he pulled back and nipped my lip when our kiss got hotter. His strong muscular hands caressed my body and caused me to moan in his mouth.

From somewhere behind us the sound of someone clearing their throat pulled me into reality. "What can I bring y'all to drink? And, sir, we have a no pets allowed rule in the establishment."

Without even a glance in the direction of the voice, Julian reached in his pocket and pulled out a twenty dollar bill and passed it behind him. "This, sir, is my girlfriend's aid dog, and we would like two glasses of your best red wine, please."

"Yes, sir, and I will bring two menus," our server said as he took the money and headed back inside, with what I could guess was a giant smile plastered on his face.

The sexy man in front of me, the love of my life, continued his assault on my lips, which already felt puffy from all the havoc wreaked on them. I ran my hands down his hard sculpted back and felt his muscles flex as my hands touched every muscle.

"Rosie, I love the feel of your lips on mine." He leaned in closer. "I would love nothing more than to take you here on the balcony." Our kiss intensified as Julian grabbed my ass and squeezed.

Before I could push him away, my stomach growled. I bowed my head and smiled with a hint of embarrassment. "Come on, honey, you know there's plenty of time for kissing and fondling," I said, and directed him to the table. "Let's have a seat."

The forlorn look that coated his face almost made me giggle, but as soon as it appeared it quickly disappeared, and he smiled at me. He leaned down, "Of course, anything for you, cher" and kissed me on the nose. Damn, the touch of his lips sent electrical tingles down my spine. He pulled me towards the table and pulled my chair out. I watched him walk around the table and wanted badly to forgo the food, but by stomach growled once more in protest. He sat, reached across the table, took my hand, and began to trace the lines on my palm. Shivers continued to plague me from his touch, and his mesmerizingly green gaze proved how much he loved me.

"Cher, you are the most beautiful and amazing woman I've ever known. I missed you so much while you were gone." His eyes lowered at his confession.

A slow wave of heat crept across my face. My hand still in his, his touch lingered as his emerald eyes held my gaze.

"Oh, Julian." I wondered silently how I had gotten so lucky to have such a man as this. His fingers moved up from my palm to my arm and sent fiery sparks through my body. Before I uttered another word, we were interrupted by glasses clinking on the table, and my gaze shifted up as a menu was slid in front of me.

"I'll give you a few moments, sir," the server told Julian.

Julian nodded, rubbed his temples, and leaned back, his long lean legs stretched out under the table.

"Julian, are you okay?" Concern was etched throughout my voice.

"Cher, I'll be fine; nothing to worry your gorgeous head about." He smiled and used his charming skills to keep me off guard.

I shrugged, flipped open my menu, and tried to find something to whet my ravenous appetite. When the server came back, I gave him my order. "I would like the fried shrimp appetizer, the green salad with avocado dressing, and the grilled chicken with cream sauce."

Julian grinned at me the entire time I rattled off my order. He handed his menu to the server, laughed, and winked at me. "I will just have the shrimp etouffee. Besides, I have a feeling Miss Delacroix won't be eating all her food."

When the server turned on his heel, I promptly stuck my tongue out at Julian and took a sip of my wine. *Damn, he is insufferable, but correct.* He leaned back further in his chair, crossed his hands behind his head, and bellowed out a laugh. Determination scrunched up my face and my expression must have given me away, because the wicked smile on Julian's face summed it all up.

His body leaned over the table, and his voice crooned, "You are quite something to behold." He laughed as he reached under the table to grab my foot before it made contact with his leg.

"What if it was going to be a love kick?" I joked.

"Sure it was." He winked and kept ahold of my foot and rubbed my ankle with steady fingers.

A plate of fried shrimp was placed in front of us. I popped one in my mouth.

"So Julian, how is work?"

"Work is fine," he said mid bite.

A shrimp dangled in my hand as I tried to figure out my next sentence. "Baby, I'm so sorry for the pain I caused you." The shrimp dropped from my fingers as I reached across the table, grabbed his hand, and placed a soft kiss upon it.

"Hey, what's done is done. What matters now is you're here to stay," he prodded.

"Of course I'm here to stay."

The door behind us opened, and a server with steaming plates of food upon a tray walked up to our table.

"Enjoy, and if you need anything else, please let me know." He refilled our glasses and left us to enjoy our delightful dinner.

We ate in silence and relished every bite. After I was finished with most of my food, I looked over to see Athena staring at me.

"Here ya go, Athena." I cut off a piece of chicken and offered it to her. Once she had taken it, I slumped back in my chair, satisfied. The waiter came over and brought the bill out, filled my glass, and removed the plates.

"Hey, cher, you're supposed to have that look only after I have had my way with you and you are sated." He wiggled his brows and teased. My grin was lax as sleep wanted to take hold of me. "Come on, let's get you home and tucked into bed." He hoisted me up out of the chair and took my small hand in his. He dropped a few ten dollar bills down on the table and shifted the candle holder over the edges to keep them from flying off.

During the walk home, I leaned into Julian's body, his arms wrapped around me like a blanket. When I spotted a mule drawn carriage sitting along Decatur Street, I tugged on Julian's sleeve and inclined my head towards the mule. "Before we go home, can we please go on a ride?"

He looked at me. "Are you sure you aren't tired? You aren't scared of the mules?" he asked.

"Yes, I'm sure; it's been long enough, and I have no ill will towards these animals for my accident. After all, it was an accident."

We both strolled across the street and Julian headed to the carriage driver. They spoke for a minute or two, Julian handed the grey haired gentleman some money, and then helped me into the waiting cushions of the carriage. The driver helped Athena in since she snarled at Julian when he tried.

"Hello, my name is Louis. So where would y'all like to go tonight?" This man's voice gave off an air of formality.

"We would like to experience a tour of this beautiful city so we can finish our romantic night," Julian replied.

"Sure thing, sir," Louis said as he held the reins in his hands, and the mule ambled down the street.

Wrapped in Julian's jacket, I snuggled against him while a slight breeze blew around us. The mule's hooves clip-clopped as we made our way through the French Quarter.

"It's a beautiful night to enjoy a carriage ride," Louis said.

"It sure is, sir," Julian replied, and pulled me closer to him.

The night air was cool and the streets were packed with people everywhere I looked. When our ride was over, Julian tipped Louis well for his kindness.

As Louis helped me out of the carriage, he looked at me. "I remember you, young lady, though you were much younger."

"You do, sir?" I questioned with shock, and tried to remember if I knew him.

"You look as if you've healed well." He winked and hopped back into the cab of his carriage.

Within moments I recognized him...well, not him but his voice.

Louis headed off in the direction of the French Market. I turned to Julian and watched as he stared after the man.

"Oh Julian, he was the man who helped calm me when I had my accident with the mule," I remarked, and smiled in the direction the man had gone.

As we walked the few blocks to my apartment, Julian draped an arm over my shoulder and held me very tight against him. We walked through the dark tunnel and headed inside my courtyard. Athena bounded up the steps with more ease this time; she tumbled once. When she was at the top, she barked at me, and a flutter flowed through my head again.

"Goodnight, cher."

After a long, lingering kiss goodnight, I turned on my heel and scurried up the steps. Before I stepped over the threshold, I glanced over my shoulder. Julian stood there leaning on the rail, looking up at me with a devilish grin.

"Get inside, Rosie."

A small laugh came out, and my Guardian and I scooted inside and shut the door. I pulled the tiny half curtain back and peeked out the window. When I turned back around, my back leaning against the door, my fingertips touched my puffy lips and I savored the taste of his mouth on mine.

"Come on, Athena, let's go get some rest." She bounded off down the hall straight for my bedroom.

CHAPTER 6

Dressed in jeans and a pink cami, I pulled my hair up with some clips and let a few loose strands fall from the arrangement and frame my face. Since my birthday plans had been interrupted when Athena arrrived, Jahane insisted we go to my favorite club. A deep bark resonated through the apartment at the knock on the door.

"Hold on, I'm coming," I yelled.

I hurried and finished clasping my bracelet to my wrist, grabbed a tube of lip gloss, and plopped it in my purse as I headed to the front door. When I flung the door open, two goofy ass grins greeted me.

"Happy birthday to youuu, happy birthday to youuu, you live in a zooo." Both Jahane and Julian sang off key like a pig was being slaughtered. I cringed and stepped back. When Athena began howling in unison with their song, I couldn't help but laugh.

"Here, these are for you," Julian said, handing me a bouquet of pink flowers.

"Julian, these flowers are so beautiful. Thank you." I tippie toed to reach him and gave him an affectionate kiss. The bouquet in hand, I walked to the kitchen and arranged the flowers in a vase, then turned to the still singing Jahane. "All right, guys, let's go before you have the police called on us." I laughed and pushed her towards the door.

"Oh, Rosie, we aren't that bad, are we?" Jahane asked with her lips turned into a pout.

"Jahane, you made the dog howl, which is never a good sign," I joked, and cocked one eyebrow at her.

Julian's lips twitched at my joke. The three of us and my Guardian left my little apartment and stepped into the now muggy air. "Wow, this weather never stops surprising me."

We boarded the street car to "Les Bon Temps Roule." The ride was quick, and at our stop, we all bustled off and strolled to the club. The heavy wooden door opened, and I came face to face with my favorite bouncer, Derrick. He stood as tall as Julian but with more muscles, which served him well in his job. He had a massive frame, and you never could tell where his shoulders ended and his neck began. His skin tone was the color of well brewed coffee.

A grin crossed his lips when he noticed me. He lumbered over to me, lifted me, and held me in a bear hug.

"Derrick, I can't breathe," I squeaked out as my feet dangled in the air.

When I slid down and my feet once again touched the floor, I stared up at him, wide eyed.

"Rosie, it's been too long since you've been here."

"I know, but I'm back."

He leaned into me and whispered in my ear. "Sorry about your mom."

"Thank you," I replied as his body engulfed mine, only this time I stayed grounded.

Before he stood back up, I spotted Jahane coyly focused on Derrick's ass while she held on tightly to my dog's leash. "Jahane, what the hell…?" Derrick pulled back, and my eyes darted back and forth between the two of them standing there all googly-eyed at each other.

"Uh…uh…it's…," she stammered.

"Okay, guys, spill it, what the hell is going on with…?" My hands firmly planted on my hips, I tapped my foot and demanded an explanation. But before I could get my whole sentence out, Derrick scooped her up and kissed her flat on the lips. My friend had held out on me, judging by the blatant public display of affection. "Um, bestie, Derrick is your mystery man, huh?"

Julian tapped me on the shoulder. "I'll go get us a table, Rosie." He winked at Jahane and Derrick over my shoulder, but it was not missed by me.

Once Jahane was back down on the ground, she grinned up at her beau with a tint of pink in her cheeks. "I've never seen you blush before," I said.

"It happened after you left, Rosie," she replied as she gushed at Derrick.

"Well, if it had to be anyone, you picked a winner with Derrick." His grin covered his entire face at my blessing of their relationship. "Uh, huh you two, I'm off to find Julian. You two make sure you come enjoy the show with us." I took Athena's offered leash from Jahane.

Derrick reached down to pet the dog and squared his shoulders. "Anyone give you shit about your dog in here, you come let me know." His voice boomed and some of the people in the club glanced over at us.

Headed in the direction of the stage, I saw Julian at a table, so I made my way through the tables to where he sat with an Abita beer in his hand. I watched him as he took the lime sitting on the edge of the bottle and squeezed it down the long neck. When he was done he pushed it through until it plopped down into the carbonated liquid, where it bobbed up and down a bit. Finally, he noticed me standing there, and he turned to stare. With his attention diverted, the bubbles slowly crawled up and overflowed down the sides of the bottle.

"Rosie, come sit." He smiled, and without ever taking his eyes from my body, he picked the bottle up, placed it to his mouth, and took a swig. His lips let go from around the bottle to hold the lime that had previously danced around in his beer. He sucked hard on it and smiled up at me. With his other hand, he reached over and scooted my chair out for me.

Taking my seat, I began my interrogation. "So, how long have you known about those two?" I inclined my head at the couple still by the door.

Before he could answer, an Abita beer was placed in front of me. The condensation slid down the brown bottle and onto the napkin underneath. I took a sip as he settled an arm around my shoulders, and I leaned into him. From Athena's position under the table, a low rumble shook the table.

My shoulders shrugged at her apparent dislike for Julian. "I really don't know what's wrong with her."

He chuckled. "Maybe she's jealous of the attention you're getting from me."

All of a sudden, the lights dimmed, and Jahane and Derrick joined us at the table as two men stepped onto the stage. One of the men, dressed in a suit and hat, tapped the microphone. "Hey, y'all, let's get this party started. Shorty and I have heard we have a birthday girl in da house. So without further ado, let's wish Miss Rosie Delacroix a happy birthday."

"You did this?" I whispered to Jahane.

"Uh, duh, anything for you, my bestie." Her arms squeezed around me.

Everyone in the crowd turned and started to clap as the two musicians placed their trombones to their lips and blew. The jazzy tunes flowed through the room, the tempo intensifying with every note.

The crowd sang along, and the urge to join in overwhelmed me. Next to come out of the brass instruments was a sweet sultry tune, and soon my body swayed to the melody. The dance floor bustled with people.

"Come on, Rosie, let's take a spin out there." Julian offered me his hand. With no hesitation, I followed him onto the dance floor to be spun around. We moved in unison to the sultry horns and other jazz instruments. When the song ended, he dipped me and a tender kiss found my lips, and I smiled when he lifted me up and ushered me back to the table. When we arrived, it was full of drinks and snacks. I grabbed for one of the cheesy goodies that littered the table, and the table bumped up. Under the table, I saw Athena lick her paw, followed by her muzzle.

A deep sigh escaped me. "Jahane, what did you feed my dog?"

"She was hungry, Rosie." She licked cheese from her lips.

"Cheese fries, really?" I shook my head.

Athena stuck her head out from under the table and placed it on my lap.

The nagging flutter hit my brain again. She stuck her tongue out and wiped a bit of leftover cheese off the top of her nose. I laughed and petted her.

Julian's arm wrapped around me and pulled me closer. "Do you want to get out of here, Rosie?" He breathed into my ear.

I nodded to him and turned to my friends. "Jahane and Derrick, I think I'm exhausted and need some sleep." A big yawn escaped my mouth.

"Uh huh, bestie." She grinned at me. When she hugged me, she whispered to me. "Now go take advantage of that tall glass of water."

The anticipation of tangled sheets with Julian heightened as we walked home. We approached the door, and Julian's gentle push had my back up against it. His mouth claimed mine, and his hands cupped my ass, so I wrapped my legs around his waist. *Damn, this man smells scrumptious; his woodsy scent entices all my senses.*

With a breathy sigh, I said, "Julian, let's take this inside."

He let me go, and my hands fumbled with the keys at the bottom of my purse. After a few attempts with the key not making contact with the knob, he took them from me and pushed the door open. Inside, Julian's best weak-in-the-knees gaze made me stumble and smolder long after he'd looked away. Taking careful and deliberate steps backward, I giggled and dashed into my room. Julian's steps stalked me, and he closed the door behind him slowly. But before the door closed, I saw Athena out of the corner of my eye, curled up next to the front door.

"Rosie, I need you now." Julian's voice was husky and deep.

My lips curved into a wicked grin. "Is that so?"

My fingers curled around the hem of my shirt, and in methodically slow movements, I slipped it over my head and tossed it to the floor. As he stood there, Julian's arousal bulged at his zipper. Next, I eased my own zipper down, and an audible moan exited his mouth.

"Don't tease me, Rosie," he pleaded.

Before the zipper hit the bottom, his hands grasped either side of my hips and pulled me against his arousal. His hands moved around to grab my ass. He hoisted me up, and my legs wrapped around his waist again. His teeth nibbled on my ear. "Rosie, you are beautiful," he whispered to me.

He set me back on the floor and traced a finger right above the lace on my bra. With every gentle touch, small electrifying tingles coursed through my entire body, my nipples included. I heaved a sigh, wanting his hands on me, and my breasts begged to get out of their constraints. One strong hand reached around and unclasped the hook, and they bounced free as he removed my bra. His brows rose as my nipples tightened into taut buds.

"Julian, you are way overdressed."

"Oh, am I now?" A mischievous grin widened on his face.

He tugged at his shirt and slipped it over his head. Julian shook out his long brown hair, and it cascaded slightly over his shoulders. He pulled the metal zipper on his jeans down, and his erection begged to be released from his boxers. With his fingers laced in the belt loops of my jeans, he slid them down my thighs. Once I stepped out of them, he turned his attention to my breasts. He took each nipple between his thumb and forefinger and twirled and tweaked them until they felt like they could cut glass. Looking up at me, he once again took control of my mouth. A deep moan escaped me when his tongue took hold of mine and our kiss became more passionate.

A sudden crash and a loud growl caused us to break apart. Arms and legs instantly flew, trying to redress. I ran out of the bedroom, covering my chest with my shirt. A glass bowl lay on the floor in broken pieces. Athena crouched low with her hackles raised. She continued to growl even as I strained to calm her, and out of nowhere, she pulled from my hold on her and lunged at Julian. In my peripheral vision, I saw a hazy dark shadow in the corner of the room, but my attention suddenly refocused on my Guardian.

"Athena, no," I screamed.

Julian jumped out of the way just in the nick of time, but he lost his balance and fell onto the cold hardwood floor. Clutching his head, he rolled over, the sweat pouring from him. I scrambled over to him on my knees and ran a hand down his clammy face. His beautiful green eyes were glazed over and rolled back in his head as he passed into unconsciousness.

"Julian, Julian." My hysterical cries echoed through my apartment.

My hair cascaded over his body as I lay my head on his chest. He didn't wake, but his breaths were stable. I didn't think I could sleep for fear of his well-being, so I snuggled up close to him. But after a few moments I fell asleep whispering, "Julian, you'll be okay."

CHAPTER 7

oud snores reverberated from somewhere close and nudged me awake. My hand lay gently over Julian's chest, and after a few moments of feeling his chest rise and fall, I reached up and kissed him. He stirred but never opened his eyes. I felt Julian's forehead with the back of my hand. He was burning up, and his skin was clammy to the touch. Pushing up on my knees, I stretched up off the floor, but before I could leave, his hand stopped me.

"Don't go, Rosie," he begged.

"Oh, sweetie, I'll be back, but I need to get some aspirin for your fever."

Heat seared my lips as they kissed his forehead. In pain, I jumped back and rubbed them, but still the burn on my lips had not dissipated. It had been like a quick touch to a hot surface. A sense of dread spread through me like a wildfire, and I hoped my worries weren't evident on my face.

"What's wrong, Julian?" I asked him.

His muscled arms covered his face and he stuttered, "I have no idea."

Once I had given him some aspirin, I paced around the room, worry inching inside my body and taking control. Finally, sitting down in a chair not far from Julian, I could see the sheen of sweat glistening on his head, his hair matted around his beautiful face. I dropped my head into my hands and cried softly. "I can't lose him, too," I muttered under my breath. "I'm sorry I left you with no word and no reason." A thought popped into my head, and I knew one person who could help me, so I ran into my room to get dressed.

Julian stood wobbly in the doorway of my room, his fist clenching the door jam. "Rosie, my sweet Rosie, will you tell me?" he begged. "Why did you leave and where did you go?"

The back of my hand wiped at my tear stained face, and I shook my head and finished tugging my shirt over my head. "Not yet. I need you and Jahane both in the same room when I tell you." A deep breath expelled from my mouth, one I had no idea I was holding in. "But for now, we need to figure out what's wrong with you."

I watched him stumble toward my bed. Instinctively, I ran to him as he collapsed on it. When he curled into a ball, I covered him up, and with an exasperated sigh, I jumped from the bed and sprinted for the door, the whole way ignoring the protests from Julian. I ran down the steps two at a time and through the courtyard, where the cast iron gate swung and scraped against the brick wall behind me as I rushed through it. I ran the few blocks through the Quarter, skidded to a stop, and scanned the Square for Madame Claudette's table.

My body spun around in a tizzy as I searched, and when I saw the familiar purple table cloth, I raced over to her. Suddenly, regret began to surface at my decision to seek out the fortune teller instead of a doctor, even though deep down I knew she was the only one who could help. She must have the answer. My fingers clasped the amber teardrop shaped amulet hanging around my neck, and my legs shook as I sat down at her table. "Child," she asked with a grin, and eyed my amulet. "How may I be of service to you?"

"My…boyfriend. He's ill," I stuttered.

Her elbows on the table and her fingers steepled, she leaned into me. "I know, child, but it is not my place to tell you what I know. I must speak with him, and soon."

The urgency in her voice caused me to knock over the chair as I stood up instantly. It clattered, scraped, and bounced off the pavement as it hit the ground. Total disbelief spread across my face as she leisurely stood up. "What in the world are you waiting for?"

"Let's go, my dear."

My nails dug into her arm as I grabbed her and pulled her down the street in a flurry. Questions needed to be answered as to what Julian was experiencing, and now. Even when she tried to slow down, I refused to until I stood before my apartment. Bent over, my breaths ragged as I sucked in a deep breath, I spoke.

"We are here, Madame Claudette, please help him," I begged with heartfelt determination in my voice.

Madam eyed the building from one end of the street to the other. It gave me the heebie jeebies. She tightened the shawl around her shoulders and clambered up the steps to my apartment. At the top, the door was wide open, with my dog curled up in the front hallway, licking her paws.

Tears threatened to slide down my face as the thought Julian is gone swam through me. My knees hit the floor hard as I reached my dog. "Are you okay? Where's Julian?" I laughed nervously when I realized I'd asked Athena where he was. It wasn't like she could answer me.

The strange flutter churned through my head as I petted her soft fur. When I knew my Guardian was okay, I raised from my position and ran through each room, gripping the wall as I called out for Julian. "Julian, where are you?" I hollered as my panic rose.

With no sign of him, and with my head down, I wandered back to Madame Claudette, who was still outside my front door. She never stepped a toe over the threshold, but muttered under her breath and raised her hands high over her head. A slight breeze blew through my hair and danced around my shoulders. I couldn't make out the spell she'd performed.

"This is not good, my child, not good at all," she said to me.

"What is it?" With a heavy heart I slumped to the floor next to my dog, who in turn placed her head in my lap for comfort.

After a slight hesitation, the fortune teller walked inside, laid a gentle hand on my shoulder, and squeezed. Her touch was welcomed, since I needed the comfort.

"You, my child, must go see the voodoo queen."

Dazed for a moment, I stood until shock and horror consumed me. "But she is dead! She has been for years."

Madame's quiet laugh awakened a sudden anger in me, and I gawked at her.

"No, my dear, she is quite alive, and in some form or another...well, living here in New Orleans."

"But...but...," I stammered.

She tilted my chin up and looked into my eyes. "Dear Rosie," she told me. "You must go to the tomb of Marie Laveau."

With a vigorous shake of my head, I said, "It's not possible. I can't. I know voodoo is powerful, and with all I've learned about myself, I can't take any more right now."

"Yes, you must, and soon. Be brave like your mother." Madame Claudette smiled kindly as she patted me on the shoulder.

"What, you knew my mother?"

"That is for a later time. First Julian, my dear."

Later, after the fortune teller left, I began to wear a hole in the floor as I paced back and forth. Still with no word from Julian, my heart plummeted as the thoughts of what could have happened rushed at me. I plopped down into the soft cushions of my couch and tried to disperse my fears of what could have befallen him. My phone was still clutched in my hand from all the phone calls I'd made to local hospitals, but no one with his description had been admitted in the past hours. Quickly, new thoughts invaded my senses at the idea of visiting the tomb of Marie Laveau.

"You know, voodoo is a powerful religion you don't go messing with." My Guardian's tail thumped on the ground as her blue eyes stared up at me. A tiny twitter surged through my head, and I shook it, trying to dislodge the feeling. *What in the hell is wrong with my head? It doesn't hurt, just a weird sensation.* Worries poured through me at how adamant the creepy fortune teller had been I go see the queen of voodoo.

At the sudden knock on my door, I lurched off the sofa. Athena's hackles rose, and the floor reverberated from her growls.

"Hush!" I said, my annoyance evident at her rumbles. The door opened to reveal Julian, who just stood there. Anger bubbled and intensified deep inside me. "Where the hell have you been, Julian?"

His long wavy hair tangled as his hand brushed through it. Fear and confusion were etched on his otherwise beautiful face. His square jaw dropped in a sheepish expression, and his eyes dipped down in embarrassment. *This is not the confident Julian I know and love.*

"I don't know what's happening to me, Rosie, and it's scaring the hell out of me. I wake up and can't remember where I've been."

I grabbed his hard, calloused hand with my small one and pulled him into the living room. "Julian, come sit down, we'll figure this out together. I'll call Jahane and Derrick and see what we can figure out. Besides I think it's time to get some stuff out in the open. Maybe we can figure out how to deal with both of our problems. At my touch, he dropped his head into his hands as he crumpled into the sofa.

Fifteen minutes later, the four of us sat in my living room. Athena kept a constant vigil on Julian and snarled anytime his body shifted on the sofa. I ran my hand over her soft fur in hopes of calming her, but with the sudden resurfacing of my worries and nerves, my foot tapped on the floor, shaking the sofa.

"Rosie, what's the matter?" Jahane asked me.

"Oh, nothing at all." A heavy sigh left my mouth, the tapping stopped, and my folded hands relaxed in my lap.

Julian reached over and gently covered my hand with his large one and linked his fingers with mine.

I stuttered a bit. "Something is wrong with Julian."

"What do you mean Rosie?" They both clamored at the same time.

"He's been having headaches and...well...Madame Claudette was here...she said I needed to go see...My voice wavered.

Julian tightened his hold as he whispered in my ear. "Cher why don't you tell us your secret, mine can wait."

Nervously I smiled at him and whispered back. "Are you sure?"

He nodded so I began trying to calm voice. "Okay well...umm... there's another reason why I called you over here. It's time for me to tell everyone why I left. I have to stop putting it off." "Cher, it's all right, we're here for you." His deep voice soothed me enough for me to pull my big girl panties up and get my secret off my chest.

"I'll be back." Athena followed close on my heels in the direction of my room. On my hands and knees, I peered under the bed in search of a box I'd hidden there. My Guardian crawled under the bed to assist me, and pushed the ever present dust bunnies aside with her wet nose.

"You're a good girl." The box was hidden behind another box, and so I tugged it out from under the bed, lifted the top, and laid it on the floor beside me. Warm tears formed and slowly trickled down my face. Athena examined the contents of the box as it was propped up on my knees. I lifted out the smaller box containing the items I had found the day my momma went missing, then slid the other box back under the bed. With a heavy sigh, I mustered every bit of my courage, stood up, and carried the box back into the living room.

Once back in the living room, I pushed a strand of my dark hair from my face and positioned the box on the coffee table. Jahane eyed me suspiciously, opened the box, and looked at the objects.

"Rosie, what is this?" she exclaimed as she riffled through its contents.

"I found these the day my mother vanished, along with a note. Well, before she disappeared, I kept having these nightmares. They foretold my mother's future, which was she would die by the hands of some kind of creature. The message…." I began to sob. "Was clear…tell no one. I left so I wouldn't put y'all in danger." Tears streaked my face and dripped onto the box. Jahane's face was painted with worry about my situation.

"Girl, don't be silly, we are all here for you…and if you're in danger, so are we. We'll go into the depths of hell for you." She laughed. "Besides, what the hell do you think friends are for?" She spun me to face her with her hands on my shoulders and stared at me. "If I could kick the bullies' asses in school for picking on my best friend, well, it stands to reason, then, that I would be there for you no matter what, right?"

"Yes." I wiped at my face and nodded.

Once my confession was out, we all stared in awe at the objects in the box.

"So, anyway, these items were found not far from the cryptic note on the counter, but in different spots throughout the store," I said. Jahane touched the bone, but passed over the voodoo doll and the empty little gris gris bag.

"Rosie, what do you think this all means?" Julian's deep baritone voice boomed.

"I have no idea, but we need to figure it out."

Jahane interrupted us. "Yeah, but the burning question we all want to know now is, where did you go when you left?"

I chuckled. "I went to Savannah, Georgia and worked in a quaint little bookstore. I know, I know, the perfect place for a bookworm such as me."

Jahane tried to hide her shocked look but changed the subject. "So, with the cryptic message you received in your dreams, why did you come back? Not that we aren't glad."

"Well, I realized it was time for me to come home and stop being scared and face my demons. Also, I needed to find out the truth of what happened and who did this to my momma."

The other three in my living room looked at me. "Well, it's about time," my bestie said. Jahane high fived Derrick and Julian, then turned to me and declared, "Well, sista, we are behind you the whole way." I giggled when she started to shake her ass.

I leaned down to Jahane. "Hey, can you keep an eye on Julian for me for a few minutes? I need to run down to the shop and take a look in my momma's old stuff to find out more about my family." She nodded, and I kissed Julian as my keys jangled in my hand. "Come on, Athena." The dog bounded past Julian and growled one last time before she followed me out the door.

Athena's nails scratched on the back door as I stuck the key into the lock to open the shop. My mother had some books hidden in the storeroom of the shop, and as we stood knee to shoulder in the door of the room, defeat overwhelmed me as I glanced at the stacks and stacks of boxes before me. Sighing deeply, I sat down crossed-legged on the floor in the middle of all the different sized cardboard cartons.

"Okay, girl, how in the world are we doing to find a needle in a haystack?"

She barked loud, and a small flutter surged through my brain.

"Well, girl, let's get started on this." I opened the first box and watched as the dust sprayed and settled all over the place. When I managed to rid my throat of all the dust, I riffled through the other boxes, pulling books out one at a time.

Athena sprawled on the floor with her head on her paws, looking intently at me. "Yes, I know this is taking forever." She barked at me in agreement.

With my shoulders slumped, I leaned against the wall, and defeat erupted and surged through me. The scattered books around me brought no comfort. An abrupt burst of nervous laughter escaped my mouth, and out of my peripheral vision, I saw another box further back by the wall, made of an antique metal. I stood and dusted the dirt from my hands and blew a loose strand of dark brown hair away from my face. The closer I stepped to the antique bronze colored box, the more excitement seeped into my soul. This has to be the one.

My hands clutched the ornate chest, and carefully, I slid down on the floor with my legs circling it. "What do we have here?" The pads of my fingers traced the intricate markings on either side of the box. Athena bounded over to me and barked. "Well damn, girl, there's a lock." I flicked the tiny lock and thought, *where did I see a key*?

Frantic, I shoved the books on the floor around until I saw a shiny, silver key dangling from a rabbit's foot keychain. Enjoying the irony of this situation, I spoke aloud to the empty room. "Gosh, Momma, how cliché is this?" I could hear the sound of her laughter in my head. *You know, we must all have some form of good luck charm, Petal.*

As I stuck the key in the lock, the mechanisms turned and clicked open, and I observed Athena. Her tail steadily thudded on the floor. The top of the box popped open, and she barked and wagged her backend. "What, girl, I'm getting to it. Sheesh, be patient." Once again, the flutter went through my head, this time different though, like her bark sounded in my head.

Inside the box was a book with very intricate designs and raised drawings on the cover curving around to the binding. I heaved the book out, and a piece of paper floated to the floor. My fingertip traced the raised designs. The book thudded to the floor as I reached down and grabbed the slip of paper. Within an instant, I recognized the beautiful handwritten script. This time, curiosity played with my emotions as I sniffed and held my composure while I unfolded the paper and read out loud.

My dearest Petal,

If you are reading this, I am no longer with you in body, though, my dear, I will always be with you in spirit, guiding you through your life. I trust Alina has told you who you are. It was my wish to tell you the truth myself, but I hope you have received your Guardian by now if you have turned twenty-seven. I've planned for her to be delivered on your birthday. She will be with you for a long time. By now you know she is not just any Great Dane."

At the mention of her in the note, my dog came over and laid her head on my shoulder. I stretched a hand over and stroked her floppy ears.

This box holds a precious gift. It is your Crescent Grimoire, a book for witches. It will help you through the troubles and trials you must and will deal with. This was predestined for you before you were born. There are evils out there that want you for their own purpose, because if Alina has spoken to you, you know you are one of the most powerful witches alive. You must practice your gift and go to her for help with anything. You will find people want to be your friend. Some will be honest, others, not so much. You will also find an allegiance with someone; but be careful, you will be tied to her forever. My dear Petal, make wise choices. And trust in your Guardian."

As I sat back against the wall, I fiddled with the note until it was folded back along its creases. My mind ran around in circles as it contemplated all I had learned today. Without any hesitation I picked up the book, placed it back in the box, locked it and scooped it up. I raced out of the store and locked the door behind me.

My Guardian and I took the steps two at a time to the apartment. My door flung open to laughter ringing through the house. My friends were all positioned around the table playing Bourre.

"Mease up, Jahane," Julian barked out at her with laughter.

"Julian, speak English, man," she replied to him with a snort.

The smile creased his face and shone bright even from where I stood inside the doorway. "Ante up, Jahane; make your bet."

"I'll raise your five with ten."

His laughter boomed and followed me through to my bedroom as she flung curses at him. I shoved the box with my Crescent Grimoire under my bed. When I returned to the living room, Jahane was sulking.

"What, did Julian take all your money? You should never, ever play Bourre with him; he's a Cajun card shark."

Her bottom lip poked out, then she smirked at him. "True dat, Rosie."

Before I entered the kitchen, Julian's hand popped me on the ass. I jumped at his playful touch and rubbed my backside. In the kitchen, I poured four glasses of sweet tea and popped slices of lemon on the edges of the glasses. I walked back in, making two trips, hands full of glasses. When I handed Julian his tea, his long legs pushed his chair back and he patted his knee. I nestled onto his lap and took a huge gulp of sweet tea.

"Who's ready to lose more money?" I shuffled and dealt out the cards.

I leaned down and whispered, "This game is mine."

He chuckled as his breath tickled my neck. "We'll see."

CHAPTER 8

T he next morning, down in the store, my lazy dog slept next to the counter while I flipped through the torn and tattered pages of my Crescent Grimoire. With a tender, careful touch, I tried not to tear the delicate pages. The bell above the door tinkled, and my head popped up when a beautiful woman with skin the color of fresh brewed latte glided inside.

"Ma'am, may I help you?" I asked.

"No, dear," she replied with a hint of a French accent.

"If you need any help, please let me know." I reverted back down to look at the book. "Damn it, there is nothing in here to help with my Julian problem," I mumbled.

"That, my dear, is because you won't find any answers to the problem with your boyfriend."

My head jerked, and I jumped at her unexpected appearance in front of me, but quickly regained my composure. Astonishment and bewilderment laced my next question. "But ma'am, how do you know about my problems?"

"Never mind, child. In due time, you will come to find the answers you are looking for."

She turned on her heels and headed for the door, and at the same time, a tall ebony god sauntered in and held the door for her. "Thank you," she said, her white teeth showing. He tipped his head down and did an about face in my direction.

Still puzzled at this strange woman and her knowledge of my situation, I stared after her as the door closed behind her.

"Ma'am?" A male voice pulled me from my stupor as I stared at him, slack jawed. "Miss?" He tried again. "Miss?" I shook my head, and Athena's tail thudded against the counter. A shiny, dark bald head lightly dusted with black hair blocked my view of my dog as he knelt down and petted her. In those ten seconds it took him to pet her, she had become a traitor.

I tugged on her collar until she moved with reluctance at the loss of the scratch behind her ear. Once she was behind the counter, I pointed at her. "Stay," I commanded.

She whimpered low and relaxed on her haunches. My focus returned to the man before me, and my breath caught in my throat. He was extremely tall—almost as tall as Julian—and his cotton t-shirt clung to his perfect six pack. This man was oh, so sex-on-a-stick. His abnormally dark blue eyes for a man of his race raked over my face, and a slow curve tugged at his lips. From his skull trim with a hint of black hair to his light mocha colored skin, he was gorgeous. His features hinted of creole and/or Spanish in his bloodline.

"Yes, sir?" My mouth tried to open and shut in cohesive words as he stared at me.

He brushed a hand over his trimmed goatee and said, "Well, miss, I'm looking for a job and an apartment."

"I…uh…," I stuttered. "I do not…." But I shook my head and remembered what my momma had said in her note. *Some want to be my friends and others want to use me.* My gut told me he was a good guy, and not just because he was sexy as hell. I had a sense about him, and felt it was right to go with my instincts. With my hands on my hips, I stood my ground. "Well, sir, do you have a name?"

"Oh, yes ma'am," he replied. "Where are my manners? My name is Remi Louviere."

With a chuckle, I stuck out my hand, and when his hand touched mine, a jolt pulsed through me. "Well, Remi, it's nice to meet you. My name is Rosaleigh." I shook my finger at him. "But the ma'am crap is making me feel old, and I'm probably the same age as you."

He shot me a wink and grinned. "Hmm…I'm a little older then you; and as for the 'ma'am crap,' as you so fondly call it, blame my momma. She taught me manners."

I quirked a brow at him. "Remi, I do have a vacant apartment, and rent is cheap since it's small. The shop owners left me a key just in case. But I'm not too sure what type of work I could offer. Maybe something around here." My shoulders shrugged nonchalantly.

"Anything is good, Rosaleigh. I'm making do until I can get my house back up to code after the hurricane. It seems to be taking forever to get it right, and I'm tired of living off relatives."

"So, where do you live?" I inquired.

"Down in Tremé," he replied.

"Tremé? Wow, what a small world. You may know of my best friend, Jahane Olivier," I said with a smile.

He laughed. "Little Jah…yes, I know her; she is an old family friend."

"Wait, what? Hey, how come I have never met you?" I asked, my suspicions getting the better of me all of a sudden.

He laughed at the look on my face. "Because I never hung out in Tremé, though I did see you one time with Jah; it was after your accident. And, if I recall, Jah was always down here with you in the Quarter. But everyone in Tremé knows of you and Jah's friendship. The neighborhood was ecstatic Jah had found you for a friend. She didn't have many friends… she's kind of pushy and bossy, you know." He leaned back and laughed at the shocked look on my face.

I cocked a brow at him. "Really?"

"Yes really, Rosaleigh. I know what you're thinking. Even though you and Jahane are different races and come from different cultures, it doesn't stop you from being good friends. You both give each other something."

Quickly changing the subject, I asked. "So what have you been up to then?"

"After the hurricane, I left for a bit to go to culinary school." Confidence stoked his words.

I sat on the stool behind the counter, becoming more interested. "Culinary school?" My curiosity became more evident with my next question. "So, how come you're not working in a restaurant?"

"Oh, well, the local restaurants aren't hiring right now."

"Hmm, I can talk to someone for you. It doesn't hurt to help someone who knows my best friend. Wait until I see her. Speaking of seeing her, what are you doing tonight, Remi? We are going to the Orpheus parade. Want to join us?" My words all babbled out at once.

He laughed. "I would love to, but I have plans tonight. Maybe I will see you around, Rosie." He winked at me.

"Wait, hold on, let me get a key for the apartment out back. And by the way, Remi, only my friends are allowed to call me by my nickname." I told him, and winked back.

He took the key I offered and feigned mock hurt. With a hand over his chest, he said, "Hey, Rosie, I thought we were friends." A pout spread across his face.

The door to the shop opened, and a low deep growl resonated from the floor as Julian stood in the doorway. His glare shot through me. Remi walked over to Athena and whispered low in her ear. In a second, she settled back on the floor behind the counter. Shock coursed into every fiber of me. "What, now you're a dog whisperer, too?" He shrugged his shoulders at me.

Julian took up the entire frame of the door, and turned his glare to Remi. "Julian," I said, "stop and come meet an old friend of Jahane's." He strolled in but never took his vicious glower off Remi.

"It's nice to meet you, Julian," Remi said as he shook Julian's hand, ignoring Julian's evident dislike for him.

"Come by the store tomorrow and I'll see what you can help me with.

I'll also talk to a friend of mine who owns a restaurant."

"Thank you. I'll be back later." The door closed with a click, and Julian grabbed me and pressed his lips to mine with such passion and fervor that my breath hitched. He kissed me like he wanted to devour me. Both of us in a heated embrace, his mouth inches from my beating pulse, he growled low in my ear, "Rosie, you are mine."

I pushed him away. "Oh hell, no; do not get all territorial with me, Julian."

As I walked back behind the old wooden cypress counter, my long skirt caught on a piece of wood jutting out from the side. While I struggled to detangle my skirt, Julian casually walked over, untangled it, and spun me around in one swift move. His eyes glowed a deep hue of green as they bored into me. "Rosie, I'm sorry. But I can't stand other men ogling my woman."

Aghast at his caveman comment, I nudged him with my elbow. "Seriously? You know I only have eyes for you, and my heart...well, it belongs to only one man. Besides, he isn't even my type. Let's close up and get ready to meet Jahane and Derrick for the parade." Athena's leash in hand, I bent down and clipped it to her collar with a click and we headed upstairs.

"Julian, make yourself comfortable. I'll be back after I change."

Before I knew it, he was in front of me. "Do you need help?" His grin was laden with lust and his heavy lids relaxed.

My head down, all I saw was his glorious chest, and with a slow upward glance, my gaze rested on his. In an instant, he grabbed me and his lips met mine with such force it almost knocked the wind out of me. The moment our lips connected, a shudder escalated through my entire body. Emotions and memories flooded my head in a swirl. My sensations hit the mother lode as my heart beat wildly, and Julian crushed me against his broad chest. A tsunami of rattled nerves hit me as I remembered I hadn't had sex for six months.

Before we entered my bedroom, Julian turned to me. "Cher, don't be nervous," he said, winking at me.

"How did you know?" I blushed.

"Rosie, the grip you have on me is indication enough." His hand turned the knob to my bedroom and he led me inside. We inched inside my room, and my back hit the wall as his kisses grew intense. His need for me pressed against my abdomen as his fingers grasped my hair.

My nervousness disappeared as I purred seductively. "I know you want me…." My own lust-filled eyes scanned his body. "But I think you have too many clothes on, Julian."

With a wicked leer, he removed his shirt and tossed it to the chair beside my bed. "How about now?" His eyes crinkled at the corners.

"Let's see." My gaze moved up his chest down to his erection straining against his jeans. The urge to trace down his chiseled abs with my fingertips was powerful, and I paid close attention to every detail of each ridge. His muscles constricted at my gentle touch.

"Umm." I ran my tongue over my lips, and raising my eyebrow seductively, I shook my head. "Yeah, still too many clothes." Once my fingers had traipsed down his abs to the waist of his jeans, I popped the top button. My hands reached for the pull on his zipper, and with each movement slow and concise, I pulled it down. *Holy hell, Christmas came early…he's gone commando today.*

"Rosie," he hissed at me.

I reached out and touched the tip of his erection and traced around his shaft. He shuddered at my gentle touch. Heat spread down my face and continued down my body as he pushed his pants down and stepped out of them. A quick toss of his jeans left him standing before me, the epitome of a Greek god in his entirely nude splendor.

"Now, Rosie, it's you who has too many clothes on," he chuckled.

His hands eased up either side of my body, taking my shirt with them. Shivers spread through me as his fingertips grazed my sides and ran the length of my curves. He lifted my shirt over my head, and it joined his on the chair. Running his hands down my pale arms, he circled them back to the front of my bra and traced the lace around the top of my breasts. His touch sent tiny vibrations through my entire body. My chest heaved when he reached around me to unclasp the hooks separating him from his early present, and a hiss escaped his mouth when my breasts popped free of their restraints. He knelt in front of me, and his hands trailed down in sync with my jeans being pushed down my hips and legs. I stepped out of them, and he tossed them to the same spot where his lay. In nothing but my lacy thong, a strong feeling of vulnerability came over me. As I smiled down at him, I remembered the long, ugly scars covering my legs. Even though he had seen them before, the instinct to cover them overpowered me. In an instant, my hands dropped from my breasts to cover my legs as much as possible.

"No, cher, don't do hide them," he whispered to me as he knelt down. He traced gently along the jagged lines as he removed my hands from the grip they had on my legs where I tried to cover the ugliness and pain I had endured.

Julian's sensual, erotic, and loving touches sent a wave of emotions through me. His strong hands took hold of my leg, and his fingertips glided down the length of my scars. Then he bent down, and with his soft lips placed feather light kisses on each jagged line. His touch made me weak in the knees, the loving touch soothing the pain and sadness I had experienced for so long. Instinct took over, and my hands reached around to the back of his head. I ran them through the silkiness of his long, dark brown hair, and moaned at the incredible feel of his lips touching the sensitive, serrated marks on my leg. Love poured from him, not only for me but also for my scars.

Julian stood and I had to stand on my tiptoes for my lips to reach his. While I moved my body closer to him, the kiss intensified, and for one moment, our bodies melded into one, full of pleasure and passion.

He pulled away from our embrace with urgency. "Rosie," he breathed, "you are so beautiful." He dipped his head down, and his long hair brushed over my shoulder. His tongue skimmed across the swell of my breasts and I shivered.

When he picked me up in one swift movement, the instinct to wrap my legs around his waist astounded me, and I closed my eyes and enjoyed the feel of his flesh against mine. His hands grabbed my butt, and his fingers dug deeper with the intensity of our kiss.

He effortlessly carried me into the bathroom. The skin to skin touch of our bodies had my desire burning for him even more. Once in the bathroom, still in his arms, I opened my eyes and kissed every piece of his skin I could reach. He placed me on the floor, and the slow descent down his body ignited every sensitive spot on mine. Our eyes met, and his held a look of pure, unadulterated lust in his heavy lidded gaze. He leaned down, and my mouth opened to invite him to savor me. With our tongues intertwined, the temperature rose in the room. Our passion began to slow, but when he broke the kiss, I nipped his bottom lip in silent protest.

Julian's face lingered close to mine, and the smugness on it dared me to stop. I wanted to oblige him but had other wicked thoughts in mind. I pulled away for a brief moment to turn on the shower, and as I did, his hand friskily popped me on the ass.

"This thing, right here," he said while he played with the strap over my hips, "has got to come off." His finger slid in between the thin strap of my thong and my skin.

With a slight tug, the thong ripped and the soft silky material slid down my legs and landed on the floor. His sexy, throaty laugh excited me as he nuzzled my neck. My hand reached under the water to check and see if it was warm enough.

"Julian, the water's ready." I crooked my finger at him to follow as I stepped into the glass encased shower and pulled him in with me.

My gaze scanned him up and down as the water droplets rolled down his glorious, sexy body. I dipped my head under the falling water, and when I came back up, he cupped the back of my head, leaned into me, and lowered his face to mine. The hot, steamy water poured over both of our bodies and his lips on mine made my legs buckle. His arms wrapped around me to prevent me from becoming a puddle on the floor of the shower. As my hand reached out for the loofah, he took it and lathered it up with body wash.

"Rosie, I have this." He dragged it across my collarbone and headed down between my breasts, taking his time with slow methodical movements. His arousal throbbed and touched my belly button. He spun me around and pulled my arms up so they were braced against the shower walls. This time he poured more body wash into his hands, and rubbed them together until they became lathered. Taking his time, with tender touches he washed my back, then reached around and massaged my front. I shook from the pleasure of having his hands on me again. His other hand reached around me and cupped my chin, and his lips found their way from my lips to my neck, then down to my collarbone. Letting the water fall down on me, the soap slide down my body. His lips found their way across my chest right to my breasts, and he cupped one in his hand. A slight moan rose from my mouth as he took my already tightly budded nipple and placed his mouth around it. The sucking sensation on my breast and nipple sent me almost over the edge.

With his hands, lips, and tongue, he had me in need of so much more that in no time at all my body had a mind of its own in response to him. "Julian, I need you. Now." The sound of my voice was husky and almost unrecognizable.

He laughed. "Rosie, cher. Not yet. You are not ready yet."

His hand moved lower down my flat stomach and traced every curve of my body. He continued his assault and trailed a finger from my belly button to the sweet spot between my legs, and I trembled at his touch. When he inserted a finger, I gasped loudly.

"Rosie," he breathed out against my neck, sending shivers up and down my body.

It took all my energy to remain on my wobbly legs; if he continued his ministrations, I didn't know how much longer it would last. The water

continued to trickle down our slick, wet bodies, and I grabbed hold of
Julian's shoulders while he lured me closer to the edge.

"Julian," I gasped. "Now! Now! I need you this minute!"

He continued to tease me with his capable fingers. "No, cher, I still
don't believe you are ready."

His wet hair fell down my shoulders when he pressed closer to me,
and I grasped the wall to stop me from my downhill slide. When his hand
moved between my legs once again, I moaned in pleasure and arched my
back, pushing against him, wanting all of him inside me. I lowered my
head when the pinpricks of electricity unfurled throughout my body and
made my legs wobble, and almost lost control to the percussion of a well-
deserved orgasm. I knew the moment he felt me fall over the cusp when
he spun me around to face him and took control of my mouth, like he was
thirsty for water.

"Rosie, do you want it now?" he asked with a wicked smile on his face.

By this time my mouth wasn't able to form a coherent word, much
less a whole sentence. He grabbed one of my legs and raised it, teasing
with the tip of his arousal. I grabbed ahold of him, wrapped my other
leg around his waist, and pressed my body closer to him, daring him
not to enter me. With a smile on his gorgeous face, the tip once again
tormented me. I inhaled deeply as I felt him enter me, and I moaned while
he mimicked his body's movements with his tongue. His thrusts went
deeper, and our bodies rocked back and forth in unison. When our moans
went from sensual to frantic, our lovemaking became harder and faster,
and we felt each other reach a point of no return. I continued to rock my
body with his as the sensations of him filling me shoved me over the edge

into an orgasm leaving me breathless. When we were done I let my head fall against his strong muscular chest and let him hold me up.

"Rosie, I love the way you feel wrapped around me," he breathed in my ear.

A quake rushed through my body as his breath tickled my earlobe. Nothing else mattered at the moment but the awareness of our bodies and souls connected together.

Fully sated, I slid slowly down from his body, finding my legs weak. He held me up as I breathed out, "Damn, Julian," my brain not able to form unified sentences.

He kissed my forehead. "Rosie, I'm glad you're back. I've missed you and have missed this." He placed a tender kiss on my nose and ended it at my lips. "Now, let's get you cleaned up. We have a parade to attend."

I smiled and laughed. "Oh no, you don't. That is how this all started." I snatched the mesh loofah from him. "I can handle this; if not, we'll never get out of here." I laughed as he placed a hand over his bare chest and acted hurt.

"Rosie," he whispered, skimming his finger up and down my hip, "what is this mark? It resembles a small tear drop." He bent down to get a better look as I bowed my head down and saw it. My fingers pressed it and squeezed it.

"Wow, I never noticed it." But the sense I knew what it meant evaded me. "I don't know, sweetie, but we don't have time to worry about it," I said, and hurried to wash my hair.

CHAPTER 9

My long flowing skirt twirled around me as I strolled out of my room. My hair hung in ringlets down my back, and I felt a hand sweep it off my shoulder as we headed out the door. The gaslight lamps swung above our heads in the slight breeze and lit our path with flickering hazy shadows as we headed down towards Canal Street. My head tilted up at Julian, and he smiled and laced his fingers with mine.

Down the street we spotted a rowdy bunch of tourists, their drinks sloshing out of their plastic cups. When we passed by them, they bumped into me and caused me to stumble. Julian grabbed hold of me as my face and the pavement were about to become personal acquaintances. He righted me, and a growl rose from deep within his chest.

He blocked my view of the group, but I peeked around his shoulder and saw fright on their faces as he glared at each one.

"Sorry, sir." They all clamored together and ran down the street. The moment was forgotten by the time they reached the end of the block, because the rambunctious group continued to sing off-key.

He turned to face me, and I tried to mask my shock at seeing his eyes turn red again for a brief moment. With a shake of my head, I squinched my eyes tighter and hoped it had been my imagination. As worry seeped through me, I popped open one eye and then the other, and saw Julian's eyes were, once again, their dark green color. The instinct to ask overpowered me. "Julian, what is wrong with you? I swear your eyes were red."

Before he could answer me my head whipped around to Athena. She growled as the drunken group continued to move away from us, their voices even louder and more off-key.

My agitation rose rapidly at both of them. "Oh, now you two are going to bond." I stalked off towards the parade route.

Julian caught up with me, stopped me with his hand, and turned me around. "I'm sorry, Rosie, I couldn't help it. You could have been hurt." He held me close to him, and the comfort of our bodies pressed against each other soothed my annoyance, but only some.

I pulled away from him. "No, Julian, you know how tourists are; it's part of the season. Everyone gets drunk and rowdy."

His strong arms encircled me, and I leaned into his hard body. The smell of his body wash and our sex on him helped calm me. "All right, Julian Quibadeaux." I poked him in the chest. "No more cave man acts."

With slow and seductive movements, he stroked my cheek and his eyes flashed me a wicked smile. "Anything for you, Rosie."

Before I knew it, he had me in his arms, and his ferocious kiss made me pant and knocked me for a loop. I held onto him as my knees almost collapsed, and breathed out in a whisper, "Julian, our friends are waiting for us."

He stepped back at arm's length and looked at me. "Yes, we will continue this conversation later." He shot me a wink.

"Yes, later, much later. Right now we have a parade to attend."

We rounded the corner and saw our friends up ahead. "Jahane," I called out to her.

She turned at the sound of my voice and waved to us. When Athena noticed Jahane, she bounded ahead and pulled her leash from my grasp. An incoherent mumble forced itself into my head, and I shook my head to dislodge the nonsense. *Oh, hell, I'm going crazy again.* When my Guardian reached my best friend, she sat on her haunches in front of her and waited for us. The look on my dog's face was comical, and I cocked my head to get a better look at it.

A flutter went through my head and the jumbled, *Uh, I have been here forever. What took you so long? Played in my head.*

"Bad dog," I chastised her, and leaned down to her level. "I don't know what I would do if I lost you."

Jahane palmed the leash in her hand. "Aww, Rosie, don't be mad at her; she can't help but love me."

Athena barked at me, and behind me, a gruff voice boomed, "How's life treating you?" I turned around as Derrick grabbed me in a bear hug.

Once I was released, Jahane looked at me and must have seen the color painting my cheeks. She grinned like the cat who ate the canary, leaned into me, and whispered, "Looks to me like someone had a little bow- chick-a-wow-wow before they showed up and met us." My elbow made contact with hers as her ass shook seductively.

Derrick's head played tennis at our back and forth whispers. She leaned in a hair's breadth away from me and whispered, "It's okay, sweetie, it's about time you let your freak flag fly." She chortled and bumped me with her hip.

A slight heat burned my cheeks when it dawned on Derrick what my bestie had insinuated. I tried to hide my face, but Julian leaned down and took my face in his hands. "I like that color on you." Before he stood back up, a gentle kiss caressed my earlobe. The touch of his lips sent delightful shivers down my spine.

The blare of horns from the fire trucks alerted us the parade was about to roll down the street. The tune of a Mardi Gras mambo thrummed and stepped up the tensions around us; it was time to party.

A slight breeze blew around and a horrible feeling of uneasiness settled in my gut. My head whipped around at the eeriness surrounding me, and I saw Madame Claudette poised on the other side of the street. My hand suddenly grasped the amulet around my neck. She nodded her head, mouthed "good girl," and smiled at me. For a split second, I turned away to watch the first float roll closer to where we stood, and when I looked for the fortune teller again, she had disappeared.

The parade was in full swing...beads flew, doubloons twinkled and spun off the ground, plastic cups sailed overhead, and the crowd screamed for more throws. Julian pulled me against him protectively, a move I loved so much. I was surrounded by the protection of a well sculpted body, one

I wished to do wicked and tantalizing things to. The more I leaned into his embrace, the more I enjoyed the heat coming in waves from him. Meanwhile, he caught a handful of beads and slid them over my head. Light, tender kisses fluttered on my shoulder, and when he removed his lips, the lack of intimacy left me bereft. The realization hit me, and my thoughts flooded through my brain like a sieve...*I do love this man. How in the world could I have left him for so long?* The memory of my dreams marched like an army and invaded my thoughts with the message, *Tell no one or you and your friends will meet the same fate.*

After my thoughts settled, I shuddered from the memory, pushed it deep down, and refocused on the parade. With a shake of my head, the past was forgotten, and I maneuvered out from under Julian's arms and started to jump up and down, yelling, "Throw me sumthin, mister!"

Jahane and Derrick jumped in the air to catch beads, and my head swiveled around to Athena, who was covered in an array of beads of all shapes and lengths. Stifling a laugh, I muttered, "Damn, that dog must be strong, because there is no way she should still be standing with all the beads she has draped over her." As if she knew I was talking about her, she looked at me and wagged her tail, and the sudden movement sent beads flying through the air.

We stood next to the parade route until my favorite part finally approached us.

"Go ahead, Rosie."

The flambeaux carriers marched beside the gaudy double decker floats. Secured to them were huge poles lighting up the night sky with red and orange flames. The men's faces were masked as skulls as they twirled their torches and danced down the crowded street.

One of the men slid his mask up, and the familiar face of my visitor from earlier winked at the crowd. "Remi!" I yelled his name over the chaos. His head turned at my voice and his face lit up his face. Pushing through the throngs of people, I reached him before the parade rolled again. "Hey, Remi, how 'bout you do a little move here for this coin?" The coin flipped between my fingers, and I tossed it at him as he danced and spun around. He caught the coin midair and boogied down the street.

"Thanks, Rosie." His voice trailed off as he left.

When I returned to our little group, Jahane's mouth flapped open. "How do you know Remi?"

Beyond amused, I wrapped an arm around her shoulder. "Well, he came into the store today looking for work, little Jah." I laughed some more as she elbowed me in the side.

She muttered under her breath, "I can't believe he told you that stupid nickname."

"Aww, I think it's cute," I teased.

When the parade wound down, I grabbed Jahane's arm. "Come on, let's go get a bite to eat." I turned around and realized Julian was nowhere to be found again.

"Damn it, Julian," I said, exasperated.

Jahane looked at me in confusion. I dismissed her look with a wave of my hand. "Never mind, let's go get a drink on Bourbon Street." She nodded her head vigorously as I grabbed my bead covered dog's leash and headed back towards the Quarter. Maybe Julian would find us; if not, I was too aggravated to care.

By the time we had reached the Cat's Meow, most of my steam had diffused. But in my heart, I knew Julian and I needed a little tête-à-tête about his repeated disappearing act.

The three of us walked into the bar together, followed by my Guardian. "Hey, bestie, wan' to sing a song?" Jahane turned to me and laughed.

I knew her plan was to goad me, but what the hell? They went to get us some drinks from the bar, and I went in search of an empty table close to the stage. While I waited for them to come back with our drinks, I heard a voice from behind me ask, "Hey, is this seat taken?"

My head whipped around to face Remi. The sexy grin on his lips sent a shiver through me, and his eyes dazzled me as he held my gaze. I patted the seat next to me. "Not at all."

Derrick returned to the table I'd secured, alone, with bottles of ice cold beer. He placed them on the table, and the condensation slid down the bottles to the table, making the napkin underneath catch the water.

"Derrick, this is Remi, an old childhood friend of Jahane's." They shook hands and knocked bottles together.

"Ahhhh!" The soft smooth liquid slid down my throat as I took a swig of my beer.

The waitress sashayed over to the table, so we ordered another round of long necks. When she returned a few minutes later, I'd finished my first bottle and I picked up another one from the table. The bottle was still wet from being in the fridge, and I chugged it down.

Jahane strode toward us and, with a nonchalant flip of her hand, she tossed the karaoke song book on the table as I set my third beer bottle down. "A few more of those and you will be ready to sing." She tossed her head back and her curls bounced as she laughed and sat down in Derrick's lap. Jahane looked at Remi and said, "Well, hello there, stranger. When did you get back into town?"

The beer had begun to take effect and I had a good buzz started. Not listening to them chat, I flipped though the song book till I came to a song I thought was perfect. I pointed with my index finger to a nice bluesy tune. Jahane leaned over my shoulder, and with a haughty laugh, said. "Oh, hell, no." She shook her head and her emphatic laughter rang in my ear. "No way; I mean, hell no."

"Yes, my dear friend, you are. You wanted to sing." My chair scratched against the floor as I stood up. Book in hand, I laughed the entire way to the end of the stage, where I handed the book back to the DJ.

I sauntered back to the table, grinning the whole way. "We are next, my dear friend," I said, with a smug smile plastered on my face.

When the DJ called our names, we made our way up to the stage giggling, even though I had to practically drag Jahane. I grabbed the microphone, bumped her hip with mine, and we set out in a rendition of "I Wanna Do Bad Things With You" by Jace Everett.

While we sang our hearts out, our bodies moved in time to the melodious, bluesy tune. The song took on a sensual feel, and we emulated the sexual tune with our voices and dance moves. I grabbed the microphone stand for the last few lines of the song and belted them out. When the song ended, we stepped off the stage to a barrage of cat calls. Together, we shook our asses on the way back to the table amidst our side-splitting laughter.

Back at the table and still with no sign of Julian, I felt a sudden wave of exhaustion, and my anger resurfaced. The night's activities had caught up with me, and fatigue took control.

"Hey guys, I'm exhausted. I think I'll head home. See y'all later." I grabbed Athena's leash and headed out.

"Wait, Rosie, I can't let you walk home alone." Jahane took on an emphatic mother hen tone with me.

"I'll be fine, I have Athena with me," I reassured her. She nodded her head in dissatisfaction, but I turned on my heel and left the bar.

I walked down the dark street and almost screamed when someone touched me. Remi's deep voice calmed me and stopped me from kicking him where his future children would have felt it.

"Damn it, Remi! I could have done damage to you."

He laughed heartily. "Rosie, I doubt that seriously. Come on, let me walk you home."

Way too tired to argue, I took his extended arm, and we walked to my home in silence.

When we entered the courtyard, we found Julian propped up next to the steps, his face riddled with sadness. His gaze moved from the ground to Remi beside me, and his face went rigid.

His eyes widened when he looked at me, and I knew the irritation I felt was plain on my face. "Do not, Julian…do not get mad!" I chided him as I walked past him with my Guardian in tow. "You disappeared again, and Remi was nice enough to walk me home. Thank you, Remi."

"Anytime, Rosaleigh."

My head swiveled towards Julian. "As for you, we will discuss this tomorrow…I'm too tired to talk with you tonight." With a raging headache working itself up to full steam, I ushered Athena up the steps and inside, but before the door shut, I saw the apologetic look on Julian's face. Before I changed my mind and let him in, I clicked the door lock, then peeked out the window through a crack in the shades and watched Remi retreat down the street, followed after a few minutes by Julian.

CHAPTER 10

The next morning, my headache had dulled but sat behind my eyes. I rubbed the sleep from my eyes and rolled out of bed. There were new items needing to be priced and shelved down at the store. Muttering all the way, I threw on a pair of jeans and a t-shirt, grabbed a cup of coffee, unlocked the door of the shop, and got started.

Back in the storage room, I swiped my face with the back of my hand. "This is going to take all day," I muttered to myself. Without further ado, I opened some of the boxes. "Athena, where are you, girl?" Around the corner, I saw her with her head in a box of my new trinkets for the store. I wondered how she had opened it, but nothing surprised me anymore.

As the door opened, the bell above it sounded like a dozen tiny wind chimes. My dog picked up her head, and a silver necklace dangled from her muzzle. Once the door shut, she turned her attention back to the box.

I knew she would be no help at all, so I turned my attention to the first customer of the day.

A tall woman with ebony hair tied in two perfect pigtails stood by the window. She craned her neck around, gazing at the shelves. Her studded motorcycle boots and the elaborate tattoo snaked around her neck gave her away as the quintessential goth. As she moved further into the store, her tattoo became more visible, and I realized I could see it was a snake with its tail descending around her back and the head wrapping itself over her shoulder. The head slithered its way down her chest and disappeared under her low-cut shirt.

"How may I help?" I wiped my hands on my long flowing shirt.

"Wow, you're the spitting image of your mom," she blurted out as she stalked towards me. When she reached a hand out to touch my hair, I jerked back, but not before I felt a slight tug at my scalp.

"My name is Gabrielle Broussard, but you can call me Gabby." She reached out her hand to me, but I held my mouth agape and stared at her in utter shock. She laughed and reached up to close my mouth, and with her other hand grabbed mine and shook it.

"Rosie, it's not polite to stare," she said to me.

"But, uhm, uhm...," I stammered. "How do you know my momma?"

As Gabby walked around the store, she passed her fingertips along the bookcases and slid books out, then placed them back on their shelves. "We were coven sisters," she replied, without even a single glance in my direction.

Sitting down on a nearby sofa, the dust rose and settled, making me cough. I looked at her in disbelief. "How come I never heard of you?" My tone was full of pure indignation. I knew all of Momma's friends and coven sisters. A deep sigh escaped, and I shook my head. I was still not used to the idea my mother was an actual witch—or me for that matter—and it was no easy feat to wrap my head around this reality.

Athena came over to sit at my feet, and I glanced at her and noticed the lone necklace dangling off her ear. I plucked it off and placed it on the table next to the sofa, then reached out my hand and petted her. It always seemed to calm me and put me at ease. I could hear a slow rumble from her as she moved in closer to protect me.

Gabby eyed my dog with a mysterious, curious look, and for a brief moment, her eyes blinked from blue to a dark black. I tried not to stare at her, but she seemed to know more than she wanted to let me in on at the moment. If it hadn't been for my blatant disregard of my manners, I would have missed it.

"Rosie, is that a Guardian?" she exclaimed in a high pitched squeal. I winced, and even Athena whined at the noise.

I shook my head and feigned ignorance at the word "Guardian." "A guardian…what is a guardian?" I asked her, and added a little hesitancy to my voice.

"It's a dog of great power created for the most powerful; but I've said too much." Her gaze raked over both of us.

A deep laugh resonated from her as I continued to pet my dog, whose low rumble from deep within had turned into a low growl. I found Gabby's intent stare upon us, and I continued to stare back at her. "Nope, she is just a Great Dane I adopted from the shelter." I figured a little white lie wouldn't hurt, and it would stop her prying questions about the nature of my dog.

When Gabby sat down opposite me, an uneasy feeling settled in my gut. There was something about this woman I didn't like. It seemed like she had a hidden secret, and I didn't trust her. Again, my momma's message sounded clearly in my head.

There will be those who want to be your friends; some will be honest, some not so much…

No sooner had the thought popped into my head than Remi walked into the store. I breathed a sigh of relief, because this goth chick was seriously giving me a case of the heebie jeebies. He sauntered over to us, knelt down beside Athena, and gave her a quick pet before he stood back up.

"Well, well, who is this sexy specimen?" Gabby's flirtatious voice made me want to hurl. Her attention was poised on Remi like he was a pig at the feast of all feasts, apple in his mouth included. What about this woman made me dislike her so much?

"Gabby, this is my friend Remi." She shook his hand and giggled like a school girl, and I almost lost my breakfast. Within seconds, I had become invisible. With a huff, I grabbed my dog's collar and went in search of more boxes that needed to be brought in from the storeroom.

I had all the time in the world, so I searched methodically through several stacks of boxes in the back holding the supplies I intended to display next. Finally finding the correct boxes, I started for the front of the store, slowly maneuvering my way through the maze I called my storeroom. As I navigated blindly through, the boxes were lifted out of my arms, and a gasp hissed from my lips.

"Rosie, why didn't you ask for help?" Remi's voice was full of concern.

I waved my hands. "Uh, because you and Satan's helper were

engrossed in y'all's conversation," I retorted.

"Rosie," he joked. "Do I sense a hint of jealousy?"

I dismissed his question. "No, I don't trust her."

He gave me a quizzical look. "Why not?"

"I just don't." My gaze slid up to his face, and his expression made me weak in the knees. I dislodged all crazy thoughts from my head. I didn't want to have to go into an explanation of, "Oh by the way, I'm a witch and my Great Dane is actually not just a dog, she is a Guardian." Wow, even in my head it sounded extremely sarcastic.

"So, anyway, where did Satan's sister flash off to?" I asked in my sweetest of sarcastic voices.

Remi eyed me with a hint of humor and retorted, "She said she would be back later to talk with you."

A low mumble of incoherent words fled from under my breath. "I hope not too soon." I turned and looked at Remi as he gawked at me.

Before we continued back to the front of the shop, I punched him on the shoulder. "Come on, why don't we stop chit chatting and get some work done?" I pointed him to the back of the store room where the delivery man had placed my supplies.

I sat cross-legged on the floor and began to pull some of the books out of the boxes. I had a few things left over from the time my mom ran the store, but couldn't bear to sell them. They had all been placed in my office in the back.

My idea to revamp the store was to turn it into a bookstore. I envisioned this to be a place you could come relax, pick a book, settle on the sofa, and drink some coffee. I even had a new name picked out…

Books and Lagniappe. With a wistful sigh, I thought about how my momma would be proud and not upset with me for trying out something new with the store. Besides, I had enough of her essence in the store so it still felt like she was there.

Remi came out of the storeroom and pulled me out of my daydream. "Rosie, I think you could use some more bookshelves," he said, looking at all the books spread out around me.

I looked down at the book I held in my hand called *The Book Waitress* by Deena Remiel and sighed. "You know, you're right." I looked at the boxes surrounding me containing an assortment of genres and authors, from Rhonda Dennis and Morgan Kearns to Belinda Boring and Kris Tualla.

Remi walked over to a shelf and pulled out a book titled *Erotic Treats* by Rhonda Plumhoff, and licked his lips. He flipped through it and mumbled, "Um, yep I can do that, and, oh yes, that. Hmm, that one, too. Hey Rosie, can I borrow this book?"

"Yes, but if you think that's hot…." I reached into another box. "Why don't you try this one?" I tossed it to him.

"Hmm, *Naked.*" His leer raked over the title as he read it. "This might be right up my alley." He grinned wide, showing off a set of perfect white teeth.

I laughed at him and scoffed. "Get your mind out of the gutter. It's a love story."

He let out a chuckle as he placed it on the table. "Rosie, would you like me to make you some more bookcases?"

"Sure, that'd be nice. I appreciate the offer."

"Okay, do you have any old wood, or do I need to pick some up?"

"No, I think Momma had some old cypress wood out in the courtyard."

Remi and I settled into a nice working rhythm. While he made new bookshelves out of some spare wood, I worked on my organization of the books into categories I thought worked best together. I also found a shelf for the few trinket souvenirs from New Orleans if tourists came in.

As I sat on the floor trying to get things organized, Remi sauntered back inside and interrupted my thoughts. "Hey Rosie, you know, I could find you some nice display cases for all the new jewelry."

"Oh, great. Let me know what you find and I'll write you a check."

Once we were done and all the books were stocked and in order on the shelves, I wiped my sweaty forehead. The grime poured off me. I stifled a yawn and stretched like a cat after a long nap. Remi walked over to the table next to the sofa and picked up the book I had handed him earlier. He placed some bills in my hand and I looked up at him, shook my head, and said, "You can't afford this right now."

His deep baritone laugh echoed through the small store. "Rosie, think of it as your first sale in your new shop. Let me do this for you, okay?" he pleaded. He cupped the money in my hand.

"Oh, all right, Remi."

The closed sign hit the glass door as I flipped it around. With the door locked, I waved goodbye to Remi and watched him walk down the street.

"Okay, girl, let's go grab something to eat and get cleaned up." I swore by all things sacred I heard the damn dog talk in my head. No, this can't be real. She trotted in front of me as we entered the courtyard and went up the steps to the apartment.

Once back in my apartment, I set my purse and keys down on the kitchen table. I was in the mood for pizza, so I took one out of the freezer.

After I preheated the oven and popped the pepperoni and cheese pizza in, I fed Athena, then stripped off my clothes and got into the shower to wash off the day's funk. Once clean, I wrapped my hair in a towel, slipped into a pair of shorts and a t-shirt, and grabbed my book of magic off the nightstand.

When the buzzer went off, I pulled the pizza out of the oven and headed into the living room for a bit of light reading and dinner. Athena followed me as I balanced the pizza and a Coke in my hands. I curled up on the sofa and flipped through the book once again. I needed answers to this whole situation I found myself embroiled in, and I hoped the vellum pages would show me what I needed.

A few minutes later, the phone rang, and the caller ID on my phone popped up to reveal Julian's number. Not in the mood to talk to him, I decided to let it go to voicemail and went back to my book. I figured it would be good for him to stew some more. I picked up a slice of pizza and bit down as cheese pulled from the slice to my mouth.

Before I opened the book again, I sighed as a hint of anger and disappointment hit me. Why didn't my mom tell me I was a witch, or Miss Alina? Why wasn't I informed of my powers? Anger surged through me at the thought I might have been able to save my mother, and I almost threw the book on the floor.

Athena nudged my arm with her head and looked up at me. I felt a flutter in my head and rubbed my temples. I petted Athena, and absently my fingertips traced the design of a crescent moon on the cover of the thick leather book. I muttered to myself, "Oh well, I am determined to get my answers."

With a gentle touch of my finger, I flipped one of the vellum pages of the book and saw recipes for a few spells, but the next page was all about a witch's Guardian. I was intrigued. Athena crawled up in my lap as far as she could, and I had to wiggle around her to get us both comfortable. She seemed to be as curious as I was to find something out about her. I mumbled to her while she sat there and took up almost my entire lap. "I swear you have gained fifteen pounds."

I began to read aloud from the book.

"A witch's Guardian is a dog of great stature. Her bloodline comes from the first Great Danes ever born. A well-known Danish alchemist, Alexander Christiansen, who lived in Germany in the 1600s, began to mix in a little magic with the dog's DNA to make this special dog, and it is still known as the Guardian. Sadly, only a few of the puppies survived the transition from non-magical to magical. Those who did were trained to serve the witch they were meant to guard. They are always and foremost female. If a male is born, it will become a warrior and go to a male witch. Until her witch is ready, the Guardian will stay in her puppy form. Sometimes it takes hundreds of years for her witch to present herself."

I looked over at my Guardian and wondered aloud. "How old are you? Are you hundreds of years old, hmm?" She nudged her head under my hand and a little flutter went through my head.

I flipped to the next page.

"Only a handful of witches have ever gained the power to obtain or receive a Guardian. The witch must be born from two powerful parents. There have only been a dozen or so of these witches in history. The Guardian pup will be sent to them on their twenty-seventh birthday. While the witch begins to come into her powers, the Guardian pup will continue to grow. Even if the witch shows considerable talent at a very young age, when her Guardian arrives, she will become more powerful."

The next few lines were in my mother's script. "I traveled to Germany, where Alexander still lived, and asked him for a favor. He told me he knew of the right dog, and she had been waiting hundreds of years for you. HE knew she was destined for greatness."

With a glance at the now sleeping puppy curled by my feet, my question of her being hundreds of years old was answered by my momma's beautiful script. At the sound of Athena's soft snores, I smiled down at her. "So you're my Guardian, huh?" I snuggled deeper into the sofa and closed my eyes as my mother's words played over and over in my head. My momma's confession of making sure I was protected brought a tear to my eye. Exhaustion from the last couple of days had caught up with me, and I was asleep in minutes, with Athena next to me and my book on my chest.

CHAPTER II

The book on my chest fell to the floor with a loud thud when I rolled over on the sofa. My eyes cracked open at the loud noise. I patted the ground in search of the book, closed it, and bent a page in the process.

"Ugh, how long was I sleep?" I stretched, arched my back, and tried my best to get the kink out of my neck.

My hands fought with the strands as they brushed through my tangled hair. I hoisted myself up off the sofa and trudged into the bathroom for a quick shower, but not before I texted Jahane and asked her to meet me. Thoughts of visiting Madame Claudette to ask her why I had to talk to Marie Laveau, a dead woman, ran rampant through my head. I muttered to myself, "I can't believe it. The voodoo queen has been dead for years! How in the hell can she help me find out what's wrong with Julian?"

After I finished getting dressed, I scooped my long hair up in a ponytail. A knock sounded on the door, and when Athena scratched at it, I ran to open it. "Hold your horses, girl," I told her.

Jahane stood on the other side. The dog bounded into her and almost knocked her on her ass.

"Damn, Rosie, what the hell are you feeding her? She weighs a ton." My bestie righted herself and held onto the wall in case she was actually knocked down again.

I glanced at my dog and realized she had grown quite a lot in a short amount of time…she even looked a little taller. Dumbfounded, my friend and I stood in the doorway of my apartment, and for the next ten minutes, gawked as Athena's ears transformed from being floppy to standing straight up, like a Doberman pinscher's ears. Well, at least one did. She sat there and stared up at us, and continued to wag her tail on the floor with a thump thump thump.

When she let out a single bark, the damn flutter circling through my head was clearer this time, and a strange voice boomed through my head. *Okay, Mom, I am done with my transformation for now.* I stumbled a bit at the voice in my head and shook the cobwebs out. My eyes went wide as my Guardian spoke in my head again. *You had to believe in yourself and me. And now our powers are growing.*

I moved over to inspect her ears, and she rubbed my arm with her muzzle. I whispered so she could hear me. "You can talk to me?"

Yes, it is part of our powers. But because you were in denial, you couldn't understand me.

My body swung over to face Jahane. "Well, what do you know? It looks like my dog is magical." A low chuckle burst out as I watched her mouth hanging open, agog at what she had witnessed. On my way to grab my purse, I raised her chin to close her mouth.

"It can't be," she exclaimed.

"It is what it is. And I call it magical. And you know it's rude to stare," I joked with her. "Well, let's go see what the crazy fortune teller has to say." I turned to shut my front door and stopped. "Wait one second, I forgot something; I'll be back."

Her head bobbed up and down, still in awe at what she had witnessed. She hooked Athena's leash to her collar as I sprinted back into my room, grabbed the little blue bag, pulled out the amulet I'd been given for protection, and placed it back around my neck.

"Okay, we're ready."

When we stepped outside, the weather was perfect, the sun shone, and a slight breeze blew around us. Jahane, my Guardian, and I headed to Jackson Square. I scanned the many tables lining the Square in search of Madame Claudette's. The space her table had occupied was empty, and we ran toward the vacant spot.

"Okay, now what do I do?" I asked in exasperation.

Someone tapped lightly on my shoulder, and I turned around to look into the face of an older woman, who wore her grey hair in a tight bun. "Yes, ma'am?"

"Are you looking for Madame Claudette, child?" she asked.

My head bobbed up and down. "Yes, ma'am, I am."

"Oh, child, she is in her store today. She works there on Thursdays, and does not do business in the Quarter," she informed me.

After I obtained the directions to Madame Claudette's shop, I thanked the little old lady and watched her toddle down the street.

Jahane came to stand beside me with Athena in tow. "Where is the bat shit crazy woman?" She asked, and almost fell into a fit of laughter at her joke.

I raised an eyebrow at her. "She is in her store today."

Off we went through the Quarter. I remained quiet as we walked down the red bricks of Chartres Street. Not paying attention, I tripped on a broken brick, but caught myself before I fell. At the corner I glanced around, looked at the signs, and took a left onto Dumaine Street. Looking around, I noticed a wooden sign that swung a few feet from us. I tugged on Jahane's sleeve and pointed to a gaudy sign across the street, in big, bold purple letters, MADAME CLAUDETTE FORTUNE TELLER EXTRAORDINAIRE.

I nudged Jahane as we stepped into a large, posh anteroom. A counter stood to the left of us, as well as a door with sixties style beads that swung with the movement of air as the front door shut behind us. I cleared my throat and asked the room, "Ahem. Madame Claudette, are you here?" The atmosphere was eerie at best, and a chill climbed up my spine, so I scooted closer to where Athena and Jahane stood. I swore my dog stood prouder and taller than she had at my apartment.

"Be right with you, my dear," came a disembodied voice from the room behind the laced beads.

The store was full of knick knacks, and I shook my head, at the thought people were crazy for believing all this stuff. But again, I was there wanting answers, and I didn't consider myself crazy; or was I?

"Oh, my dear, of course they believe, and no, you are not crazy, either. There are so many things out in the world most people see and won't ever believe, and make up stuff and deny the truth." Madame Claudette laughed as she walked out through the beaded curtain. The woman was surely a sight to see with her multicolored skirt, and around her shoulders she wore a red shawl with fringe covering her chest. Her red curly hair was loose, and fell down and framed her face. She was almost pretty with it down.

I turned around in disbelief. "Uh ... uh ... what...? I didn't say that out loud." The shock resonated in my voice. I had been so deep in thought I hadn't even heard the beads move around her when she walked through them. They closed in perfect symmetry behind her.

"No, you didn't, child ... but I am a telepath, so I can hear your thoughts." She waved us over to sit down. "My powers are much like your own, though if I am right, you have yours in the form of dreams, correct? And you are so much more than I am." She smiled at me.

Panic emerged once more, but I pushed it down and replied, "How do you know all this about me?"

"Oh, I know plenty. Besides, wasn't it you who came to me for help about your boyfriend?" she asked with no malice in her voice, just a matter of fact statement.

I nodded in agreement and let out a breath I didn't know I had held. "Yes, and that's why I'm here today."

"Okay, then please believe in what I can do for you." She steepled her hands in front of her and asked, "Now, child, how may I help you?"

"You said I needed to talk to Marie Laveau. How do I speak to someone who's been dead for years? They even have a tomb for her. So how am I supposed to talk to a dead woman, Madame Claudette?" I demanded.

With a gleam in her eyes, she replied. "My dear child, you didn't think her family wouldn't carry on in her absence, did you?"

In the next moment, the front door opened and a woman dressed to the nines walked in; her black skin almost gleamed, her hair was trussed up, and her gold hoop earrings swung as she headed towards me. She looked familiar to me, but I couldn't place from where. All of a sudden it dawned on me; she had been in my store. She almost floated towards us, and her expression was full of kindness.

"Rosie, how are you?" she asked.

For a moment, I was dumbfounded by the amount of people who knew who I was. "How do...? Uh...yeah...How do you...know...about me?" I stuttered.

She laughed and looked at Madame Claudette. "She's resembles her mother, doesn't she?" she remarked. The fortune teller snorted and bobbed her head.

She sat in the chair opposite me, and took my hands in her own. "You have done a wonderful job with your mother's store. It was such a pity to lose her." I was in total state of shock because she was the woman in my store the other day. "Rosie, my name is Marie Laurent. I am a descendent of Marie Laveau. And, yes, I knew your mother."

"Are you the one I need to speak with?" A dozen emotions rolled through me at the craziness I'd jumped into since I had been back. Voodoo, the Voodoo Queen, and her descendant...I shook my head at my life.

"I am one of the people you must speak to, but the other person is for another time. But, ah, yes, your boyfriend, Julian Quibadeaux, has a story I don't even think he knows about." She patted my hand, which she held in hers. "Rosie, years ago, a young Henri Quibadeaux, who I presume would be an ancestor to your beloved

Julian visited my ancestor Marie Laveau."

Jahane and I leaned closer and rested our elbows on the table as Marie spoke.

"Henri went to Marie to ask a favor. You see, his wife was carrying a child. He wanted to protect her, but she was not of his class or his race. Henri had met her at a quadroon ball, and they had fallen in love. But, rich white men did not marry any woman with even an ounce of African blood in them. They were only there for pleasure, and if they did happen to fall in love...well, they were made into mistresses, not wives. He married her anyway, and because of this, was disowned by his family. His family consisted of wealthy plantation owners. Once disowned, Henri and his wife moved into a small cottage in the Quarter. They were in love and did not mind being poor. They had each other."

As Marie paused in her story, Jahane and I looked dumbfounded. "What did Henri ask of Marie?" I asked.

"All in good time, my dear," she replied, and continued with her story. "Henri was forced to endure some death threats, because he was to have been married to a well-to-do lady from a neighboring plantation, and her brothers did not take it well their sister had been dumped for a creole woman. They threatened Clara's life, and so, because of fear for his unborn child and his wife, he went to Marie Laveau for help."

Jahane leaned in closer, enthralled with the story we were being told. I turned my attention to Marie and interrupted her. "But, what does this have to do with Julian?" I asked.

Marie cleared her throat and said, "Okay, now let me finish my tale, child." She looked at me with a quirk of her brows, which signaled for me to allow her to finish her whole story, and if afterwards I had questions, she would be happy to oblige me with the answers.

She continued. "Well, as you know, once you make a deal with my great-great-great grandmother, you must stick to it. He made a deal with the devil, so to speak, in this case. She could be kind, but if you rubbed her the wrong way, you were doomed. In order to protect his wife and unborn child and rid his life of the death threats, he would have to take the life of the brother who had placed a bounty on his head, to pay Marie for her services. Marie had told him this was the only way to rid himself of the threat. Once the deed was done, he was to bring the body to her so she could perform a ritual, so no one would know the man had died at the hand of Henri.

"Henri was all set to do this, but his father intervened. So, Henri decided to trick Marie and make it look like he had accomplished what he had set out to do, which caused dire consequences. After Marie had been duped, I can only imagine she prayed to one of the Loa and they guided her to the decision she made. It was not until his second child was to be born that he was summoned to Marie, and when he arrived, he had to pay for his slight. The penalty was every first born child of his blood line, at their twenty-eighth birthday, would become a monster and change into what you know as a Roux ga Roux."

I inhaled sharply, and Athena jumped up from her position under the table, placed her head on my lap, and whined. Marie's face changed in a flash from shock to apprehension, and she grabbed her throat at the sight of my Guardian.

She turned to me and placed a fake smile on her face, and asked, "Rosaleigh, is that what I think it is?"

I nodded. "Yes, ma'am," as I held tighter to Athena and petted her head.

Jahane interrupted to ask. "What is a Roux ga Roux?"

The woman regained her composure and continued with her story. "Ahh, my dear child." Marie spoke in a hushed tone. "A RougaRoux, or LoupGarou, is the Cajun werewolf. In the legends of the Cajun people, the creature is said to prowl through the swamps of neighboring bayou parishes all the way to the Greater New Orleans area. It is also said to have been seen in the fields and the marsh areas. Its body resembles a human with the head of a wolf or a dog, similar to the werewolf legend. When it stands on its hind legs, legend says it is almost eight feet tall. The Roux ga Roux has red eyes that can pierce right through you. It is said if you happen upon it and shine a light in its eyes, it's something you will never forget seeing."

While I watched the other two women at the table listening intently to Marie's tale, panic ran rampant in me at the thought of Julian turning into such a creature. My thoughts were interrupted by a loud gasp from Jahane. Marie placed a kind and gentle hand on Jahane's arm and finished her story.

"Other legends, or stories, like this range from trying to instill fear and obedience in children, to suggesting the beast would hunt Catholics down and kill them if they didn't follow the rules of lent. It was believed by many if you were to break the Lenten rules seven years in a row, you would be turned into a Roux ga Roux. One legend even includes blood sucking. The monster is said to be under a spell for one hundred days, but once the time elapses, the last human to be bitten by the bloodsucker will have the curse fall upon them. During the day the Roux ga Roux returns to his human form, and although he acts sick, he will abstain from telling anyone what has befallen him.

"As we all know, only strong witchcraft can bring about this long suffering, indelible curse. And, as you well know, my ancestor was considered to be quite powerful in her day. So with all we know about her—and I have heard this through the family—Marie Laveau was the one who enacted this particular curse, of course with the help of the Loa." Marie finished her outrageous story and folded her hands in her lap. She looked like she had just been telling the three of us the most delightful tale, when in reality, she had explained my Julian was doomed.

I asked, "So is this what's happening to Julian, and how do I stop it?"

Her laugh was soft and subtle. "My child, there is no help for him; he is doomed and will make the change." She placed her hand on my shoulder and looked at me with sorrowful eyes.

I sniffed back my tears and placed my head in my hands. I felt the familiar touch of Jahane's hand on my shoulder, and I let go with no hesitation, and tears poured down my face. "But...uh...there has to be a way!" My words tumbled out of my mouth like a waterfall. The continual wringing of my hands was the one thing keeping me sane.

Jahane moved over and knelt in front of me. "Rosie, we will find a way," she tried to assure me. Madame Claudette handed me a tissue, and I wiped my eyes. The presence of Marie loomed behind me.

"Child," she said, "there may be a way." She eyed Athena and continued. "You have a Guardian, which means you are a very powerful witch in your own right. What are your powers, dear?"

I looked up at her through tear stained eyes, with my nose a bit stuffy from crying. "Ma'am, I don't know. Before I came back home, I had no idea about any of this." I hiccupped.

Madame Claudette and Marie passed glances between each other, and I knew there was something they weren't telling me. I sat up in my chair and tried to make my voice not squeak. "What are you two not telling me?" I asked with an indignant tone.

Madame Claudette stood, walked over, and sat next to me. "My dear child, not only can you see the past, present, and the future in your dreams, but you have the power of resurgence, or in layman's terms, you can heal. Which means you can pull a person or animal back from the brink of death. And only one with three powers like yours gains a Guardian. We know time will show your third power. But for now you have two out of three." The fortune teller glanced down at my lap. My skirt had been ruffled, and the scars on my legs were now visible. With the swiftest of movements, I pulled the skirt back over to cover my scars.

Dismayed at what I was told, I turned to them and said, "What do you mean I can heal? I can't heal anything. I'm not a doctor or a magician."

Jahane pushed up from her position. "Uh, Rosie? Yeah, I think you can."

Pure unadulterated shock and disbelief crossed my face and continued with my next question. "What are you talking about?"

"Rosie, don't you remember the little pigeon in the Square you found one day a few weeks after your accident? It was almost dead, and when you picked up its little lifeless body in your hands, with the slightest of your touches on its wings, it stirred. By the time we made it back to the shop, it had perched itself on your shoulder and tried to fly around."

The memory of the pigeon hit me like a ton of bricks, and my mouth went slack. "Oh my gawd, this is unbelievable. I don't think I can handle much more." With Athena's leash in my hand, I stomped out of the shop. The tinkle of the little bell sounded above me as the door shut behind us.

Jahane jogged after me, pulled me to a stop, and forced me to look at her. When she pulled me into a comfortable hug, the tears streamed down my face. "This can't be happening." My chest heaved as I pulled away from her. "I can't lose Julian. I don't want him to turn into a monster. How can I do this? I'm not strong enough. I ran away from home when it got bad because a dream told me not to tell anyone," I cried.

"You won't lose him; we'll come up with an idea."

I sighed, and with Jahane's arm wrapped around me, we ambled back towards Jackson Square.

CHAPTER 12

A rm in arm we strolled for a while in silence as I let all the information soak in.

"Rosie?" She interrupted the silence and looked over at me. "We'll figure it out."

"I hope so." With my head hung low, we continued back to the shop. "I don't know what to believe anymore, Jahane. Julian is supposed to turn into a monster from an old folk tale our parents told." I shook my head in disbelief and continued. "This can't be real ... and why does Julian not know about all of this?"

Jahane stopped and turned me to face her. "Rosie, I don't know about the Julian situation, but I can tell you this much...I do believe them when they say you can heal."

Shock and fear spread through me. A sudden flashback of the zoo incident played in my head like a slow moving movie. The leash dropped from my hand, and my head replaced it. "Jahane, when I went to the zoo the other day with Julian, there was an incident with the tigers. They were in an uproar, like they wanted to rip us apart, and there was a little girl…" My words came out in a rapid babble.

"Take it easy, Rosie … come here, sit," she said in a calm tone, and led me to a bench. I sat and Athena placed her head on my feet. The instant comfort I felt with my Guardian and my best friend consumed me. Their presence eased all the tension I had built up inside me.

Once I had become calm enough, I continued my story about the zoo. I relayed to her how the tigers were eager to escape their enclosure, and about the little girl who'd collapsed. "I touched her, and one moment she had a very weak pulse, and the next her heartbeat was strong."

Jahane nodded at me. "Just like with the pigeon. I'm sure there are other incidents. Ones we don't remember right now."

The folds of my skirt moved as I shifted on the cold bench, and my gaze fell along the zig-zag marks peeking through the folds. The scars made me sad and angry. Tears brimmed at the corners of my eyes as they focused on my legs. Without even looking up at Jahane, I asked, "Why can't I heal my own legs? What good is having this power of resurgence when I can't even help myself?"

Tears trickled down my chin and landed on my exposed skin as I continued to trace the jagged scars. The whole time Jahane held me, her comfort soothing the pain and heartache and trying to pull it free from me. My best friend pulled back from our embrace and watched me trace the raised skin of my scars. She cupped her hand over mine and drew along the jagged edges along with me. In a hushed whisper, she said, "Rosie, have you ever thought maybe you were not meant to heal your own body? Maybe they are a reminder to help you be stronger."

Athena whined in my head. She picked her head up and placed it in my lap. With an absentminded action, I petted her and looked up at Jahane. "What do you mean, it makes me stronger?" I asked indignantly.

Jahane's curls bounced as she shook her head at me. "Rosie." She removed my hands, and with a light touch traced along the serrated scarred lines that wound around my right leg. "These marks have made you stronger by helping you cope with life. Hell, look what you have accomplished in life. At one time you couldn't walk, and look at you now. Let me tell you a story of a beautiful girl who turned into an even more beautiful swan."

My head raised up and I began to say something, but she stopped me with her hand. "No, Rosie, I know what you're going to say." My head dropped once more, not able to believe a word of what my bestie said. She lifted my lowered chin, and I looked at her, scared.

"Look, I remember the day of your accident like it was yesterday. We were only fourteen years old. I remember my mom coming to me, screaming for me to get my ass in gear, because you had been hurt. I nearly passed out from fear at the possibility you could be dead." Jahane stopped to wipe a tear from her face and continued. "When we got to the hospital, your mother was already there, pacing back and forth. My mom ran over to her and swore to Marie Laveau herself your mother was going to wear a hole straight to the devil as much as she was carrying on."

My friend's worries and fears about me swirled around me like a hurricane as her words tumbled out of her mouth.

"I remember how your mother had to lie her ass off to get me and my mom in to see you. I swear those nurses almost had a heart attack when she told them we were family. But because your momma was so strong, those nurses never stood a chance against her, even when they were faced with a white woman having had a black daughter. She refused to take no for an answer, so they were forced to allow us in." Jahane stopped for a moment, taking a breath to regain her composure. "I remember how you looked, lying there in the hospital bed."

My hand went to her knee, and with one look, I willed her to stop.

Warmth radiating from her face surprised me. "No, I must finish. You need to hear this." She winked at me and continued. "As I was saying, when I saw you in bed, it tore my heart out. Your poor leg looked mangled. I ran to the bed and held your hand. I could barely hear the doctors over the sounds of all the machines in the room. I even climbed into bed with you and held your hand as long as they would allow me. My mother told me later, at home, the doctors weren't sure they could even save your leg, or if you would ever walk again. They said the mule and carriage had almost taken your entire leg off. When they were able to get the spooked mule to stop, the back wheel of the carriage was stuck between the bones of your thigh. But, you proved everyone wrong. You, Rosie Delacroix, proved everyone wrong."

She pointed at my leg. "These are your battle wounds and ones you should be proud of. You, my dear friend, beat the odds. Even if I had not been there when the kids at school made fun of you, you would have survived. I had your back; but you, my best friend, have been and always will be the strong one." Jahane finished and hugged me tight.

The tears glistened and fell down my cheek, and I smiled up at my best friend in the whole world. "You are correct, Jahane."

Athena barked and pranced around in agreement. When I ruffled her fur, she barked in my head. I know, Athena, I know I am powerful.

Jahane stood up and dragged me from the bench. I stumbled from her hurried movement. "Geez, Jahane, no need to try to make more scars." My skirt fell back down and wrapped around my legs, and a light breeze blew it around to twirl. Magic was in the air, and I could feel it surround me and infuse all through my bones.

She raised her brow at me. "Come on, let's go find some awesome costumes; you know it's Mardi Gras, and its partay time." Her shrill laugh pierced my ears, and Athena howled in protest, then barked once again in agreement. Jahane's gaze moved between my dog and me. "Well, it's settled. Let's go," she commanded.

Before we headed to Canal Street we made a stop at the jewelry store to pick up the items we had ordered on my first day back. "Oh no; look, Jahane, they are closed."

"It's all right, we can check back another time. I'm sure it's because of the parade tonight. Come on, let's go costume shopping."

We crossed over the neutral ground on Canal Street towards a local costume shop. On a major search for the perfect costumes, we stepped inside the small store. When we entered, my bestie made a beeline to the back wall, where she picked up a costume. She dangled it up in front of her and squealed in delight. "Look!" All I saw were thin strips of material that would never come close to covering any of Jahane.

"Yes, I see it. It will cover...uh, yeah, about two centimeters of you," I replied.

"I know, and don't you think Derrick will love me in this deliciously erotic outfit?" Shse giggled and winked at me.

"I do, honey, although I don't think you will last long out partying. An early evening in is what that costume screams."

On a mission to find the perfect costumes for Julian and me, I continued around the store. By the far back wall I found the perfect dashing pirate costume for Julian. I fiddled through some more and found a cute, sexy number for me.

With the costumes draped over my arm, I wondered where my dog had gone. I glanced around and saw her with her nose sniffing through a basket close to the floor. I watched in awe as she hooked a rainbow colored feather boa over her shoulders and continued to rummage for a few more minutes. When she seemed satisfied, she moved over to me with a mouthful of things and the feather boa trailing behind her.

I kept a close eye on the shop owner, as I didn't want him to kick us out because my dog was moving through his merchandise...or worse, call the cops. I noticed the manager glance over in our direction, and I nervously grabbed the items from her shoulders and her mouth. One glance at what she had picked out had me doubled over with laughter. "What the hell is this, Athena?" I asked as I flipped over the parrot's mask.

She cocked her head at me. *Duh, Momma, it's my costume.*

"Well, at least you'll fit in with us pirates," I laughed.

We paid for our purchases and stepped out into the bright sun. Oh yeah, it was a great day for carnival.

On the way home we both sent texts to our guys. I needed to make up with Julian. I missed him, and now with my new found knowledge of what he was going through, I needed to be there for him. Tonight would be fun, and the idea I didn't need to worry about certain things, even if for a few minutes, had me giddy. "Wait, let's stop at the neighborhood bakery to get a king cake," I said. We both trudged off down another street headed for our favorite bakery.

Once home, I placed the cake on the table, and we giggled all the way to my room to change. A loud bark resounded in the living room, and we knew the guys had arrived. Our high heels clacked on the floor as we entered the living room. Jahane and I were still in a fit of giggles, and I wasn't paying attention and ended up colliding with a brick wall, namely Julian.

"Whoa there, cher." He held me at arm's length, and his deep green eyes sized me up from my head down to my black pumps, but fixated on the skin showing through the slit in my skirt. He licked his lips, crushed me towards his hard chest, and captured my mouth. His tongue darted in and I moaned into his.

My hands braced on his chest, I leaned back, and his heartbeat throbbed in sync with my pulse. "Julian, my dear, ye should be changin' them threads or else ye be walkin' the bloody plank."

He snapped his heels together and saluted me. "Aye aye, Captain."

As he slid past me, he playfully smacked my ass. Startled, I jumped, giggled, and rubbed my backside. Jahane handed Derrick his costume and pushed him with both hands in the direction of the other bathroom to change.

Cat calls and whistles exploded the moment Julian stepped out of my room. Julian looked every bit the part of sexiness, right down to his belt and leather boots. I crooked my finger at him, and when he stood in front of me, my legs almost buckled at his statuesque figure. His strong hand wrapped around my nape and pulled me closer to him. The instant our lips met once again, a fire surged straight to my core. When he broke the kiss, his tongue lingered and caressed my bottom lip.

"You two, go get a room, will ya?" said Jahane.

Still wrapped up in two muscular arms, I leaned my head back and saw Derrick. "No, bestie, but I think you will."

Jahane's head turned to the side, and Derrick sauntered out, standing tall and straight. The pirate outfit he wore fit him like a glove, from his black leather boots to the handkerchief on his head. Jahane cleared the distance in two steps, and clenched the front of his shirt in her hand. "Well, hello, sexy." He took her in his huge muscular arms, and every vein popped as he stroked her arms down to her hands and clutched her tight against his body. The black handkerchief he had wrapped around his head slid down the side as Jahane grasped him and planted a kiss.

"Ahem; shall we be going, mah ladies?" Julian said with his hat over his heart.

"No, wait, we need some king cake and wine." I scooted out of

Julian's hold.

Derrick, still tied to Jahane, went into the kitchen, pulled out a knife from the drawer, and cut four slices of king cake. On my tiptoes, I reached in the cabinet and pulled out four wine glasses. Julian was behind me and grabbed the wine from the pantry. The red liquid swilled around in the crystal glasses as he poured the wine.

"Everyone, let's toast to carnival." All four glasses clinked, and as the glass touched my lips the smooth red liquid slid down my throat.

The cinnamon with green, purple, and yellow sugar scattered on the top of the cake melted in my mouth. A bit of Bavarian cream oozed out, and before I could lick it, Julian's finger wiped it off. My head lifted to see him lick his finger with a wicked grin.

Once we were all done and dressed as our merry band of pirates, Athena came bounding out dressed as a parrot. Derrick busted out laughing at the sight, holding his stomach, his hysterical laughter echoing off the walls.

"Now this will get us noticed tonight," he joked.

Jahane popped him on the arm and seized him for a kiss while her breasts pressed into his thick chest

"Okay, you two, get a room," I jested.

Derrick grinned at Jahane and headed towards the bedroom. She braced herself and stopped him, which, as large as he was, seemed a feat in its own right. "Later, you sexy, dirty

pirate. Aye mate, I will have me way with ye later." She winked at him.

By the time we had made it downstairs and to Bourbon Street, the revelers had already started to celebrate. The enthusiasm and decadence was high, and some of the costumes people were wearing left little to the imagination. The sky showed a hint of light, making it easy to maneuver through the crowds.

"Hey, do y'all want a drink?" Julian asked.

"Sure." We spoke in unison. As Jahane and I waited by the entrance to the club for the guys to bring us drinks, we caught enough boobage to make a grown man cry. The perfectly rounded breasts jiggled as more beads were tossed up to the balcony overhead. With each bead they giggled and shimmied their bodies.

I nudged Jahane with my elbow. "Looks like they have been at this for a while now; they almost have enough beads to make a shirt."

"Girl, you are so bad," she cackled, and we high fived each other.

The crowd thickened like a good gumbo roux, so my merry band of pirates headed to the closest bar to watch the shenanigans. From the doorway, I scanned the crowd, and gasped when I saw a tall figure staring in my direction. His menacing sneer held me in a trance. Covered from head to toe in black, his cowl hid all but his eyes. He stood still, his red eyes peering out from under his hood. Then he began to glide through the crowd as they separated like clouds dispersed by the wind.

My head whipped from side to side, looking for Julian, and I found him with a beer in his hand, chugging it as Derrick spoke to him. When

I couldn't get his attention, terror consumed me. My heart beat rapidly as the monster edged closer and closer to me. As soon as his body came into view, I saw through his open cloak as it billowed in the nonexistent wind. Thick, coarse hair covered his entire body, and his head reached almost to the overhang above me.

I backed up until I hit a hard object with a thud, the creature still inching closer to me. All of a sudden, it was just the two of us standing there in an empty street. Before he made it all the way to me I pulled my amulet from under my shirt and grasped it. His teeth dripped saliva as he closed in. When he was in close proximity to me, my fear registered and my reflection mirrored in his eyes.

With a nervous glance around the empty street, I wondered where everyone had gone. "What do you…want…with me?"

His mouth was a dark abyss with two yellow stained teeth. His long dirty fingernail dragged down the side of my face, and a chill raced down my spine. "I want your powers," he hissed out, as spittle formed on his lips and dripped down his hairy chest.

The amulet clenched in my hands, I held it out in front of me and shoved it in his face. He stepped back and hissed. All of a sudden, my Guardian appeared beside me, and power surged from her and into me.

"You can't have my powers." Bravery and a magical essence coursed through every vein, bone, blood cell, and nerve in my body. My Guardian and I stood side by side and emitted a power I hadn't known was in me. With the blink of an eye, the street was once again crowded, and all I heard was the distant sound of an evil laugh and the words "We will be back for you." My hand still clenched the amulet, and my fingers hurt from the tight hold. I regained my composure and slowed my breaths. When I looked around, I saw Jahane staring at me.

"Girl, what's wrong? You are paler than usual, even for a white girl. It looks as if you've seen a ghost."

I sighed after I counted to ten. "Jahane, did you see the creature? It stood there in the middle of the street."

"No, Rosie, all I saw was you, still as a rock. You reached up to your neck and pulled out your amulet, and Athena sidestepped closer to you." Her frenzied words spilled out of her mouth.

"This can't be real. I swear, I saw an old bayou folktale come to life here on the streets of New Orleans. It's not possible. I think all this partying and drinking has gone to my head." But a nervous laugh came out because I knew what I had seen was real.

"What the hell are you talking about, bestie?"

"Oh damn, Jahane, we'll discuss this later. Hey, where are the guys?" I inquired.

"Behind us." I knew she wouldn't let it go, but for now, I needed Julian.

Julian's presence enveloped me as I yearned for his warmth and comfort. His hands brushed through my hair at the same moment I leaned into his body. The five of us headed down the street to another bar as the horns and brass of Mardi Gras Mambo drifted through the street. The later it got, the more we had to shuffle through the cluster of people. Booze was thick in the crowds down Bourbon Street.

The wind carried a familiar voice to me as we shuffled through the crowd. I whipped my head around to see who'd called my name. "Oh my gawd, Rosieee," the voice squealed out.

A head full of ginger hair popped up and down through the sea of people. I smiled when I recognized my old friend. Finally, the crowd parted, and he broke free of the throngs of people. He practically threw himself at me, and I stumbled backward into Julian's arms. A hard chest caught me and arms blanketed me as I fell.

"OMG, I am so sorry, Rosie and Julian," he said. His eyes lit up, and his freckles showed even more at his embarrassment.

"It's all right, Andre." I grinned at him in his Hugh Heffner outfit and snickered at the thought of a red headed Heffner.

"You like?" He spun around and stopped to puff on his cigar. His caught sight of my costume. "Girlfriend, you look totally hot. I think someone has planned on a little action tonight?" He wiggled his eyebrows.

"Good gracious, Andre, you're as bad as Jahane," I teased.

"Oh please, girlfriend. Who do you think taught your bestie all she knows?" he whispered to me. "Now, don't go tellin' her I told you." A sly smile crossed his face. I made a motion of zipping my lips to him as he grabbed me in a long deserved hug and looked over his shoulder to Julian. "Don't be a green-eyed jealous monster, honey! You know she's not my type; but you, on the other hand, are looking sexy as ever." Andre winked.

"Andre, please, why must you flirt with my boyfriend?" I teased him.

"Because, he's all kinds of sexy."

I didn't dare turn around to see Julian's face. Thankfully, Andre changed the subject. "How the hell have you been, girlfriend?" Andre inquired.

"Oh, I've been good. I reopened my momma's shop. It looks like you're doing great." With a nod of my head I indicated the guy dressed like a bunny headed in our direction.

"Yes, I am. Oh Rosie, I think I have found *the one.*"

"I'm so happy, Andre, you deserve it."

When the guy stood in front of us, I noticed he was quite handsome. "Robert, these are some of my best friends in the world." Andre slung an arm around his shoulder. He shook our hands and the group of us headed down the street to get another drink.

Three in the morning came fast and exhaustion took over. Before Andre and his new man left us, he turned to me. "Rosie, I'll come visit you at the store. I'm sure you could use some help in the fine art of design."

I laughed and shook my head as I hugged Jahane and Derrick goodbye. Julian and I walked hand in hand on the way home.

CHAPTER 13

The next day, Remi hammered and nailed out back, since he'd decided I needed a new countertop for my shop. I flipped through the pages of the newest magazine I'd purchased with items for the shop. The pages of the magazine contained different pieces of jewelry and accessories I wanted to sell, but my mission was to find the perfect ones. Highlighter in hand, I circled yellow around the items I thought would do well and earn a profit, then dialed the number to order. After I placed my order I hung up the phone.

Outside, the roar of a motorcycle diverted my attention to the front door. Not for one moment did I hide my disdain for the person who walked into my shop.

"Rosie. Hey, hun, how are you?" Her studded biker boots thudded on the hardwood floor as she sauntered inside. She shook out her ebony pigtails as she removed her helmet.

With all the energy I could muster, I put on my best fake smile and crossed my arms over my chest as she approached the counter. "Hello, Gabby," I retorted, and looked back down at the magazine in hopes she would go away.

"Look, Rosie, I think we got off on the wrong foot the other day. I know I must have freaked you out when I came in here talking about your mom. And I know you won't trust me overnight, but eventually, I would like for us to be friends."

"Mmm hmm, yes, you did, Gabby." My voice took on a sarcastic tone.

She leaned over the counter, and I looked up from under my lids at her. Her position showed me a better view of the tattoo encircling her body, though it looked to be in a different spot than last time. As I stared at her, the tattoo began to move. I gasped, but stopped myself from screeching. With her low cut blouse, I could see my instincts were correct...the head of the snake dipped down lower on her breast.

She eyed me inquisitively. "Why don't we go get something to eat? I can also fill you in on how I know your mom and the symbolism behind my tattoo." She winked at me. Even though I had tried to hide my curiosity about her tattoo, she knew.

I was still apprehensive, but I thought it would be beneficial for me to find out more about her. I'd always heard to keep your friends close, but to keep your enemies closer. My smile was almost too sweet. "Yes, sure, we can talk. Let me get Athena and we can head out."

Out back, Remi was still busy and Athena was with him. I knew it was a good idea to let someone know where I went in case the she-devil was up to no good and this was a trick. Around the corner, the tap tap tap of the hammer was steady.

"Hey, Remi." I stopped dead in my tracks. His shirt was off, and his dark skin glistened in the sun. Sweat dripped down every delicious ridge. His muscles rippled as he picked up a board and placed it in the position he wanted it. He turned and picked up a towel, and I watched as he wiped the sweat from his brow, and the erotic way he made sure to pay attention to each crevice of his six pack abs.

As he put the towel down, he squinted up at me. In a hurry, I regained my composure, but not before he had caught me gaping at him. His smile was proof he had noticed my display of lust.

"I'm almost finished here, Rosie."

I nodded and tried to grab from my brain why I had come outside. Oh, yes…mental face palm. "Remi, Satan's bitch is here and apologized for her recent bomb about my mom, and she also wants to talk to me."

"Are you sure, Rosie? I thought you didn't trust her." His tone was full of concern.

"Eh, I'll be fine. Anyway, I'll have my trusty companion with me. I think I need to find out what her deal is and what she wants. "

"If you need me, text me."

"Sure will; please lock up when you're done. Come on, Athena, let's go." I patted my leg, and she bounded up to me and licked me on the face. "Ewww," I snorted as I clipped the leash to her collar.

Once back inside with Athena in tow, Gabby's back was turned to me as she made tea at the counter. "We're ready." My voice was a little louder than I meant.

She jumped, spun around, and almost dropped the tea cup at the sound of my voice. I covered my mouth and laughed. The little satisfactory giggle made me giddy.

"Oh my goodness, you shouldn't scare a person like that," she exclaimed as she held onto the teetering china cup.

I waved her off. "Oh please, Gabby. I'm so not scary. Now this one, she's a different story." I pointed to the Great Dane and burst into a fit of giggles at Athena, with the tip of one ear up and one down as her tongue lolled out the side of her mouth.

With a shaky hand, Gabby placed the cup down and strode towards us. "You're right, Rosie." She followed us both, and before she stepped outside, she ruffled the dog's ears. My Guardian's hackles rose a tad then instantaneously went back down.

"Okay, let's go." I held the door open and the three of us stepped into the bright sunshine and rounded the corner to the Square. As I spotted the local lucky dog cart, I turned to face the she-devil. "Hey, Gabby, have you ever had a lucky dog?"

She shook her head. "No, Rosie, I can't say I have."

Shock registered on my face. "Oh, you have got to be kidding me," I scoffed. "Well, you are in for a treat."

Athena padded off to the cart as we followed. "Hey, Raul," I hollered as we got closer. The short, squat man turned around, smiled a toothless grin, and waved.

"Miss Rosie, how are you today?" he asked.

Athena sat down on her haunches, and the movement of her tail swishing caused a mini tornado. The look shared between Raul and my dog made me wonder. "Nice looking dog you got there. Miss Rosie, how can I help you today?"

"Oh, you know, the same ole same ole. I'm great, Raul, but my friend here has never tasted the scrumptious treat of a lucky dog."

"Oh no, she hasn't? Well, we'll have to change that now, won't we, Miss Rosie?" he exclaimed.

"Make it three lucky dogs with mustard and relish."

"At your service."

He dipped his metal tongs into the vat of boiled weenies, plucked one out at a time, and snuggled them into their buns. My stomach growled as he layered them each with a huge glop of relish. "Here you go, Miss Rosie," he said. When he bent down to eye level with

Athena, she took her treat gently, not even nipping Raul. "Good girl." I would have sworn he winked at her. I finagled around the items in my purse and grabbed a few dollars. After I slipped them to the vendor, we sat on a nearby bench.

Between bites, Gabby turned to face me. "I'm sorry I freaked you out the other day. I didn't mean to upset you."

My hand rested on her shoulder, and the tattoo seemed to undulate and slither under my touch. I inhaled silently and withdrew my hand, and returned it to my lap. "I understand,

Gabby. But, it's been hard without her. Plus, the suddenness of her disappearance doubled the stress. Not knowing why, where, who, or how adds to my frustration." I bowed my head to hide my weakness in front of her. After a few seconds, I pulled my head back up. "So how did you know my momma?"

"Oh, I met her at a ritual a long time ago before she even had you. She was a powerful witch, and I think she was the same age as you are now. She taught me so much in the world of magic, and her death saddens me." Her voice was almost inaudible.

There was no way in hell Gabby was any older than I was, but my best move was to nod my head.

As if she could read my mind, she spoke. "I know what you're thinking…I don't look that old. But," she smiled at me, "I have great genes."

My eyebrows cocked upward at what I deduced to be a lie, but I nodded and looked wide-eyed at her. *Yeah, more like maybe a ton of facelifts.* The thought drew an instant smirk to my face.

I glanced at the tattoo once again. I was sure my curiosity was written all over my face, and she chuckled. "Well, as for my little pet here…" She reached down, and when she touched it the skin of the tattoo rippled. "Snakes are considered protectors of magical entities and sacred knowledge. A Roman warlock from the old country—who, I may add, is quite talented in the art of tattoos—gave this to me. He said it would protect me from harm."

As I sat on the bench and stared at her in silence, I contemplated all she had told me. There was something amiss here.

I was pulled from my thoughts by the sound of the familiar voice of my best friend. "Rosie, Rosie."

I jumped up from the bench and ran to her. "Hey, girl, what's up?"

Jahane looked at me, and then her gaze stopped on the goth chick on the bench. Athena sat beside her and licked her paw with a slurp. *Silly dog,* I thought to myself.

DIANA MARIE DUBIOS

"Jahane, come meet another coven sister of my momma's, or better known as Satan's bitch." I whispered the last part with raised brows. "Gabby, this is my best friend, Jahane."

"Nice to meet you." She took Jahane's offered but apprehensive hand.

I faced Jahane. "So what has you in such a tizzy this morning?"

"Well, what has me in such a tizzy, as you call it…," she air quoted and whispered, "is you need to find out more about your powers. I think we need to go and see Alina. She can help you deal with all this, and maybe tell you more about them. I also thought afterward we could make a stop to see if the jewelry store is open." My head swiveled over to Gabby as she sat back on the bench stoically.

"Hey Gabby, want to come with us?"

She nodded, jumped up, and followed us. "Sure, why not?"

Athena's leash dragged along the cobblestone street as we headed to Alina's with Gabby in tow. Jahane's breath tickled when she leaned in and whispered low in my ear, "Do you think she's trustworthy?"

With a slight shake of my head, I replied under my breath without much faith, "I don't know, but my goal is to find out, or at least discover what she wants."

I was the first to walk through the door, and my entrance made the bells chime above it.

"I'll be with you, dears," a muffled voice said from the back.

I flung myself into one of the comfortable chairs Alina had dispersed throughout the shop. A chocolate chip cookie scent floated to my nose, and it twitched to find the cookie. I looked around and saw them on the table beside me. It was as if Alina had known I would be there today. "Here ya go, girl." I grabbed one and tossed it to Athena, who caught it midair. "Miss Alina bakes the best homemade cookies."

As I sat there, I was deep in thought about all I had been through in the past. The loss of my momma and this new situation with the love of my life sent emotions running amok in my head.

"Rosie." A familiar voice pulled me back into the room and away from my thoughts.

Greeted by a soft hug from my momma's dearest and oldest friend, I snuggled into her embrace. Alina pulled back from our hug and gazed around at the people in her shop.

"Jahane, it's nice to see you again, sweetheart."

Pure hatred crossed her face when she saw Gabby, who stood with a fake smile on her face. "Gabrielle, it's nice to see you as well." Her tone was cold and unfriendly. "You still have that thing with you." She pointed in disgust at the tattoo slithering around Gabby's shoulder.

My gaze followed from Miss Alina to Gabby and then to the snake. Its forked tongue flicked in and out. I shook my head and wondered why Miss Alina hated her so much. *Ahh, maybe because the she-bitch has a weird ass snake tattoo that came alive on her.*

Miss Alina edged back around the counter, and her long skirt flowed around her legs. The look in her eyes and her demeanor towards Gabby did not go unnoticed by me. If I could get her alone, I would get to the bottom of who Gabby was; and more importantly, why Miss Alina's hatred for her radiated through the shop as she stared at Gabby.

"Umm, Miss Alina, may I have a word with you for a second? I have to ask you something about Athena." I tried my best to get her in the back to start my bombardment of questions.

"Sure, Rosie." She looked at both of the girls. "Jahane and Gabby, y'all make yourselves comfortable. There are cookies and tea on the counter." As she scanned the room, she gave the stink eye to Gabby, and I secretly chuckled to myself.

"Come on, girl." At my command, Athena jumped up and trotted behind us. I gave a look to Jahane, telling her to keep an eye on Gabby for me. She shook her head as our silent words passed to each other.

Once we were in the back, I sat at the little antique table, and a platter of pralines and hot tea were placed in front of me. I picked up a praline, and when I bit into it, the concoction of butter, sugar, and pecans exploded in my mouth. "Mmm," I mouthed. "Alina, this…oh wow, I have no words; this is the best I have ever tasted."

She laughed. "I'm sure it is. Rosie, it's your mother's special recipe." I took another bite, savoring every bit of the sweetness, and popped the rest into my mouth. Memories of my momma flooded through me with the delicious treat.

"So, what is it you would like to talk to me about? I know it has nothing to do with Athena, does it?" She winked at me and reached down and stroked the dog's ears from bottom to tip. "Well, aren't you growing fast and coming into your own powers as well?" Athena barked once in agreement. "You must be what now, sixty five pounds, and will continue to get bigger."

I watched the interaction between Alina and Athena with amazement. Alina must have sensed me watching them because she turned to me. "Rosie, she's a very strong dog, and she has grown in a small amount of time. No worries, she will stop growing when she's done, and she won't be overly big, though I suspect big for a Great Dane."

I nodded and sipped from the tiny china tea cup in my hand. "Well anyway, Miss Alina, the reason I'm here is because I've found out what my powers are and I need help." The words finally out of my mouth, I sank deeper into the chair.

"Oh, sweetheart, that explains a lot, and must be the reason Gabby is here. She must have felt a force pull when you received your Guardian and got stronger."

I sat up and my nails dug into the arms of the chair. "I knew I couldn't trust her, but…." I stammered and glanced at Athena. "How come my Guardian hasn't growled at her?" With a shake of my head, I whispered, "You know, every time Julian is in the room, she growls at him."

"I'm not sure, but I suspect a charm or a spell has been placed on Athena. It was a matter of time before you received your Guardian. Since she knew of your mother's powers, and maybe yours, if she came around, Athena would sense who she was. The consequences of her coming around without some spell to keep your Guardian from sensing her magic…" She waved her hand. "But I digress. Has she told you she and your mother never got along?"

"No, she didn't. Why didn't they?" I asked.

"Well, my dear, once you try your hand at dark magic, it's hard to come back to what you were before. And it was too late even after your mother found out. Still, we have no proof she dabbled, but our suspicions were strong." The disdain on her face was evident for the woman who sat out front with my best friend.

"Oh no!" I cried with sudden worry for my best friend.

"No worries, Rosie, sweetheart. Gabby will never show her hand prematurely, because she's here for a reason, one which we must find out soon. And Jahane is secure with the wards I have set up around the shop," she indicated with her arms.

I relaxed a tad in my chair. "You know, I knew something was off about her."

Alina smiled at me. "And that's why you're keeping her close to you?" She winked at me. "You have always been smart, haven't you, sweetie?" Her smile was one of a proud mother, one I wished was on the face of my mother. A tear slipped from the corner of my eye and slid down the side of my nose at the thought of her. "Oh, dear, don't cry. Your mother would be proud of you. And what she was supposed to teach you, I'll do now; it is my bound duty as her best friend and your nana."

"Oh, speaking of my momma, I wanted to show you what was left after she went missing, but the items are at my house." My face fell for a split second.

"No problem, honey, you can bring them next time you see me."

Alina stood behind the counter in the back and packed a few dozen little burlap bags. I sniffed back tears as I watched her with curiosity. "Thank you, Miss Alina." Her hand gripped mine as she handed me a canvas bag full of the little individual ones. As she let go, I wiped a stray tear from my eye.

She nodded at me. "And as for your Julian problem…" I looked at her in shock. "Yes, I know all about that issue. Claudette called and spoke to me after you left her place. She thought she may have been in the wrong for talking to you. I assured her we would all get together with Julian and discuss this situation. So please don't worry now."

"Yes, ma'am. But before I go, there's one more thing. Uh I, uh yeah…I noticed a small mark on my skin the other day."

"Ah, I had expected this would happen, but was not sure. So, where is this mark?" I pushed the waistband of my skirt slightly down my hip. "Ah yes, Rosie, this is a gift from your mother, a spell, and shows how powerful you are indeed. A small part of Athena has merged with your body. I didn't know for sure, but I had an inclination your mother visited Germany before she…" She stopped and shook her head, sighed, then pushed her white bangs back and continued. "Your mother visited Alexander, and if you have found your Crescent Grimoire, he is mentioned in it. But I've gotten off track. Your mother must have met your Guardian and put a spell on her so the moment you two came into contact, you would have a part of each other. Does she have a mark?"

"Yes, ma'am, and Momma mentioned a trip to Germany in my book." But, I was vexed at the realization my momma had placed a spell on Athena and me. I tried to remember when this could have happened, but was interrupted by Athena's head nudging me. Her broad chest came into view, and upon it was a dark red rose I had never noticed. I touched it, and it turned a multitude of colors in her fur. Heat leapt to my fingers and flowed through my body to my hip. The teardrop on my skin glowed, and after a few seconds, both marks dimmed.

Alina clapped her hands together. "Now you both are bonded in more than one way. And if anything were to happen to either one of you, or you happen to go somewhere without her, she would always be with you." She scooted off the chair and stood. "Now, wait to get home to go through that bag, and don't go through it under any circumstances in front of Gabby. You and Jahane can go through it together." Her tone was stern.

Back in her ever familiar embrace, I sniffed, and the smell of lavender surrounded me. The three of us came out of the back, and Athena bounded ahead. I looked around and saw Jahane on the sofa. She popped another cookie into her mouth, and there was a magazine in her lap. "Where did the she-devil run off to?" Sarcasm iced my words.

She stood up and dusted the remainder of the crumbs from her shirt. "She said she would meet up with you later at the store."

"I bet she did," I grumbled. "Come on,

Jahane, let's get back to the apartment before Satan's spawn finds us again," I retorted with a snort.

"I knew you didn't trust that bitch." She smiled at me as she linked her arm into mine. We promised to come back soon and waved goodbye to Alina.

CHAPTER 14

T he door to my apartment clicked open and swung back. Athena marched in and sat in front of the TV. I shook my head when Jahane sashayed into the kitchen and grabbed two wine glasses and a bottle of red wine from the pantry, then skipped back over to me. The flute shaped crystal clinked as it hit the bottle when she placed them on the coffee table. Pillow hugged to her chest, she propped herself on the sofa.

"Okay, Rosie, what do you think is in the bags?"

"Not sure, but she said to look at it with only you and Athena. Her instructions were clear, the she-devil not know the contents."

"Ah, well, now I'm intrigued." She flung her head back in laughter.

After my bestie poured the red wine, I curled my finger around the stem of the glass and sat across from her. I dumped the contents of the bag on the coffee table, and our eyes widened at the wrapped pralines.

"Go ahead and take one." She nodded and unwrapped it and savored the buttery delicacy.

The instant I saw the other items spread across the table, I inhaled a deep breath. In front of us were an assortment of stones, herbs, some personal effects, and coins. As I shuffled more of the objects around, I came across a few little bags in different materials like flannel, chamois, and leather. Jahane sat cross-legged on the floor and picked up a few crystals in her hand, flipping them back and forth. She also noticed an amulet similar to the one I wore around my neck. "Look, Rosie, there are even carved stones, what looks like good luck tokens, and a letter."

My hand trembled as I reached for the letter. The flaps wavered as I tried to unfold them. The familiar script of my mother's hand came into view.

Dearest Petal,

My beautiful girl, if you have received this letter and the contents of the bag, I must assume evil has come to the city. Be very careful, but keep this person close so they don't know you are on to them. I had Alina prepare for you the necessary items to make your own gris gris bags for protection. She, along with Claudette and another, will help you in what you must do. The amulet is for Jahane...she will likewise need protection. When you make the gris gris bags, you must be careful to follow the directions and don't leave a single step out. You will not need one, even though I made one and gave it to you through Claudette; but you are powerful in your own right. Yes, dear, I know the thoughts that have invaded your mind as you read this letter. The amulet hanging around your neck I made with the strongest of spells. Be careful, black magic can disrupt the order of such spells. Now, you must set up a meeting with Claudette, Alina, and one other I mentioned. I hope you have met her but, if not, perhaps a relative of hers. Like I said, make wise choices in your decision to align yourself to her. She is a strong ally but can also be dangerous.

I love you, my flower petal,

Mom

At the mention of my amulet, I clutched the teardrop object against my chest. A single tear slipped down my cheek because, no matter what, my momma would continue to watch over me. Quickly, I wiped it away with the back of my hand. Jahane caught my eye and I nodded at her.

"Yes, let's get these bags made."

We separated the items so each bag would have one of each. I read the directions, and in no time had a dozen made. After we were done, I murmured the spell written on a separate piece of paper.

Carefully crafted pieces selected.
To keep the possessor always protected.
Respected are these powers so great.
Guide their will and guard their fate.

I handed Jahane the gris gris bag I'd made for her, as well as the amulet. She placed the round amethyst caged in silver around her neck. Her smile lit up her face as she traced the beautiful stone. The moment she touched it, a light purple glowed then dimmed.

"Okay, let's get down to the shop and place the remainders around." I grabbed a handful of the little bags and the leftover pralines.

Athena bounded over to the door, nudged it with her muzzle, and it unlocked. I wondered when I would ever get used to the fact my dog was magical. Jahane's mouth flopped wide open, and I walked over to her and nudged her. "I guess she is magic after all. There's no denying it now, is there? Anyway, it's not like you haven't seen this before." I laughed at the still shocked look on her face.

"Uh huh. I swear Rosie, if I had not grown up here in New Orleans and had not been privy to the crazy shit going on lately, I would think I was going bat shit crazy and not believe a single bit of this." She turned to me and laughed. "But you know, that dog of yours could come in handy. We could have her grab us Cokes from the fridge." No sooner had the words come out of her mouth than my dog stood there, tail thumping the floor over and over, with Coke bottles dangling from either side of her mouth.

"Holy crap, Athena!" I exclaimed, and sent out a mental message to her. *Stop messing with Jahane; do you want her to go to the looney bin?*

No, but I thought she wanted a Coke. She sat down on her haunches and continued the movement of her tail. Her lips turned up and her teeth held on to the bottles. I gently took one from her mouth, wiped off the drool with the hem of my shirt, and popped the top to take a swig. The Coke burned my throat as it quenched my thirst.

Jahane stood gaping at the both of us. A loud laugh escaped my mouth at the priceless look on her face when my faithful companion nudged her hand to give her the bottle. "Jahane, before I send you off to the looney bin, let's get down to the shop." I grinned at her as she took the drink and shook her head.

Laughter echoed as we bounced down the wooden steps, discussing all the things Athena could do. Once in the shop, the lights flicked on but my finger had not touched the switch yet. I gasped quietly...I didn't want to freak Jahane out any more than she already was, so I pretended to flick the light switch.

Another gasp came out when I saw the new countertop created out of cypress and marble. On closer inspection, I realized the marble was, in fact, jade stone. The base was a beautiful yellowish brown cypress wood that engulfed the store in a fresh cut tree smell. Excitement consumed me, and I ran from the new counter to the new glass display cases. All the jewelry and magic items were displayed on velvet pedestals. In my peripheral vision, I saw a brand new Keurig machine with an assortment of little individual flavors of coffee and tea. A shiny new cash register was positioned by the left side of the counter. Underneath was a spot for my laptop, and I noticed my Internet had been installed. A sense of awe struck me while my eyes darted back and forth through the store. Remi came out of the store room, followed by Derrick and Julian.

I stuttered as the three men came out. "How did y'all do this?" I managed to get the words out.

Remi's all-white-teeth smile beamed, then followed my gaze to the other two men. "Well, after the countertop was built, I went to pick up the display cases, but figured I would get these two involved in the surprise. The other items Julian and Derrick paid for." He inclined his head in the direction of the two, who had smiles on their faces as if they had eaten the canary.

Happiness surrounded me. I had all I needed...a new store, great friends, and the love of my life. Even though my mother wasn't there, I knew her essence was. A rush of adrenaline flowed through me, and I knew I would be all right.

The clean aftershave Julian wore hit my senses before his arms wrapped around me. I leaned into the body of the man I loved and would do anything to help. Shivers ran up and down my spine at the soft words in my ear. "I love you, Rosie."

I spun around in his arms, my lips found his, and I whispered against his mouth, "I love you, too." I leaned back and smiled at my new store and my family.

"The surprises aren't over yet."

I squealed in delight. "Ooh, there are more surprises?"

His head spun in Remi and Derrick's direction. Both guys turned on their heels and went to the back of the store.

A question burned and the opportunity to ask it presented itself while Remi was out back. "So spill it...why are you being friendly to Remi?"

"Well, my cher, I would do anything for you, and since Remi asked for my help, I didn't feel like I could deny him as it was for you. And, yes, I admit he isn't such a bad guy. Besides, I know you only have eyes for me and my sexy body." His wink took on a mischievous glow.

"Oh, you do, huh?" I returned the wink and stood on my tiptoes to kiss him on his collarbone.

"Yes, I can see how much you want to devour me." His passionate kiss curled my toes and sent electrical pulses through every inch of my body.

"Later, Julian...I want my surprise now, and we can have the other surprise later and christen this new shop." I winked.

Julian's arms were interrupted while wrapping around my waist when the two guys grunted and carried in a huge metal sign in the shape of a fleur di lis. My excitement ran rampant, and I dashed over to them. When they turned the sign around, I inhaled sharply at the beauty.

"Oh my goodness, it's beautiful!" I gushed at the same time my finger traced the letters on my new sign for the shop. The scrolls and curly Q's of the new name Books and Lagniappe were designed with a gorgeous flair. I wondered if Andre may have had a hand in this beautiful design. It looked like it could be his work.

I turned to my friends, Jahane included. "You knew they were doing this?"

"Duh, of course. Remi texted me and told me you were out with the she-devil and to get Julian's number, so I knew to keep you out as long as I could. But, I never dreamed Alina would play into this." She laughed. I wondered how she'd known to keep us out as long as she had.

"Oh, trust me, she knows lots of things." I hugged her hard, then stepped back. "I love you, Jahane, thanks for this." Making my rounds, I hugged Derrick and Remi, and both returned the hugs.

Derrick cleared his throat while Jahane and I both did another run-through of the store. "Who's in the mood for pizza and Hurricanes, guys?"

Our heads bobbed in unison. After the guys left, Jahane and I started up our chatter again. She threw some of the books on the shelves. "Is this book any good, Rosie?"

I grabbed the book out of her hand and looked at the cover. Shoving it back into her hand, I cocked a brow. "Yes, Jahane, it's good. But let's get these bags up and around in the shop." After all of them were placed in various spots, I made us both a steaming cup of hot chocolate. My eyes lit up when the steam danced above the rim. "Thank you, Momma," I whispered to the air. In the next instant steam shaped into a perfect heart over my chocolate, and the air around me was warm and inviting.

An hour later, the door opened to our fit of hysterical laughter. The guys strutted in, arms laden with pizza boxes and Hurricanes. "What in the world is going on with you two?" The deep boom of Julian's question stopped us mid giggle, and we doubled over with laughter again at the looks on their faces.

"Sounds like these two have already had enough to drink; what say we keep these drinks for ourselves?" Derrick joked.

Jahane jumped off the sofa. "No sirree," she quipped as she grabbed the two large Styrofoam cups from his hands, headed back to the sofa, and handed my cup to me.

"Hey, no fellas, I think they are on a sugar high." Julian indicated empty praline wrappers scattered on the table and chocolate encrusted mugs.

"Damn, girls, did y'all eat all those pralines? And how many cups of chocolate did y'all drink?" Remi's question was laced with sarcasm.

"Not sure, man, but I'm sure it's their weight in sugar," Derrick quipped. All three started high fiving each other.

I scoffed at their immature behavior as Remi placed the greasy pizza boxes on the table. "Come on, how many pralines did y'all eat?"

"Uh…" We both looked at each other and giggled. "All of them," we chortled, and fell into another fit of hysterical laughter. The guys looked at us and all rolled their eyes in unison, which sent us into even more laughter.

The top of one of the pizza boxes was propped open, and I pulled a piece out. As the cheese stuck to the box, I pulled at it until there was a long string attached. After I took a bite of the slice, I sipped my drink slowly. For hours we chatted, laughed, and ate.

Once all the pizza was gone, I felt a nice little buzz from the alcohol. Things were a blur as Jahane hugged me. Derrick picked her up, tossed her over his shoulder, and carried her out of the shop. My eyes heavy, I watched Remi and Julian shake hands. Before Remi turned to leave, I did a little three finger wave to him.

Julian closed and locked the door, then turned to me. Before he made it all the way to me, he closed the blinds on the big picture window. I never took my eyes off his languid, sensual body. I loved the way his body moved, the way his tendons in his hands moved with every twist of the closure of the blinds. He stalked towards me like a jungle cat, his seductive long legs carrying him closer. I waggled my brows at Julian and gave him my best "come hither" stare till he stood over me and leaned down. My breath hitched in my throat as his dark emerald stare gazed into my soul. But behind his eyes I could see his soul as well. "I want you so bad right now, but I don't want to seem like I'm taking advantage of you," he confided to me.

"Julian, you could never." I fisted the collar of his shirt in my hands and pulled him closer to me. "I'm not drunk…a bit buzzed, but I know what I'm doing." His forehead rested on mine, our lips inches from each other, almost touching. I smiled as he claimed my mouth.

In an almost magical movement, Julian swept me off the sofa, and his muscular arms hoisted me up. Instantaneously, my legs wrapped around him, my feet locked together to hold me. The entire walk to the counter, his lips and his tongue were like fire on mine. The moment my bottom hit the cold stone, a wicked grin flashed on his face. "Cher, how would you like to christen the counter?"

"I would love nothing more," I breathed out, and my breasts heaved.

With his arms still around me, he pulled me to the edge of the counter, then bent down and slipped off my shoes. The softness of his lips started at one of my ankles and continued up my leg. He grazed a finger lightly on the bottom of my foot as his lips whispered back down and moved to the other leg. When finished, he moved up to my thigh and pushed my skirt up to reveal the crisscrossed skin. Julian's hair fell down around my legs, and his soft kisses on my scars sent an explosion through my body. My hand brushed through his long, wavy, dark hair. "Oh damn, Julian, that feels great,"

"You like this?" He purred, and his hand moved a little further up my leg. Tingles exploded through me the moment his finger traced the lace of my panties. His touch exuded all he wanted with a burning fire. Gently, he lowered me onto my back, and even though the marble was cold, my body was on fire. His steady hands moved up my legs and he brought his head down to my thigh. The instant he tugged at the edge of the silky lace,

I moaned again. I squirmed when I felt his teeth graze my legs and pull the thin material down slowly. The silky panties and his hot breath on my soft, cool skin was intoxicating to all my senses, and it had me quaking at his touch.

"Rosie, you are beautiful; these are beautiful," he murmured against my leg with a bit of the fabric between his teeth as his finger traced over the red lines that zig-zagged around my thigh. The silkiness of my panties being pulled down by his teeth made me whimper for more. Before I knew it, a blast of air hit me and they were on the floor.

My legs spread automatically when his lips moved back up. As his mouth went to where my legs opened, my body trembled and invited him in. Feather light kisses caressed my thighs before his tongue delved inside me. My hands gripped the edge and I strained against the counter as his tongue kissed and teased me.

"Julian," I breathed. "I need more."

When he came up for air, his kisses moved up my stomach. Without taking his tongue and lips from his current endeavor, his hand reached up and massaged my rounded breasts through my cami. The more he pressed and rubbed, the more my nipples budded until they ached. I arched my back and begged for more.

He gripped my shoulders and pulled me up to face him. Even though I sat on the counter, his stature towered over me. "This," he fiddled with the straps of my shirt with his finger, "needs to find a way off." The smell of sex was heavy in the room, and I knew if my clothes weren't removed he would rip them off. But, I decided to tease him a bit.

"Not before yours," I bantered with a grin.

The intense look he gave me made me shudder, and with ease I pulled his shirt off over his head, then dipped my head down to kiss the taut muscles of his body. They flinched with every kiss. My fingernails grazed over each divot of his lean, sculpted body, and I kissed up to his collar bone, then moved to his earlobe. When I felt him tremble under my touch, I gently nipped it and breathed deep into his ear.

"Julian, I want you. I want your hands all over my body."

Calloused fingers rubbed my shoulders and reached around my nape. Quickly, he untied the straps and my cami fell down to reveal my breasts. I quivered under his lusty gaze. My chest rose and fell with my every heavy breath, and my breasts conformed to every movement. A slight hiss from him did not go unnoticed, and made a smile crease my lips.

"Rosie, oh my, you are so gorgeous." And I knew at those words he was ready to devour me.

The instant our bare skin touched, we both shivered in sync, and the contact made my nipples harden. "You like, Julian?"

"I do like, cher," he growled deep in his throat, and I sighed as he cupped a breast in his hand. With my nipple between his thumb and forefinger, he rolled it back and forth. The outcome was even more tautness.

"More," I breathed. "I need more." I arched my back and pushed my breasts further into his hands.

My hands moved around and held tight to his back and pulled him closer to me. I wanted all of him; I needed all of him. I grabbed a handful of his thick brown locks and whimpered at the touch of him.

On the brink of letting it all go, he grinned down at me. "Are you ready for more?" he said through clenched teeth.

I nodded, because the words could not find my mouth. He spread my legs with his hips, grabbed my ass, and pulled me closer to the edge. He pushed into me, and I felt his erection strain to be set free. Fervor took control as our mouths staked claim on each other. I reached down to pop the button on his jeans, and the zipper slid down with ease. In the next second, his erection was let loose to have its way with my body.

"Rosie," he said, his voice husky. My heart beat fast as he pushed his pants down. This man was impressive as he stood at attention for me. I reached down and wrapped my hand around him, and he shuddered at the feel of my hand affectionately moving up and down. He cocked a brow at me as he rubbed his hands up and down my thighs and moved his body closer into me. I felt an eagerness beyond my control at the opening of my legs, and arched my body when I felt him glide a finger into me. He rubbed until I wanted to scream in ecstasy. With all his sexual prowess, he dipped his head down and our tongues danced at the same time in rhythm to the movements of his finger. I moved closer to him, wanting him inside me. Once again, heat and passion consumed us, and I returned his kiss with one as fierce.

Finally, I breathed out, "I need you now, Julian."

He pulled back and smiled, and I bit my lip as I recognized the lust in his gaze. With his erection still firmly in my hand, I guided him inside me. I waited with bated breath and let out a sigh when I felt his hardness thrust inside me. When he placed a palm between my breasts and gently pushed me back, I writhed under his touch. I clenched my muscles around him, and he growled low in his throat. He grinned down at me, and I watched as his hand trailed down my flat stomach. His hands squeezed my thighs and moved around to grip my backside, where his fingers kneaded deeply into my flesh as he squeezed tighter. My legs gripped his hips tightly, and as he pushed into me, his thrusts were matched with the rocking motion of my hips. When he sensed I was about to go over the edge, I felt him get tighter inside me, and I clenched all my muscles to keep him at his task. Ecstasy threatened to consume me, and it was about to happen fast. He pulled me up, and the sensation of him inside me as I sat up made my breath hitch. The shock waves rolled off my body, my arms wrapped around him, and my nails scored his back. His hands found their way around me, he grabbed the back of my head, and our mouths melded together in heat and passion. This man knew how to multitask, and never once was one part of my body not ravished.

"Julian. Oh gawd, Julian," I screamed out.

"I know, baby, I know, baby…try to ride it out." With a final thrust, I climaxed and he followed soon after.

I breathed hard as I hit the maximum level of ecstasy and fell limp into his arms. Well sated and with an elated breath, I watched him pull his jeans back up. Then he wiped away the sheen of sweat I felt on my face and tucked a stray hair behind my ear. Scooping my limp form into his arms, he turned off the lights and headed out the back door. Comfort wrapped around me as I cuddled in his strong, well-built hold.

Before he went up the steps, he stopped, and I peered into his dark green eyes. He said, "Rosie, I have never felt this contented with anyone but you."

"And I you, Julian. You are everything to me." I held onto him with everything I had and kissed him. Before I realized it, I was immersed into everything that was Julian. He pulled back from our kiss and dropped light kisses on my nose, and continued to my forehead as he carried me up the steps and unlocked the door.

We entered my apartment, and he pushed the door closed with his boot. He turned the knob on my bedroom door and stopped in his tracks. I looked up from his chest to see what had him at a standstill. Athena was sprawled from head to foot on the bed, with her damn head on my pillow.

"Rosie, is she snoring?" he asked.

The rise and fall of her chest could be seen from the doorway where we stood. A deep rumble came from her as she rolled over on her side. I nodded at him and said, "But, hey, that's not even the real question. How in the hell did she get up here in the first place? I never saw her leave."

With a deep sigh, he shook his head and shifted me up in his arms. While I was jostled, I yelled. "Athena, get out of the bed!"

She turned her head in the direction of my voice, blinked, stood up, and jumped off the bed.

The last words I heard in my head before she padded out was one of a spoiled teen. *Geez, Mom, you didn't have to scream.* We both watched her turn three times and curl up. She was asleep within seconds, and her loud snores continued.

Julian entered the room, walked to the bed, and laid me down. He sat on the edge and removed his boots and jeans. As I sank into the soft mattress, he crawled in next to me. His hand brushed a strand of hair back, and I sighed as his arms engulfed me and pulled me to his hard body.

"Goodnight cher, Get some rest." He curled around me and nuzzled my ear before kissing my cheek. Exhaustion took hold of me, and soon I was out cold.

I ran through the cane field faster as the rain pelted down on me. The stalks snapped back in place as I plowed through them. I weaved in and out of the field and the material of my long, flowing skirt caught on a stray stalk or a rock. I tugged and tugged without a backward glance until the material ripped free, and I almost stumbled at the force of my pull. The need to keep moving drew me forward; I had to get away. My bare feet slapped in the mud and tossed the brown sludge up to my legs.

When I emerged at the edge of the field, my breathing was still ragged. I dashed for an old oak tree I saw in the distance, and once I reached it, I bent down and breathed in the fishy scent of the water surrounding me. I rubbed at my face and reached a hand to brush back my drenched and tangled hair. As I leaned against the tree, raindrops bounced off the top of the deep, dark waters of the bayou in front of me and developed into larger ripples. I sensed an evil closing in around me. Glancing around, all I saw were the cypress knees poking out of the dark murky water. A light breeze blew and the moss fluttered seductively in the trees. An eerie scream in the distance drew closer to me. I knew it would catch me soon, and my heart beat faster at the danger looming towards me. Wet strands of hair stung my shoulders as my head whipped back and forth, searching for an escape route.

My own scream echoed in the still air of the bayou as I felt the wet, hairy fingers emerge from the darkness. They wrapped around my arm and pulled me in. It was too late…it had me in its clutches. And the only things left were the leaves and Spanish moss blowing in the silent wind.

My screams woke me as my arms flailed around, and my eyes popped open to see Julian's concerned face. I began to breathe hard as I tried to remove myself from the sweaty, tangled sheets wrapped around my body. "Shhh, cher. Calm down." His strong arms unwrapped me from the tangled restraints and pushed my hair out of my face as he held me tight until I stopped screaming.

Molded to his body, I began to calm down. He whispered in my ear, "Shhh, cher, it's all right, it was a bad dream."

I pried my tear infused eyelids open again to stare into his mesmerizing emerald eyes. His smile soothed me. I burrowed deeper into the comfort of him and sighed, and we became one seamless body. The sensation of him drawing circles on my back had me comfortable and back to sleep in no time. I once again drifted into a dream, though this one was different … this time, I seemed to be invading someone's privacy.

I focused on what the female, who seemed familiar to me, was doing. My hand instantly went to my mouth to stifle a loud gasp. Her black hair was not in her usual pigtails, and she sat in front of an altar draped in black. I inched closer to her out of curiosity. The moment I was behind her the snake on her body turned and hissed at me, and I almost toppled over from fright.

I regained my stance and saw the altar was adorned with an assortment of items. I blinked my eyes, hoping what I was witnessing wasn't true. A picture of me when I was younger lay neatly underneath a dead rat. Glasses on each side were filled with what looked like blood, though I shuddered at the thought.

I tensed as she started to chant,

Trust to be given rather than earned.
Spoken words of a spell once learned.
Trust in me with all your might.
Trust in mind not in sight.
Spell unknown when you awake,
A binding so strong never to shake.

As soon as the voice stopped, the figure swiftly turned toward me to reveal her familiar face. Her red eyes stared coldly through me. She turned back around and lit a piece of paper with a match, and when she faced me once again she blew the ash at me, obscuring my vision.

I woke suddenly, not sure why, but found comfort in the man snuggled beside me. I curled into the confines of his body as he pulled me closer to him.

CHAPTER 15

The next morning I woke with Julian's arm around my waist, his hand cupping my breast. I wiggled more into the curve of his body and pressed my butt up against his now waking erection. My memories of the previous night's nightmare swiftly dissipated. His laughter tickled my ear as I nestled in deeper. The feel of his lips sent little fiery hot tingles along my spine when he breathed against my hair and whispered, "Good morning, cher." His voice had a just woke up sexy tone.

I rolled over in bed to face him. He propped himself up on one elbow, and a slow smile crept along my lips. "Morning, sexy," I breathed out. "Would you like some breakfast?" I nuzzled into his chest and smelled a subtle hint of his cologne.

He tipped my chin up and brushed his lips across mine. "Of course. I'm famished after last night's exertion." He winked.

When I rolled out of bed, he stopped me and pulled me on top of him. "Maybe we could have a repeat of last night," he quipped.

"Sure, maybe after breakfast. I need the energy to keep up with you." I grinned and jumped out of the bed, and his hand popped me on the ass. At the pop, I grabbed my robe and wrapped it around me.

"You know, Rosie..." He scooted to the edge of the bed and reached a hand out. Before I could stop him, he tugged on the sash of my robe. "I enjoy you more without this on." He winked up at me.

"I know, Julian, but I can't cook naked, now can I?"

He pulled me back onto the bed. "Of course you can." He untied the sash and parted my robe. His hands found their way inside and brushed down my abdomen until he reached the spot that made me ache for him. Julian's hands moved up to caress my breasts and pulled me back on top of his body, and I straddled him.

With gentle, soft touches along my shoulders, he slipped the robe off. His tender touch moved down the swell of my curves, down to my hips. My body shivered in reaction to every slight movement of his hands. Swiftly, he rolled me over, and with a mischievous smirk, he kissed down my body, dipping his tongue into my belly button, which made me squirm even more. He pulled my legs apart with his hands, his quest obviously to tease my body with his tongue, and the anticipation made it hard not to cry out at his every touch. My breathing became more labored as he continued on his mission of driving me insane.

"Oh, Julian, Julian," I breathed, trying to get my breaths to return to normal.

I thought we were done when Julian moved up my body with a wicked gleam in his eyes. "Not done yet, cher," he said, his voice gruff.

When he moved up, I rolled him over, sat astride him again, and positioned myself to accept him fully. I splayed my hands on his chest and felt every ridge and every muscle as he moved me up and down. His hard erection filling me up inside, I moaned with pleasure. Slowly at first, I rocked my hips, and then the rhythm became faster. My Julian was a master at lovemaking, and he always made sure to pay complete attention to me. Ecstasy hit me and I was on the verge of exploding. Instead, I eased back a bit and groaned at his touch. I wanted more, as always.

His hands moved back up and gripped me around my waist flipping me under him as he pulled out. Once again, I felt his hardness slip between my thighs. "Oh gawd, Julian," I breathed out.

The tip of him entered me and I was ready to accept him fully once again. His mouth claimed mine as his rock hard erection entered me and pulled back out. I knew Julian liked to tease me, to push me to the edge of insanity.

"Rosie, you feel good," he said through clenched teeth.

He pushed deeper inside me, and I cried out. Skin to skin, I clutched my body even closer to his. When he pulled his broad chest from me and looked into my eyes, they showed how much he loved me. He pushed back against me and I felt his broad chest press against my breasts. We ravenously synced the rocking of our bodies as he took possession of me. He balanced himself on one hand as he rubbed one nipple, then the other, into tight little buds. He dipped his head down and sucked ravenously on each nipple until they were perfect pink buds, and his long hair touching my sensitive skin almost sent me crashing over the proverbial cliff. I curved my back more, wanting him to devour me even further. He slipped one hand between my legs and rubbed me as he thrust inside me at the same time. The sensation of his finger rubbing me and his hunger thrusting in and out almost made me topple over once again. I grabbed ahold of the sheets with tight fists as I began to feel myself slip over the edge of consciousness. I screamed out Julian's name in the throes of the most perfect orgasm, and I felt him shudder as he climaxed and thrust one last time to finish.

"You stay here." He leaned down to kiss my nose. "And rest, and I will whip something up in the kitchen to perk up your expended energy." As he got up, he showed off the most perfect backside I'd ever seen.

When he turned around to place a final kiss on my lips, I got a great view of the V curve of his hips before he slipped on a pair of boxers. I smiled and gave him my sexiest smile.

Once Julian had headed off to the kitchen, I curled around in the big empty bed and reveled in the fact I loved him so much, and I knew I had to help him out of this debacle. As I lay in bed, the smell of sex was in the air and I was feeling well sated. Delicious and wicked thoughts invaded my brain, but were interrupted with thoughts of how to help Julian.

Before I could finish my thoughts, he returned with a tray of food. My mouth instantly watered at the delicious smells rising from the tray.

"Here, cher." He smiled and sat on the bed, and I scooted over so he had more room. Sitting back in bed with me, he placed the tray with the delicious smelling food down in front of me.

My mouth watered as I took a fork of fluffy, cheesy eggs and bit into the spiciness. "Ooh, what is your secret ingredient?" I asked as I fluttered my lashes up at him.

"Oh, a little milk, cheese, cracked black pepper, and a dash of Tabasco sauce." He laughed as he wiped a string of stray cheese from my chin.

"This is quite delicious." I finished eating and wiped up the rest of my eggs with the last bit of toast. The mug he placed in my hand was warm to the touch, and the chicory coffee slid smoothly down my throat.

Once I was done eating, I got up to get dressed. I pulled my hair back in a ponytail and sat back on the bed, sighed loudly, and then plugged on. "Umm, Julian, I may know what's wrong with you, and I know someone who can help us."

He slumped down on the bed next to me. Sadness and fear creased his sexy features simultaneously as he looked me straight in the eye. "You do?" Concern laced his words.

I nodded. "I do. And bits and pieces of the story, but you must come with me. They want to talk to you."

"Mais, I'm not sure, Rosie."

"Come on, you'll be fine; because I'll be with you the whole time."

After we were dressed, I grabbed his hand and ushered him towards the door. Athena padded out in front of us, barking for us to hurry. As the door opened seemingly by itself, I glanced behind me to Julian, and grinned at the priceless look on his face. "I'll explain later, honey," I told him as I pushed him out of the apartment and locked the door.

He shook his head in disbelief. Deep down, I wondered if he had even a tiny inkling of what was happening to him, even though he couldn't fathom any of it to be true. We headed down the street to Madame Claudette's, where we would also meet with Miss Alina and Marie Laurent.

The entire time we walked, Julian's mood was subdued, and I knew he was nervous about what he would soon find out.

Julian opened the door to the fortune teller's shop, where we were greeted at the door by Madame Claudette. "Come on in, my child," she beckoned. I sensed Julian's immediate hesitation and his urge to bolt from the unknown.

"Ah, this must be the man who's the topic today." Madame Claudette took Julian's hand and introduced him to the other women. He stood and didn't move. Marie sat at the table, and with a wave of her hand, two chairs scooted back from the table. "Have a seat, my children, we have many things to discuss."

Julian looked to me and the women. I sat, indicating it was safe, and he followed suit.

Marie looked different today; I was not sure what it was, but it was different. Her perfect hair was coifed and tied up. She sat opposite us and took Julian's hands.

"It's going to be fine," she said to calm him.

All he could do was stare around the table and mutter, "What's all this?" as the women sat there and gawked at him as if he were the newest science experiment. Alina came around the table and pulled a chair in front of him and took his hand in hers. He stiffened at her touch, and I placed my arm around his shoulder to try and ease his tension.

Marie looked at Julian and was the first to speak. "Julian, first I want to ask you, have you been having memories flood your mind, ones not your own, and have you experienced headaches?" In a matter of seconds, his expression went from slack to wide-eyed, and he rubbed his temples. But before he could open his mouth to speak, Marie placed her other hand over his and spoke in a soft, kind voice. "I know you have, it's what has happened in the past. All of the other men in your family have experienced these memories from past relatives. And I'm afraid the headaches will get worse."

"Happened before? What the hell do you mean?" he muttered.

"Julian, I'll tell you a story, and it's a true one. Your great grandfather six times removed, Henri Quibadeaux, made a deal with my ancestor, Marie Laveau." At the look on his face, she patted his hand. "Yes, the one and only.

"So, I'm not sure how much of your family history you're familiar with. But, it's one of deception, trickery, and love. You see, your ancestor, Henri, fell in love with and married a woman who was below his status and one he was forbidden to marry. Because of this, when she became pregnant, he had to protect both her and the child. He went to Marie Laveau and asked for her help. But, because he didn't follow through with what he promised he would, he paid a high price. The price for his trickery was he and his entire bloodline would be cursed to turn into a Roux ga Roux on their twenty-eighth birthday, and the punishment fell to the first born son of each generation. Now, only a couple of the Quibadeaux men have experienced memories in the form of dreams. It's a power I'm not sure of, but maybe you can ask my ancestor. She may be able to help you. She sometimes knows more." Marie finished her story and waited for Julian to say something.

Julian sat there, slumped into his seat at the information he had become privy to.

"Baby," I stammered. "Say something, sweetie." He sat still, frozen in place.

Julian finally stirred, and when he spoke, his voice sounded gravelly. "I do know my uncle was never around, and I know he was my father's oldest brother. My father died at a very young age. It almost killed my mamere. Mais, my father never spoke of his brother. He disappeared one day and was never seen again. When I would ask him about my uncle, he became very agitated and quiet. Mais, I've been having memories of a man and a creature, both entwined, their souls knotted together. I thought I was going crazy," he said with an air of disbelief.

Marie turned to Julian, patted his hand, and looked deeply into his soul. "Son, this can all be alleviated with help from Rosie."

His head whipped around to me and he stared at me, shocked. When he took my face in his hands and kissed me, all I could muster was a weak smile. I sensed he was trying to soak all this in. The urge to help him overcame me. I knew I needed to help.

"How?" he asked with all the confidence of the Julian I knew and loved.

Marie sat up straighter in her chair. "She must vow her life to my ancestor, the voodoo queen Marie Laveau, and do whatever she asks of her. If she agrees to this, she will be forever indebted to my family. But she alone must make this decision." She watched Julian's face with curiosity and leaned in close to him and spoke low, barely above a whisper. "You must have your suspicions of Rosie's powers. She is a very powerful witch, and we could use her. We have ways to protect her."

He stood abruptly, and his chair clattered to the ground. He pulled me to him and looked at the women. "Hell, no; you told me my family was cursed because they went to Marie Laveau. How in the hell can you expect to put her life in the hands of the woman who did this to my family?" he yelled.

Athena growled as her hackles rose high on her back. From my peripheral vision I saw Alina pet her to calm her. The knowledge she had my Guardian, Julian, and me in her best interests soothed me since I didn't want this to get out of hand, because I knew Athena had reacted on instinct.

Julian spoke low and soft to me and never looked in the other people's direction, but kept his gaze on me. "You will not vow your life or anything to anyone because of me. I will find a way out of this. I can't put you in that position. I can't have you do this, not for me."

"But, but…Julian, I would do anything for you, go above and beyond the end of the world for you," I persisted, and tried to get him to understand me.

He knelt down and enveloped me in his arms, his head resting against my stomach. As I laid my chin on his head, I ran my hands through his hair and sighed deeply. He looked up at me, and his dark green eyes sparkled. I felt safe in his arms; I just didn't want him to be cursed and have this over his head.

He stood back up. "Oh, Rosie, I don't want you to sign your life away and be indebted forever. No, we'll come up with another way, cher." He trailed his finger down my cheekbone and placed his hand behind my head, then tilted my head so all I saw was those gorgeous eyes. When his lips met mine, a fire exploded like I had never felt before.

Athena padded over to Julian and nudged his hand. I could tell he was hesitant at first, but he knelt down to where he was eye to eye with her. "Hey, girl, so you don't hate me after all, huh?" He reached out a steady hand and ruffled her straight ears. I almost died when my Guardian stuck her tongue out and dragged it down his face. Julian sat back on his heels as he wiped the drool off and laughed.

I gasped in utter shock at what I had witnessed. She always growled at Julian. Miss Alina walked over to where we stood and placed a hand on my shoulder. Her smile was kind and comforting to me.

She said, "Well, it seems your Guardian has listened to everything we've discussed here, and it seems she knows Julian will never ever hurt you. She was doing what she was created to do, protecting you. She knew something was off about Julian, but could never quite put her paw on it."

Athena sat back, her massive paws in front of her as she cocked her head from side to side at us. My Guardian looked proud of herself at the moment. She spoke in my head so I leaned over, touched my head to hers, and whispered in her ear, "I swear you will never cease to amaze me. Thank you for being my Guardian."

You're welcome. My job is to protect you, and I will with my life. She nudged me with her head.

Marie walked over to me and said, "Child, may I have a word with you?" I nodded and followed her to the back room.

"Rosie, if you do decide to do this and help Julian with the curse, you must go to the tomb of my ancestor at St Louis Cemetery. There you will find the answers and the help you will need for this to work." She smiled and kindness exuded from her. She grabbed a small bag and placed it in my hand. "When you're ready, you'll need to bring this with you."

I nodded and hugged her goodbye. I brushed past the curtain of beads to find Julian waiting for me, and walked straight into his arms.

Before we left, I told Alina I would come back to the store for some lessons, and she hugged me goodbye and said under her breath, "Your mother would be so proud of you, but please be careful if you choose to see the voodoo queen."

The three of us left, and with my fingers laced in Julian's, I knew what I needed to do, and my decision was made. But I hoped he knew together we would overcome anything. We were stronger together. I turned back to wave to the three woman as we headed down the street back to my apartment.

CHAPTER 16

After the meeting the other day with the three woman, Julian had become quiet and solemn. When we were together, it was like he was a different man. I refused to push him, because I knew his thoughts must be running rampant through his head. I had worked on my plan to get to the tomb of Marie Laveau, but Julian was adamant I shouldn't go.

One night after dinner, Julian asked to stay the night. I knew he had all types of emotions hammering in his head. After we cleaned up the dinner dishes, I led him to my room and curled up with him in my bed. Pressed up against him with my back to his front, I felt his heart thumping through his chest, and it reverberated off my back.

He nuzzled my ear. "Thank you, Rosie, for loving me." Even through his words I could tell he was deep in thought, and my heart ached for his pain.

When his hand reached around and cupped one of my breasts, I let him because he needed the intimacy I could provide. I accepted his touch and caresses so he could get what he needed from me. Julian never could keep his hands off me, and I never had a problem with this. I pressed further into his solid muscled body as he held onto me like he never wanted to let go.

"Julian, it will all be okay, I promise," I said, relaxing into him.

His soft kisses on the back of my neck sent goose bumps all over my body, and he pulled me closer. I felt him relax as his fingers traced loving circles up and down my thighs and my scars. His movements got slower and slower, and I knew he had begun to drift off to sleep. Before much longer I followed suit.

It was dark and eerie; I heard a sound in the distance, and looked one way and then the other. Holding my breath, I hoped I could hide or disappear…I didn't want them to find me. I let out a breath, very slow and steady. My heart pounded in my chest, and I tried to get ahold of my fear.

Ahead of me I could see the swamp with the giant cypress trees. The fog rolled in and hovered above the murky water.

A figure of what looked to be a woman emerged from the depths of the bayou, her movements slow and meticulous. When she stood on the embankment, she stopped, and I saw a snake slither around her feet. I stared in disbelief and blinked my eyes repeatedly. She pointed to me and spoke, but I heard the words in my head. Come to me, child, before it is too late.

I woke up with a start, and my hand went straight to my chest. As best I could, I tried to calm my breaths. I pulled myself up to a sitting position in bed and tried in earnest to focus on the darkness of the room. In the distance, two eyes peered out at me. I jumped and almost screamed until recognition hit me it was Athena.

With every bit of self-control I had, I crawled out of the bed, careful not to make a single sound. With the realization of what I was about to do, I placed a tender kiss on Julian's forehead, then grabbed a pair of sweatpants and pulled them over my hips. I wrapped a band around my hair to produce a messy ponytail, and tiptoed out of the room after Athena.

My kitchen was inviting as I put a teapot on the burner and turned it on. The whistle of the kettle pulled me out of my thoughts of the dream. I ran over and pulled it off the burner, hoping it hadn't woken up Julian. I pulled a mug from the cabinet and a tea bag from the container on the counter. My thoughts once again had me distracted as I dipped the tea bag in and out of the mug.

I sighed. "Athena, I know I am going to have to go to the tomb of Marie Laveau." My dog walked over to me with my tennis shoes dangling from her mouth. I looked down at her, smiled, and took them from her.

With my laces tied and the hot tea settling my stomach, I thanked her and said, "Are we ready to go see the voodoo queen?" She let out a quiet bark to tell me she was indeed ready.

"Okay, well, let's get going before Julian wakes up," I whispered.

Without making a sound, we both slipped out the door and made our way through the courtyard. A chill ran down my spine when I heard murmured whisperings as we stepped through the iron gate and out into the quiet streets of the Quarter. I grabbed Athena's leash with a tight grip as I began to get spooked.

We had succeeded in going maybe five blocks when I heard someone following us. Their footsteps thudded behind me, and as I quickened my pace, so did the person behind us.

I turned around and said, "Who's there?"

Only the sound of the wind answered me, which creeped me out since it was not usually windy this time of year. As I headed down a dark street, the smell of urine almost made me gag. My thoughts took hold of me, and I was deep into them. Farther ahead, I almost stumbled over a bag of garbage lying in the middle of the sidewalk. As I sidestepped it, I braced myself against the wall to stop myself from tumbling head first. I heard evil laughter, but when I looked around, I saw an empty street.

I positioned myself back down the sidewalk, and when I turned the corner, I bounced off a large body. Athena began to growl so loud it hurt my ears. Glancing up into the eyes of pure evil, I gasped and stumbled backwards, landing hard on the brick street. I tried my best to scream, but I couldn't find my voice. The smell of blood hit my nostrils, and I looked down at my scraped hand.

The creature loomed over me with a glare so menacing I shook in fear. It stood about eight feet tall and had the body of a man, but the head of a wolf.

"No," I cried to myself. "It can't be, it can't be." I glimpsed at my dog to the left of me; she bared her teeth, her hackles rose, and saliva dripped from her teeth as she stood her ground with the creature.

"Athena, come here, girl," I cried out, in fear of what the monster might do to her. My Guardian backed up to me until I could place my hand on her soft fur.

The creature stared at me with its cold, dark red eyes. When it began to stalk me like its prey, I scrambled backwards towards the wall, leaving blood stains on the brick sidewalk. "Wha…what…do you want with me?" I said as fear flowed through me.

It reached a long hairy finger towards me and touched my face. I shuddered as he dragged a finger down my cheek, and shrank back at the coldness it left. When I took another look at him and looked deep into his eyes, I knew this was not the being from my dreams.

I whispered, "Julian, is that you?"

He looked at me with recognition in his expression at the sound of the name. From behind him, I saw a flash of light which illuminated the buildings. I covered my eyes from the blinding light as it came closer and closer and lit the street.

"Back away from her, evil," the intangible voice said.

I looked down the street, and Marie Laurent stood in the middle of it with her hands up in the air and with the bright light all around her. Her dark skin was lightened by the brightness she emitted. She was adorned with a necklace of bones around her neck, and she chanted as the creature looked from her to me. He stood up and ran off, but before he rounded the corner, he turned back to me with sadness in his eyes. I watched as a single tear slid down his dark fur. I blinked back tears, and when I opened my eyes back up, he was gone somewhere in the darkness.

Marie's dozens of bracelets and bones jingled as she ran over to me. "Are you all right, dear?"

I curled up my legs and pressed them tight to my chest, as I sat on the ground and stared after the creature in my heart I knew was Julian. Now I knew more than ever I needed to get to the cemetery, and soon.

Marie's soft voice pulled me back to reality. "Child, we must get you back home," she said as Athena barked in agreement.

I looked up at her and asked, "How did you know I was here and in trouble? How is it possible you have bright lights coming from your body?"

"Oh, child, I know all. And as for my powers, that is a discussion for another time."

"But, Marie, I need to get to the cemetery, and now." My voice took on an air of determination.

"No, not tonight. It can wait for another day. Right now, we need to get you home."

"But," I argued, "that was Julian, and he needs my help."

She helped me up, looked me straight in the eyes, and placed her hands on my shoulders. "I know, Rosie, but we need to get you back home. If he has made the complete change, it could mean another evil is here, and we need you safe."

Back at home, Marie walked in with me, and my suspicions of the creature being Julian were confirmed when he was nowhere to be found in the apartment. The emptiness smothered me. I trudged, heavy footed, into my room, and my bed was vacant of his body, the quilt and sheets in a tangled mess.

I sighed as Marie helped me into bed. The bed dipped down as my trusty companion joined me and curled up at the foot. I was fast asleep before the blanket had been pulled up to cover me.

CHAPTER 17

The next morning, I woke to the light of the bright sun peeking in through my curtains, and a faint sound of knocking on my door. I heard Athena as she padded around in circles, anxiety coming from her in abundance. Her patience was thin while she waited for me to answer the door, so I rubbed the sleep out of my eyes and removed my tired and achy body from my bed.

"Hold on, girl, I'll be there in one sec." In a rush, I brushed my teeth.

When I walked into the living room, the door opened, and Julian stood there, disheveled. His eyes were circled in red as if he hadn't slept at all the previous night.

"Julian, please come in," I said as I headed into the kitchen to put on a pot of coffee.

As I pushed the button on the machine, I expelled a deep sigh. Waiting for the coffee to finish brewing, I pondered what had happened last night. Could it really have been Julian I'd encountered? An overwhelming mystical sense played havoc with me, and I felt something bad was about to happen. I inhaled deeply for fear of what he was there to tell me, but did my best to dislodge the negative thoughts from my head. With my back to him, I scooped a few cups of dog food into the metal dog bowl, and before the last kibble fell to her bowl, Athena ambled over to it and started to crunch on her food.

Once the coffee was done, I poured it into two mugs and watched as the steam wafted around me. Carefully, I walked with both in my hands and placed one in front of Julian, then stood and looked down at his forlorn and sheepish form. His head barely moved from its drooped position to look at the coffee. Sadness emitted from him as he sat at the table and played with the handle of the mug.

"What's up, baby? What's wrong?" I asked, my voice mixed with unease.

He brought me down to sit on his lap, my t-shirt rising up my thigh. He held me like I would disappear from him at any moment. Then the feeling he was there to tell me bad news overtook me again, and I choked back a sob. He crushed me to his chest, and his chin rested on my head as he sniffed my hair. I placed my palms on his chest, feeling the muscles constrict as he tried to keep me close to him. I struggled more and pushed against the steel arms that encased me as my anger boiled to the surface.

"Julian, honey, what's wrong?" I asked with my voice muffled in his hair. "Julian, please tell me what the hell is wrong. You have me scared. Just blurt it out."

He pulled back a smidge, but still remained close enough that I read the sadness in his eyes. "Rosie, my Rosie, you are beautiful. I fell in love with you the first moment I laid eyes on you. You are the breath to my lungs." His voice was strained and the sadness in him was dark.

Fear tunneled through me as I held him; I knew, but I couldn't admit it. He was…planning…before I could stop myself, I grabbed his face and pulled him to me for a passionate kiss, in hopes he wouldn't do what I felt in my gut he was about to do. When I pulled back, his eyes were downcast. "Damn it, spit it out, Julian."

"Cher," he said as he absentmindedly trailed his fingertips down the ragged scars on my legs without ever glancing back up to look at me.

Like a volcano, the anger I'd held in exploded. I shoved off him, pushed his hands off my leg, and pulled my t-shirt down to cover myself. His head flung sideways at the loud crack from my hand when I slapped him. For a split second, his eyes turned black when his head whipped back in my direction. The lethal glare he received from me made the color change back, and a single tear slid down his cheek. The look on his handsome face broke my heart…it was as if his world had fallen apart and crashed around his feet. But I couldn't stop my anger from rising. I took a sip from my coffee and slammed the mug down on the table. The coffee spilled and dripped down the side of the table, and I was surprised the mug hadn't broken.

Hesitancy tugged at his expression as he raked a hand through his hair. "Oh, cher, I can't do this to you. I can't put you in the way of the monster I will turn into. I could've hurt you last night."

I gasped at his confession…it was him last night on the street. "But Julian, I can…"

He interrupted me with a shake of his head. "I don't want to risk your life." He bowed his head in his hands in pain, heartache, and sadness. "Damn this headache, they are coming on faster and lasting longer." He held his fingers to his temples and tried to push it down.

At his words, my worries and fears came to life, and I knew he would not let me help him. I sank back into my chair, the tears now streaming down my face, and my heart plummeted into my stomach. The enormous ache inside my body paralyzed me. My words couldn't find my mouth; I was speechless, with no way to express how I felt. I knew my life would no longer be the same. I stared coldly into space, and not even a blink registered. I couldn't move, frozen in my chair. I had no idea when my Guardian came and stood beside me, but somehow my hand found her soft fur.

With the weight of the world on his shoulders, Julian stood. The last kiss he placed on my lips was full of passion and heat. I feared I would never feel his touch again, and I clung to him as our kiss intensified. He pulled back and turned towards the door, and with a fleeting look he told me, "I will always love you, cher; you are my life, you are my very being… everything I have ever dreamed of, and I will love you forever."

After he walked out the door, I once again found my voice and screamed, "Nooo, Julian, don't leave me, please don't leave me. Oh my gawd, please don't leave me. I can't live without you!" I knew he hadn't heard a word I said, because my voice echoed in the silence. The tears poured freely from my eyes and hit the now bare skin of my legs as I wrung my hands in my t-shirt. Still slumped in the chair, I swiped the wetness away with the back of my hand.

After a few more minutes of crying, I was reduced to the oh-so-lovely snot type of tears. I decided to go to my room, but didn't make it far. My legs weak from heartache, I fell and curled up on the floor. The tears hadn't yet dried up, and I lay heaving on the cold floor. My body curled deeper into itself as my legs found their way up and pulled to my chest. I continued to sob, and I felt my heart shatter into a billion tiny pieces. The pain became unbearable. Before I closed my eyes, I murmured, "We were supposed to do this together. We were supposed to be together."

After what seemed like hours my eyes cracked open. From across the room I heard the faint sound of my phone ringing, so I crawled back to the table and glanced at the caller ID. I was in no mood to talk to anyone, so I chucked it across the room. The force with which I threw it caused it to bounce off the wall and land in about five broken pieces.

I lay on the cold floor and sobbed until I heard voices inside my apartment. I hadn't heard them enter, so maybe it was all in my head. But the moment Jahane spoke to Athena, I knew this was reality. Strong arms lifted me up, and my heart almost jumped out of my chest, but when I gazed through slits that used to be my eyes and saw Derrick, it soon fell again. The room spun and my head hurt at the out of body experience I felt as I was carried to my room.

Derrick took extra care when he laid me in my bed. The smell of Remi's cologne permeated the room as he tugged the covers over me and sighed. At the sound of the door clicking shut, I curled into a tight ball and sobbed uncontrollably into my pillow. The crying jags came and went, and I succumbed to the numbness. The bed dipped down, and I felt the wet nose of my Guardian when she nudged it under my arm. My entire body was limp and numb as my arm lay across her body. She lay there with me as I drifted off to sleep.

The sound of Jahane and Derrick's voices pulled me from my sleep, and I rolled over and looked at them. "Jahane, what are y'all doing in my bedroom?" I didn't even recognize my voice; it was hoarse and broken.

"Sweetheart, we're here to check on you," she told me. "Um, Derrick, could you go down in the store and help Remi?"

His leather boots hit the floor with a deep thud as he headed downstairs. I rolled back over to the comfort of my dog, nestled into her soft fur, and sobbed even harder, surprised I still had tears to cry.

Through a series of hiccups I asked, "Why? Why? What did I do? I thought we could work on the curse together."

The bed dipped down as Jahane settled in beside me and rubbed my back. "I don't know, honey, but I'm sure he did it because he cares about you. He would never do anything to hurt you intentionally."

I continued to weep as Jahane settled behind me and held me. "You'll survive this and be reunited with Julian once again." Those were the last words I heard as I drifted off to sleep again.

At one time, I woke and rolled onto my side, and with an unsteady hand, grabbed my iPod. After a few tries, I placed the ear buds in my ears. My tears flowed down my face as the melodious tune of "Goodbye My Love" by James Blunt played. At each word of the song, my tears fell faster. I hiccupped at the words, the tender words of a man telling his love goodbye. My heart ached inside my chest, and I placed a hand over my heart to feel if it still existed. Once I settled myself back under the covers, the song played over and over in my head.

Tears trickled down my face and left wetness on my pillow. Before I fell into an unconscious dreamland, I felt Athena rest her huge head on my chest as she tried her best to comfort me.

I muttered under my breath as sleep took hold of me, "Why me? Why me?"

The sound of Jahane's voice on the phone woke me once again, but I didn't stir, and kept my back to her and listened. "Yes, I know, but she's been in bed for like three weeks. I know he didn't mean to hurt her like this, but he has…. I know, but, uh…she's my best friend. I know I need to let her cope and grieve. And, no, Athena has not left her side either, and neither one of them have eaten." Her voice became hushed and I tried to hear what she said. "Since he left."

I drifted back off to sleep as she hung up. Damn it, the tears threatened to flow through my shut eyes, so I tightened them.

The next morning, I woke up with a new refined outlook on life, though my pillow remained damp from tears that had flowed while I slept. I squinted through puffy eyes and didn't see Jahane, but the breakfast smells flowing through my house hinted at her location. I rolled out of bed and Athena sprawled across the entire thing. With a shake of my head, I headed into the bathroom.

When I turned on the shower, memories flooded my brain of the last time Julian and I had been in there together. The instant they hit, tears rolled down my cheeks. I stepped inside and under the hot steam. The loofah Julian had used last time to tease my sensitive skin hung from the knob. The holey material felt itchy in my hand as I began to scrub. In haste, I washed and pushed all the recollections threatening to invade my thoughts down to the deepest recesses. With my body clean, I dressed and headed for the kitchen. My mood was still a little somber, but the need to save Julian won out.

Jahane looked up from the stove as I entered. With the spatula still in her hand, she rounded the counter and hugged me hard. "Rosie, you'll get through this." I hugged her back and pulled myself up onto one of the stools. "Here, eat." She placed a plate of pancakes and bacon in front of me, along with the peanut butter and homemade syrup like my momma had made. I smiled at her. She always knew what my comfort food was. Once we had eaten our fill and cleaned up the dishes, Jahane gave me a quizzical look.

"Why are you looking at me like that?" I asked.

"Hahaha…I know you have something up your sleeve."

A smirk crossed my face as I looked at her. "Well, I'm still going to see Marie Laveau and see how I can help Julian." The courage from my words became stronger. "Even if he doesn't want me to do anything," I mumbled under my breath.

"But, Rosie, she's dead…you do remember don't you?" She walked over to feel my head. "Nope, you don't have a fever."

"I know, but everyone has told me if I want to help Julian, I need to go see her." I debated telling her about the dream I'd had the other night with the ethereal figure emerging from the water to tell me to come see her, and in a hushed voice, proceeded to recount the dream.

VOODOO VOWS

"Jahane, you know the night before Julian left? In a dream, I was in the bayou, and a woman emerged from the water. It had to be Marie Laveau. As she drifted above the water, she told me I must come see her soon. I left the house soon after, and happened upon Julian in the form of a creature."

She gasped at my story. I laid a hand on her knee and continued. "No, I know what you're thinking; he didn't hurt me, but Marie Laurent came and he ran off. The next day was when Julian left me. I don't know why I must go to the tomb, but my dream has told me to, and so has Marie Laurent. So I must go."

She nodded at me. "If you're going, so am I. After all, I'm your bestie and will be by your side always." I stood, grabbed a few essentials for my talk with Marie, and stuffed them into my purse. We both noticed Athena waiting for us at the door, so I grabbed her leash, bent down, and whispered, "Thank you for being here for me."

Anything for you, but don't forget the item you are to bring to the voodoo queen, my Guardian reminded me.

"Thank you. Hey, I'll be back, Jahane."

I ran back into the house to grab the bag Marie Laurent had given me. With ease and self-confidence, I headed back to where my friend and Guardian waited for me.

Athena barked and nudged me out the door. We walked down the steps in silence, my heart heavy and still saddened at the prospect of what had transpired, but I knew this was the right thing to do. On the way to catch the street car, I pondered the possibilities of where Julian might have gone. The quiet ride to St. Louis Cemetery took forever.

Even in the daytime, the cemetery had an eerie, spooky aura surrounding the place. The three of us walked to the mausoleum believed to house Marie Laveau's body. The dozens of X's placed all over made me wonder if the people actually had received the gift or wish they so desperately wanted. Or was she angered by the graffiti upon her resting place, and had exacted the appropriate revenge on those that dared mark her tomb? I sighed at the assortment of candles, bones and other things left behind for Marie.

Before I sat down on a bench that appeared out of nowhere, coldness surrounded me.

Jahane stood behind me with her hand on my shoulder. The comfort from that one touch almost brought tears, but, no, not today. The time to be strong was now.

I began to empty my purse when, out of my peripheral vision, I saw a ghostly figure walk around the disheveled marble mausoleum. Immediate fear and shock consumed me as I turned to her. She was dressed in a long flowing skirt that billowed around her without the hint of a breeze; her sheer dark skin shimmered in the sun. A beautiful shawl was draped over her shoulders, and the white tignon was tied perfectly around her head. She continued towards us, her fingertips trailing along the white marble of the tomb. I looked up at her in awe as her body shimmered back and forth from grainy to solid…there, but not quite there.

"Ah, mon piti," she spoke in a mixture of English, and the lilt of her accent accentuated her creole French language. "I had hoped you would come at my invitation and visit me, as your mér had. She was a brave woman, and she will sadly be missed. I valued her friendship, and I hope to gain yours, along with your trust."

She positioned herself next to me on the

little bench. Her smile was sincere and full of benevolence. When she grasped my hand, the sensation of it felt like touching the surface of the water and slowly dipping down, depending on how hard she held my hand. With my other hand I offered her the little bag from Marie

Laurent. She nodded and took it. Taking a small peak inside, she smiled and put it down beside her.

"I know why you are here, piti. You are here to save your amoureu, Julian. Do you love him? Does he love you?" she inquired.

"Yes, I love him. I know he feels the same about me." A sea of memories surged through me as I remembered the way he touched me, the feel of him pressed against me. I looked up at her as I felt the warmth invade my cheeks.

Her intent gaze pierced me, and I dropped my head in embarrassment. She chuckled softly at the sight of my cheeks and their instant change in color. "So I see, cheri. Now, how do you s'ppose you could be of service to me? Your mother was a brave woman, Rosaleigh; do you feel you're brave as well?"

I nodded my head and sat there, dumbfounded to be in the presence of Marie Laveau, the voodoo priestess. "Yes, ma'am, I do." I spoke with the utmost confidence. She placed a hand above my thigh and my skirt rose to show a hint of my scars.

"Yes, piti, I do believe you are correct." With a gentle touch, my skirt flowed back down to cover my thigh. "What are your powers, cheri?"

As I looked up at her, Athena placed her head in my lap. Marie smiled and reached a hand out to pet the dog. Athena's fur rose briskly at the light airy touch from the voodoo queen.

"Ah, what a beautiful Guardian you have. You must be powerful," she spoke, her voice soft. "Now, back to the matter of your powers."

"Well...umm...ma'am, I can heal people, and animals; plus, I get visions, in the form of dreams, of the past, present, and the future."

A slight tilt of her head told me I had sparked her interest. "Now, as for the healing, we will have to keep under wraps for your own protection." She smiled at me. "And, yes, dreams, as your mother...I'd hoped you had the same ones she did, which is why I chanced sending you a dream to come see me. So I am happy you received my dream. And I am sure you have more powers yet to come. What have your dreams consisted of, child?"

Sweat slipped down my back at the thought of retelling my dreams. "Umm, well, they always tend to be set in the bayou. A creature or someone is after me." I stopped as the dream of my mother replayed in my head, and I did my best to choke back the oncoming tears.

"Rosie, do not worry about that dream." She placed a long hand on my knee and tapped her chin. She seemed deep in thought as she glanced off in the direction of the entrance of the cemetery. I sat in silence and waited for her to speak.

"Now, if you have any more dreams, will you please get word to Marie Laurent? I think an evil is back, and one I shall have to take care of before he gets out of hand...and if I know him, he has help. So, if Julian is truly worth saving, he is in danger. But I digress. I fear this is all my doing. Henri was quite something in his day, and it seems I may have not taught him the lesson he so much deserved." Her laugh chilled me to the bone.

A slight breeze blew around the cemetery as Marie stood. Leaves fell from the trees overhead and fluttered all around us. One fell in my hair, and I plucked it out and let it fall from my hand. Her power was strong and emanated from all around her. "Rosaleigh, repeat after me these words I speak."

"Yes, ma'am." And I repeated every word with confidence.

"Hear these words my vow to thee.
My magic for you to always flow free.
Should issues arise no need to fear?
My magic will guide me forever near.
By your side with just a call.
This vow to you binds above all."

With a sudden wave of her hand, the candles at the base of her tomb flickered to life, the tiny infernos dancing to and fro. I was mesmerized by the yellow and orange flames. I watched in amazement as they were mirrored in Marie's silhouette. She placed a few bones around the base and began to chant, then tilted my chin up so I looked into her deep brown eyes. Her touch sent electric pulses through my body; fear of having her hand materialize into my chin had me quite still.

"So, as you have vowed to me on this day, so it is to be." She smiled, and an uneasy feeling washed through me.

She pulled a rumpled paper out of her pocket and handed it to me. "This, child, is a list of items you must obtain, and along with your divine powers of resurgence, this will cure your beloved amoureu. But only if you find every item. I shall also do my part."

"Thank you, Madame Laveau. You have been so kind to me." I took the paper she offered and placed it in my pocket. Athena, still sitting at my feet, lifted her head to sniff the paper.

"Dear Rosaleigh, do not take my kindness for granted...I can also wreak havoc on those you love, so take my words with caution. Before you leave, I must give you something else. Keep it with you at all times." Out of thin air a small, creamy doll appeared and danced above her hand. The legs and arms had stitching, and on its head sat a tiny crown of bones. It had one button eye and an X on the other side.

"Thank you, Madame Marie." I accepted the doll and glanced at it, and the coarse material suddenly became smooth in my hands. Before my eyes it changed colors, starting at the top then slowly moving down the body, shifting from cream to a soft rose hue. I held it close to me and the aromas of fresh herbs sifted around me. My nose wrinkled as I inhaled.

"I made this, and your momma blessed it with all the power and safety she had in her. It is for protection made with bay leaf, black snake root a dash of cinnamon, bat nut, fennel seeds, ginger root, and lemon grass infused into the doll. We knew you would need it one day. Yes, like you, your mother could see the future. She knew you would be in danger one day, and that, my dear, is also why you have been blessed with a Guardian. She'll protect you against the evil I know brews among us."

Jahane, who had been silent through the entire ritual, came to stand by me and linked her arm through mine. Marie turned to go, but before she dissipated, she looked through Jahane.

"Jahane Olivier, be careful, my dear; you will also find danger, and soon. Stand by your friend, but remember, death is a constant follower." And she disappeared before our eyes.

As she left, her disembodied voice rang out. "I'll come to you when I need you, Rosie."

Once again, the air became silent, and I took in all that had transpired. As Jahane wrapped a comfortable arm around me, Athena barked to get my attention.

"All right, girl, I'm coming." As we walked out of the cemetery, I chanced a look back over at Marie's tomb, knowing this would not be the last time I came to see her. Thoughts scrambled through my head at the mention of her and my momma together. I became overwhelmed at all the questions and answers way beyond the normal scope of things. But those particular pieces of trivia I would tackle when it needed to be done. Now I needed to try and find out where Julian had run off to and bring him back home where he belonged, so I could heal him of his wretched curse. As I walked home, I clutched my little voodoo doll to me and held it tight.

CHAPTER 18

The next morning I woke, stretched, and rubbed my eyes. Athena was hogging the bed, so I shoved her with my foot to move her. Her huge body lay sprawled across the bed, and her jowls hung open. The loud snores she emitted vibrated them with every breath. She had slept in my bed ever since Julian had left. I knew she stayed closer to me on those days I let my emotions consume me, for which I would be forever grateful. I turned to the window, stretched my arms over my head, and watched the sun shine through a crack in the curtains.

"Come on girl, what d'ya say we get up?" I prodded her with my foot.

Her head lolled to the side, as she looked at me. She stood, stretched, and jumped out of the bed. I watched as she retreated out the door, her tail wagging around the corner as she disappeared. I stretched a bit more and hopped out of bed. I dressed in a pair of jeans and a t-shirt, tied my hair up into a ponytail, and texted

Jahane to meet me at the apartment. After my text had been sent, I walked into the kitchen. I watched in awe as I witnessed Athena fill her bowl magically. I shook my head and laughed. She turned at the sound of my laughter and spoke. *Well, Mom, if I waited for you to fill it, I would starve.* I laughed again, grabbed a mug, and noticed the coffee pot brewing. I assumed my Guardian had also done this as part of her oh so many talents.

A loud knock sounded on the door. As my dog turned her head towards the door, a bite of food flew from her jowls. A few remnants hung from her mouth as she looked from me to the door. She barked and the door opened. When she dipped her head back into her food bowl, morsels of food flew on the floor.

"Athena, don't open the door without knowing who's behind it," I chastised her.

Oh please, come on, we all knew it was

Jahane. She turned her attention back to her food.

Jahane walked in, petted Athena, and sat. I offered her a cup of coffee, and we waited for the dog to finish eating.

"So, where are we headed today?" Jahane asked.

"Ah, well, we have to wait for one other person to join us." Before I finished my sentence, there was a knock on the door. The door opened and there stood Andre. He smiled at us with his hands on his hips, and sashayed in.

"Andre, where is your man?" I asked.

"Oh, girlfriend, I had to dump his ass; can you believe he cheated on me? I mean me, of all people, all this sexiness." He waved a hand down his body and smiled at me. He sat down on the sofa and crossed his legs.

Athena bounded over to him and placed her head in his lap. "Hey, pooch," he said as he petted her.

After a few moments and a ton of drool later from Athena, he jumped up and gave us a quizzical look. "Well, ladies, where are we headed? A strip club down Bourbon Street?" He laughed and moved his hips in a sexy move.

"Oh please, for heaven's sake," I goaded him.

I watched both Jahane and Andre roll their eyes, and he leaned in real close to my best friend. "Damn, when the hell has our girl last gotten laid?"

I interrupted him and laughed. "No, Andre, we are headed to Miss Alina's," I said.

Jahane leaned into him and whispered, "I think it's been forever since she got some, and she sure is cranky."

I stood and tapped my foot at their discussion. My fists planted on my hips, I stared defiantly at the two. "Okay, you two, I can hear y'all whispering about my lack of sex. Now let's go," I said with a grin.

"So, Rosie," Andre linked his arm in mine, "is it true you're a witch?"

"Um, what are you talking about?"

"Girl, don't play dumb with me."

I eyed Jahane and she mouthed sorry.

I turned to face him. "Andre, you mustn't tell a single soul. You must promise, it's dangerous for so many people to know.

He nodded and crossed his heart with his fingers. Athena sat outside the door waiting so I ushered everyone out. Her tail wagged, as she bounded down the steps. On the way to our destination, Andre bombarded me with dozens of questions on witchcraft. It was difficult to answer since I didn't have the correct answers myself.

"Andre, sweetheart, I just found out, which is why we're headed to Alina's. Maybe she can help us and give us some insight into how to find Julian and strip him of this curse," I said, and hurried my pace behind Athena.

When I opened the door to the shop, I heard Alina yell from the back, "I'll be right there,

Rosie." The mixture of looks questioning how Alina knew we had walked through the door shrouded me. I looked to my friends and shrugged my shoulders.

Alina walked in from the back, carrying a pot of coffee and pralines. Jahane's eyes lit up at the sight of the sweet confections. My two greedy friends held their hands out for the sugary pecan delicacies. Alina smiled at Jahane and Andre and watched them unwrap the treats.

She turned to me as I rolled my eyes at the two. "So, Rosie, what can I do for you today?"

"Well, I wanted to ask if you could maybe put out some feelers to see if we can find out where Julian went."

"Come sit down, Rosie."

I followed her to the sofa. "Okay, what's up?"

"I've sent other coven members out to search for him. My idea is he may have headed back to the bayou and back to his family's home. But when the coven arrived, he was gone. Through the grapevine I heard his mother passed in recent years. Since he had no family, I'm sure he had no idea. Though I have heard rumors there was a brother, perhaps a half-brother, since we know his father died when he was younger."

"A half-brother," I gasped. "But how would he not know he had a brother?"

"The rumor is Julian's father had an extramarital affair. A son was born and no one, not even Julian's mother, knew. Now bear with me, this is a rumor circulated around the bayou." She stopped to sip her coffee.

Before she continued, I asked, "Has anyone talked to this so called brother? Maybe Julian and he have crossed paths." I knew I grasped at straws, but I needed hope.

Miss Alina patted my leg. "Rosie, we will find him," she promised. "We will stop this curse."

I nodded in agreement and tried to keep my hopes up and alive. "So, Miss Alina, what else can you tell me of my powers? Anything else I don't know?" I asked.

"You, my dear, in time will become stronger and may come into new powers. But now be careful…there is an evil out there. But you know about as much as I do about the ones that exist now," she said.

A deep sigh escaped as I sat back and snuggled into the comfy sofa. "Miss Alina, do we have a coven initiation?" I asked.

"Yes dear, but now is not the time. We have bigger fish to fry, so to speak."

Frustration ran through me and I tried to quell it. I didn't know if she was putting me off or if I was angry at this whole situation. I wished my momma was there. Athena came over and crawled beside me and placed her head in my lap, her eyes conveying such sadness. Her soft fur under my hand caressed my palm as she nuzzled her head into my lap. A sudden thought popped into my head. Maybe I could get my momma's best friend to confide in me, something my momma wouldn't talk about.

In a very soft voice I spoke, "Miss Alina, can you tell me anything about my father?"

Her head spun to me in shock, but returned to its downward position, and she relinquished. "Rosie, my sweet Rosie." I sensed when Jahane and Andre came to sit across from us.

She inched closer to me and folded my hands in hers. "Your father was a kind man, and your mother loved him very much. My dear child," she sighed, "the day it happened…oh wow, it's like the day was yesterday. You were two years old when he was taken from you and your mom." Her voice became softer and sad.

"What happened?" I asked. "Momma would never talk about him much; just said he died. Whenever I would broach the subject, she would change it." I wiped a tear from my cheek as I remembered my momma.

She gripped my hand tighter. "The thought of him pained her too much to talk about him. Anyway, your mother fell head over heels for him. They met back in your hometown. He came from a rival coven of ours, but not rival like you think, dear. They never fought, they had different ideals when it came to the covens. They met at a council meeting between the two covens to vote on new members, and your father's name had been put in as a nominee. When he walked in and saw her from a distance, he was smitten with her. The instant they saw each other, they knew they were bound to be with each other. After the meeting, he took your mother out to dinner and they became inseparable. They were married after, and you came about a year later. He loved you so much and knew you would become powerful, and I know he is so proud of the person you have become."

For a brief moment, she stopped. She let go of my hand to wipe her eyes, so I reached over to the side table and grabbed a tissue and handed it to her. She took it and dabbed at her eyes.

"Anyway, as I was saying, one night you became fussy, and so your mother walked the floor with you in hopes you would be soothed. You wouldn't stop crying. Now looking back on it, you probably had a nightmare and foresaw his death. Your mother couldn't console you. Do you remember anything, Rosie?"

I shook my head.

"It's okay, dear, you were young; but it seems you had at least one power back then. Though I doubt you could remember much of it, you were so young and had no idea what was happening." She patted my hand in a comforting gesture. "But we still don't know what happened. When your father never came home, she called me to come watch you. Your mother searched everywhere but never found him. When she returned home, she found a message on the pillow on the bed, and she suspected it had been left by your father. It told of an evil that would come and for her to be careful. So she knew he had met with a fate he would not be coming back from. She made preparations to keep you safe, and so you both moved here to the city. I don't even know what all she did to ensure your safety and protection, but I know she did all she could." She finished and sighed as she leaned back in the sofa.

By the end of her story, tears flowed down my cheeks at both the lost moments I could have had with my father and because my mom cared so much for me to do whatever she could to protect me.

"So, my father did love me?" I asked.

She leaned back up and looked me straight in the face. "Both of your parents loved you very much, my dear."

"Miss Alina, do you think it's possible my father is still alive?" I asked.

"No, dear, your mother believed he had met an end he could never come back from. No one ever heard from or saw him again," she told me, sighing deeply.

"This is so unbelievable; and what is this evil everyone is talking about?" My voice raised an octave or two.

Miss Alina patted my hand and smiled at me. "I'm not sure, but I'm sure it will show itself sooner rather than later." Concern swirled around the room, and I could feel her power as she spoke.

In a sudden leap from the chair, Andre spoke up and snapped his fingers. "Hey, boo, enough of this doom and gloom! I'm ravenous, so who's ready for a bite to eat?" He stood there with his hands on his hips and laughed.

Jahane jumped up. "I second that." She laughed and practically dragged me from the sofa.

"Bye, Miss Alina."

I heard Miss Alina laugh as the three of us and Athena walked out together. I turned towards her before the door closed and mouthed a thank you. She nodded and headed into the back. Followed by Athena, Andre marched down the street with his hands on his hips, snapping his fingers like a drum major leading his band, and insisted we hurry.

Once we caught up to him, he asked, "So where do you girls want to go eat?"

I looked from Andre to my bestie. "How does The Brackish Tavern sound?" When the words were out of my mouth, my stomach growled in agreement.

They both nodded in unison, and we linked arms and headed down the street. The door opened to the restaurant and a couple walked out. I grabbed the door and held it open for my two friends, and they smiled and thanked me, and the four of us stepped in.

"Oh no, damn; what about Athena?"

Just then Mr. Jacque walked up to us. He winked at me. "Miss Rosie, the usual booth?"

"Yes, sir," I said nervously.

"Hello there, pup. Come, let's get y'all to your usual booth."

"Thank you, Mr. Jacque."

"No problem." He seated us and winked at me. We all scooted into the booth as Billy came over to our table and took our drink order. Once he had left the table, I flipped through the menu to see if maybe there was something new to eat. When I looked up from my menu, I saw Remi walk out of the swinging doors leading to the kitchen.

He smiled at me when I glanced up to see him headed towards our table. He wiped his hands on the apron tied around his waist. "Well, well, Rosie, Jacque told me you were here," he flirted with me. He shook Andre's hand and hugged Jahane before turning his attention back to me.

I smiled up at Remi, and his smile dazzled. The corners of his mouth crinkled, and he winked at me. "Okay, what will it be?" he asked.

Jahane and Andre gave their orders as Billy came up behind Remi with our drinks. I looked at Remi. "Surprise me, why don't you?"

After Billy left our drinks and Remi scribbled the orders down, they retreated to the kitchen. I turned my gaze back to my friends and watched Andre ogle Remi's backside.

I elbowed him. "You know you're not his type."

He laughed haughtily. "Rosie, he may not be my type, but it doesn't mean I can't enjoy a good piece of chocolate." With a snap of his fingers, he leaned over the table and said, "Damn, that man has some nice assets, and I bet he would look delicious wrapped in a coating of vanilla and a bit of nuts."

I covered my mouth and stifled a laugh.

Jahane held back laughter I knew bubbled up inside her. The fact Jahane turned red trying to keep it in told me it would not be contained much longer. When she let it out, we all roared with laughter at Andre's cockiness. We gossiped and chatted over appetizers that Jacque brought to the table. Before we knew it, the food was displayed in front of us. The intoxicating aromas had my mouth watering. I relished every bit of food, and my taste buds begged for more. The food tasted so delicious, and our silence and the sound of our forks when they clinked along the plates was perfect proof. After I took the last bite, I wiped my mouth with my napkin, placed my fork on the plate, and leaned back in the booth and rubbed my tummy.

"Damn, that was good," I said with an elated sigh.

Remi came out of the kitchen, and I felt Andre elbow me and wink.

"So, did y'all like everything?" he asked with a smile.

We all nodded in unison. I watched Jahane eat the last bits of her dinner. Billy came over and refilled our glasses with fresh sweet tea, and I took a sip and savored the sweetness. Once we were all done and the check was paid, Remi came out of the kitchen once again and handed us all three Styrofoam boxes filled with the most delicious aroma, and in an instant, my mouth watered all over again.

"Thank you," our chorus of voices sang.

We headed out, and Mr. Jacque stood by the door, so I hugged him goodbye. We laughed and joked all the way down Decatur Street to my apartment.

"Okay, Rosie I must be getting back to work. You know this city won't design itself." He laughed as he waved his hands in the air at his surroundings? "I know and you are a one man design show, we will see you later." He hugged us both goodbye.

We stood on the steps watching him leave, then Jahane turned to me.

"Hey, did you ever find the items Marie told you to find?"

I slapped my forehead, "No I didn't. But I think I need to get on that. Wait here, I'll be right back." I ran upstairs to my room and grabbed the little piece of paper from the back of my underwear drawer. Stuffing it into my pocket I ran back downstairs where Jahane and Athena waited for me. "Let's go."

"What's on the list?" Jahane asked.

I dug into my pocket and pulled he folded paper out and glanced at it. "Um…it says a moonstone, a piece of burlap, string and finally hair from a Rougaroux."

Jahane stood there deep in thought, "I

wonder who would have those things? Maybe we could find some at the French Market."

I shook my head, "no let's go see Madame Claudette."

We walked in silence the few block to her shop. I turned the corner and saw the gaudy sign. "Come on let's hurry Jahane." Stepping over the threshold, I got an eerie vibe but shook it off. I didn't have time for this today. The

moment we stepped into the store, Madame

Claudette came out from the back, letting the bead curtain swing to and fro.

"Good afternoon girls, how may I help you?"

I rushed toward her and handed her the list. As she looked over it she hemmed and hawed. "I think I have all of these items, minus one." She grinned at me. "Not much use for Rougaroux hair here in the city and especially in my store. I'll be back, let me see what I have in the storeroom."

I nodded and relaxed the tension I'd no idea I'd been feeling since walking into the shop. She disappeared into the back, and I slumped into a nearby chair. Jahane sat next to me, whispering to me, "We'll find him and you'll cure him."

All of her words made sense even though dread filled my heart in actually accomplishing this task. Madame Claudette shuffled out of the back with two tiny brown paper bags. "Here you go Rosie. I hope this helps somewhat. I know it's not everything you needed, but that last one is quite a doozy. The other bag is for Athena."

"Thank you Madame Claudette, I appreciate this." She patted my hand as she let go of the bag.

"Rosie I promise everything will work out, you just have to believe in it. I reached inside the one bag and pulled a dog treat out and handed it to Athena.

"Thanks again. We must head over to the cemetery and see if I can speak with Marie."

"Be safe my dears."

Once we had all the items but one, we headed back to the cemetery. The sun began to set sending the shadows of the trees to skitter across the marble tombs back to their hiding spots. Jahane grabbed a hold as we drew close to the tomb. The same little bench I'd sat on before materialized before me.

After a few seconds, Marie Laveau appeared and beckoned me to her. Before I made it all the way to her Athena bounded ahead of me and stopped in front of the Voodoo Queen, then sat and looked up at her.

"Well hello, little Guardian...or should I say big Guardian. You sure have grown." She leaned down closer to Athena and whispered something to her. My dog wagged her tail then turned to me. Jahane followed me to the bench where I sat down, glancing at Marie. Athena placed her head in my lap to encourage me.

"Um…Marie we only found three of the items; I was told the other one is rather hard to find." I handed her the bag. She took it, placing it beside her.

"No problem, piti. We will find it. I have an idea you may be finding it sooner than later."

I hung my head and sighed. "Piti, I know your heart is in such disarray. But I have seen him, your Julian."

I looked at her in bewilderment. I had to contain my mouth from opening and pouring out the dozens of questions tumbling in my mind.

"Shh, piti, he is fine. He is on his own and fighting his own demons. He is on a quest he must accomplish for himself. Now hurry back home; it's getting late and it's not safe here at night."

She patted my arm as she shimmered out of sight. When I stood the little bench also disappeared.

"Come on Jahane and Athena, let's get going." Athena bounded ahead of us chasing things unseen, though I suspected it was new found friends like those from the courtyard.

CHAPTER 19

The next evening, I walked down the steps and into the cool night air. The flowers were in bloom and made the courtyard smell and look beautiful. Though I felt a disturbance in the air as I crossed through the courtyard, I shook it off.

Before I made it all the way out, I heard a motorcycle and saw Gabby roll to a stop in front of the archway. She removed her helmet and shook her black hair out. When she saw me, her mischievous smile grew, and she hoisted her leg over the metal machine and made a beeline over to me. Her excitement swirled around her as she got closer. Ever since Julian had left I'd had this eerie feeling Gabby and I were connected in some magical way. But every time I thought about it, the feeling disappeared as quickly as it had appeared.

"Rosie, how's it going, hun? I came by to talk to you about something and maybe hang out. Got a few minutes to spare?"

"Sure thing, what's up?"

"Oh, not much, but I was wondering if you could help me. Have you figured out your powers yet?" She quirked a brow at me.

"No...well, uh, yeah." I was hesitant to tell her my powers, even though after Julian had left, we had sort of become friends. I knew Miss Alina did not approve of it, but after months of Julian being gone, Gabby had been nice to me.

She dismissed my hesitance and started to talk again. "You see, I have this friend and he needs my help. He's in a bad way. Maybe we could do a spell of some sort."

"Why me?"

"Because, Rosie, you are one of the most powerful witches I know, and you are in a coven."

"Coven, what coven? I'm not in the coven. Miss Alina said it could wait."

"The coven hasn't inducted you yet?"

"Uh, no." The instant pang of hurt exploded through me because Alina had been putting me off about inducting me into the coven. I felt betrayed and hurt all at once. I was sure the hurt showed on my face as she stared at me.

Gabby smacked her lips. "Okay, well, come on, hun...I have a surprise for you; let's go." She grabbed my arm and hurried me down the walkway to her motorcycle.

I looked back over my shoulder in the direction of my apartment. "Wait, what about...?"

"Don't worry about Athena, she'll be fine."

Funny, I wasn't worried at all. I knew I had a part of my Guardian with me always. I slipped a leg over the motorcycle and felt it vibrate between my legs when it purred to life. She gunned it and we flew down the street, with me holding on to Gabby for dear life. She turned into the gravel parking lot of City Park, and as soon as we parked, my instinct to kiss the ground overcame me.

"Damn, woman, where did you learn to drive?"

"Pffft, I wasn't that bad," she laughed.

I threw my leg over and adjusted my skirt. My eyes adjusted to the darkness as we walked in silence to the pavilion that had always reminded me of a Greek temple. She pulled off the backpack she carried. One I hadn't noticed before, and placed it on the ground. She pulled candles, jars, and other assorted items out and positioned them beside the bag. I watched in utter fascination.

Gabby turned around and bent down to place the ritual materials in a huge intricate design underneath the giant oaks. All of a sudden, she did something unbelievable in the middle of City Park in the darkness…she removed her shirt and revealed her bare chest.

"Oh my gawd, what are you doing?"

"Come on…damn, Rosie, please don't be a prude. You'll see in a second."

She continued to remove her jeans and underwear. Through the trees I saw the moon peek through the clouds, and I looked up into the sky, embarrassed by Gabby's sudden nudity. The clouds spread out in the sky to reveal the full moon, and its beams began to lighten the darkness.

A noise from my right brought my head back down. I looked over at Gabby and noticed how ethereal she appeared before me. Her alabaster skin seemed to glow even more, bringing to light the curves of her gorgeous backside. Her skin glimmered under the glint of the moon. She turned, and caught me staring at her. Her legs, long and lean, seemed almost endless as she walked into the middle of the design. As she walked, the tattoo slithered around her body. I let out a loud gasp and saw the crinkle around the edges of her eyes when she smiled at me. The snake now had its tail snaked around her thigh, its head curved over her shoulder resting there. I watched intently as the tongue seemed to move out from her skin. It darted its eyes towards me, and with a hiss, it slithered down between her breasts. She reached out and petted it as a deep sigh escaped her mouth.

"Shush, Asp." With one long finger, she stroked the satin-like scales and almost cooed at the snake. "She is our friend." Her voice dripped with sweetness. From where I stood I saw the snake continue to move around her body. I stood there, mesmerized and unable to move for a second. She padded in her bare feet across the soft grass, walking towards me, her slim legs moving stealthily. Still embarrassed, I looked back up under my lashes to focus on the trees and water around us.

When she walked in front of me, I tried not to look, but I couldn't help it. My gaze moved up her sensual form and noticed now the snake had slithered into a different spot on her. The tail and its body coiled and wrapped around her. Its tail disappeared around her backside, and its head nestled between her breasts. She floated towards me, her steps soft and flawless. I averted my eyes as she got closer to me, but she approached me and grabbed my right hand. My focus stayed on the snake tattoo and how it moved in a titillating and slithering motion. I stood there, dumbfounded.

"Do you trust me, Rosie?"

I nodded self-consciously, not sure of what to say.

"Okay now, Rosie, you must undress as well. It's our way of getting back to nature, and you can be initiated into the coven and do the spell to help my friend."

"Um, yeah, uh, I don't think so … you aren't my type," I laughed nervously.

"You aren't mine, either, but we need to do this for the initiation."

I didn't know what to think, and I became nervous, not sure if I was doing the right thing. My eyes wide, I shimmied my skirt down, followed by my shirt. "Um, yeah, is this enough?"

"Nope," Gabby snickered.

With a ton of hesitancy, I looked around the vast area for peeping toms. The last thing I wanted out there was photos or videos of Gabby and me on the Internet. I would never live the shame down. I could see the title now, "Naked Park Wiccans."

"Rosie, it's okay; there's no one else here but us." I slipped my lace underwear down my legs and stepped out of them, then my hands reached around, and I fidgeted with the clasp on my bra. I began to wonder what had gotten into me. Gabby read the indecision all over my face and nodded for me to hurry. With a hint of hesitation, I resolved the issues in my head and unlatched my bra. My breasts popped free, and I instantly crossed my arms over the soft suppleness. When the night air hit my skin, I gasped and felt goose bumps rise on my legs and extend all over my body. I blushed, stood back, and shivered, not from the cold but from embarrassment.

"Good grief, Rosie, you're a witch; no need to hide what you are. We are doing the same thing as those have done before us. Hell, I'm sure your mother did the same thing here in this exact spot." She laughed when shock crossed my face.

Through the dark, silent night of the park, her laughter echoed. The trees blew the sound back and forth through their limbs, and the Spanish moss caught it and threw it back out there.

All of a sudden, the cicadas stopped their incessant chirp. I forced myself to smile over at her. I mean, after hearing her speak of witches who came before us, it made me feel more special. After all, we did belong to a special club...not everyone was a witch. And how could I forget, not everyone was naked in the middle of the park like us...I looked over to Gabby to hurry this up, because I didn't want to be chewed alive by mosquitos, even if I was a powerful witch.

She stood in front of me and pushed my arms down to my sides. Her gaze raked over my body, and I cast my eyes down. "Rosie, there's no reason to be embarrassed about being free and what we're doing. Our nude bodies under the moonlight and under the trees blowing in the wind is our connection to nature. We must convene in our natural state to be empowered." She took my hand and led me back to the design she had constructed on the grass.

Her hands grazed the sides of my breasts as she positioned me behind one of the candles. I almost jumped out of my skin when she touched me, and she laughed. "I'm sorry, Rosie."

She stood next to me and grasped my hand. Her body began to gyrate in motion to the wind, and I became mesmerized by the hypnotic way her body moved. She turned her face to the sky, and once again, my curiosity got the better of me. She raised her free hand palm up towards the night sky. From my peripheral vision, I watched the snake tattoo move around her shoulders and down her left arm towards me. The instant I saw this, I wanted to pull away. But Gabby held tight to me when she felt me try to tug away.

The snake slithered down her arm till it reached me and flicked my fingers with its forked tongue. The tremble I felt followed from her hand to mine and through my shoulder to rest in my body. The pulsating went back and forth and vibrated through her body to mine. All at once, the vibrations stopped and the sound of her soft, melodic voice flowed through the air as she chanted a spell in a language I was unfamiliar with. With her hold on me, her body moved. All of a sudden, I found myself moving my body in sync with hers. I looked over to her, and the light of the moon hit her breasts at the right spot to make them appear even more silky white. As she arched her body, her breasts called out to the moonlight, her nipples peaking as she arched farther.

She turned to me and smiled. "Rosie, we must both be in sync for this to work…arch your back. Do as I do."

I nodded and smiled timidly, and began to arch my back and stare up at the moon. The odd sensation I felt when I arched my back had me think back to Julian and his touch. With a shake of my head I continued, and when my breasts and nipples pointed towards the sky, an electrical current rushed through my body. I felt my limbs become numb as I arched my back farther. Even though my eyes were closed, I felt the light and the heat wrap around me.

Gabby started to chant.

Gathered here our bodies bare,
Hearts open and souls to share.
To our coven we bring a sister new,
To accept the words and her vow be true.
See her true will, her power, her might,
Lift her up and guide her light.
We bring her in blood and soul,
Accept her as one; a part of our whole.

With my eyes shut tight, the sensation overtook me as my nipples budded tighter. When the electrical pulse rounded back to my body, I cried out an earthshattering cry, and my entire body convulsed. It felt like tiny pulses had touched every fiber of my body. I opened my eyes to see if anyone was around. I scanned the trees for other people, but realized we were still alone in City Park. Gabby still held my hand, but from the looks of it, she had experienced the same electrical pulse. Her breasts heaved as she took in deep breaths. Sweat covered my body, and when I chanced another look at my own body, the sheen glistened under the light showing through the trees. I held tight to Gabby as another tremor surged through my body. This one sent me over the edge and made me breathe harder. My free hand instinctively went to my chest to stop my heart from jumping out from my body. I looked up at the sky and saw a streak of lightning cascaded across it. As Gabby let my hand go, I crumpled to the soft grass and lay on my back, the soft blades caressing my naked skin. In the distance, the loud chirp of the cicadas could be heard again.

"Gabby, that was intense," I breathed out as I sat up. I slumped back onto the ground as I muttered to myself, "It was extreme."

She sat across from me and took my hand in hers. "I know, I've never felt it like that…you must be one hell of a witch. Now, for the spell to help my friend," she said as she tried to steady her breathing. One by one each tiny flame came to life on the candles encircling us.

Use this man pure of heart,
What makes him so to pick apart.
Reach his soul to twist and mold
To turn to dark and break the hold.
Guide his sight and turn his view,
With these words I speak a spell you can't undo.

After the spell, the flames extinguished themselves and all was dark again. Confusion hit me at the words Gabby had spoken, but I was too exhausted to worry now. My ass sunk into the dew filled ground. It must be late, and how had I not felt the dew falling? I wiped a hand on my glistening body and shook my head. I reached for my clothes, and after I had dressed, I stood and waited for Gabby to gather all her belongings. She threw the backpack over her shoulder and nodded for me to follow her.

On our way back to the motorcycle, she turned to me. "You're a powerful witch and now my coven sister. You've also been initiated into the coven. I still have no idea why the others didn't tell you." She shook her head and I noticed a slight malicious smile spread across her face.

My emotions and thoughts became scrambled on the quiet ride home. I felt a nagging sensation tug at me, like I had done something wrong, but I dismissed it. My mother's message and warning came to the forefront of my brain like a ton of bricks. I shrugged it off, because at least Gabby had asked me to help her.

Once we pulled up next to the curb, Gabby let me off and followed me through the courtyard. I babbled the whole time about the coven and asked if I should come to a meeting soon. But as soon as I entered the center, what I saw stopped me in my tracks. *What in the hell?* A ghost flitted past me and Athena chased after it. I gasped.

Gabby looked at me with confusion written all over her face. "What the hell is she doing?" she asked with a nervous laugh.

I realized she couldn't see the ghost like Athena and I could, and it hit me like a ton of bricks. Well, hell, she didn't need to know I now suspected my powers were growing. No need for me to spill all to her so soon.

I shrugged. "Who knows?" I laughed.

"Huh." She shrugged and shook her head. "Well, I should get home." She hugged me before she turned on her heel and headed back to her motorcycle.

I sat on the steps and watched with amusement. The ghostly shapes flashed from one end of the courtyard to the other. Athena barked at one and chased another. I laughed out loud when one dashed effortlessly back and forth, his body shimmering in and out and fluttering above the dog's head.

At the sound of my laughter, they noticed me sitting there. They flickered and shimmered over to me, and I felt one go through my body then turn its head around and look at me. The feeling was creepy, and I shook it out of my body until the shape of a man stood in front of me again.

I shook my finger at it. "Don't do that again."

He nodded his ghostly head and floated over to a flower bed. When he came back to me, he handed me a few flowers in apology.

"Apology accepted." I took the flowers and smiled.

He mimicked my movement and smiled back. The ghost man floated back off to antagonize my dog again. Athena jumped and bounded at the see through entities the whole time. When she had tired of playing, she turned in my direction on the steps. My belly hurt from all the laughing so hard at the spectacle before me. Her attention turned from the ghosts to me in a second. She bounded over to me and flopped down by my feet. Out of breath, she panted and drooled on the ground. I ruffled her ears and waved to the flickering figures as they popped out of the courtyard. The one who had offered me flowers darted back to wave once more at me. I smiled as it sheepishly disappeared.

"Okay, enough play time, let's get inside." I stood from the steps, turned, and made my way up to the apartment with Athena quick on my heels.

"Well, it looks as if you've made new friends while I was out," I laughed.

She barked as I closed the door behind us.

CHAPTER 20

J ahane and I sat in the shop with the radio on, with at least a dozen books in front of us. Our interest focused on the news and the mention of the impending hurricane that had its eye set on Louisiana. Even though we should have gotten out, we had all decided to stay in town for the hurricane.

After Remi's shift at the Brackish Tavern, he planned on helping us out at the shop.

As the weather outside began to get ugly, I turned to Jahane. "Hey, have you heard from Derrick?" I tried to focus my attention on something other than the storm headed towards us, so I flipped open a book.

"Yeah, he said he would be here soon with the wood." He and Remi were going to help board up the windows of the shop and my apartment. Even Gabby had told us she would be there. We had grown close since

Julian's departure and my induction into the coven, which I had yet to tell Miss Alina about. I was still a little perturbed at her for not inducting me. Madame Claudette, along with Alina, had enlisted some help to find out where Julian had gone. We wouldn't give up on finding him. And I still had to find the one object on my list in order to cure Julian of the curse. I felt around in my pocket to make sure the paper was still where I had put it.

"Rosie, what time does Remi get off?" Jahane asked.

I looked up from the book my fingers absentmindedly flipped through. "I think he said Mr. Jacque was letting him off early because of the storm. He's already secured boards on the windows of the restaurant."

She shook her head. "Rosie, I've known Remi from when I was a child, and he has grown into a great man. And I think he has the hots for you, my bestie." She winked at me.

"Oh, yeah, right, Jahane; you know I'm in love with Julian. You know I only have eyes for him. And anyway, I think Remi and Gabby are dating." I laughed without ever taking my eyes off the book.

"Rosie," she laughed. "I didn't say to fall in love with Remi, but I'm sure he would not mind letting you scratch that itch you desperately need scratched. And besides, I don't think Gabby has anything on you. I mean, she is okay, but she's not you. When was the last time you had sex and let your freak flag fly? You know you want some mocha lovin'." She laughed and good-naturedly punched me on the shoulder.

I glanced away from my book and looked at her in utter shock. "Geez, Jahane, you are so gauche." I smirked at her before I returned to my book. "I want to get my freak on with a certain tall Cajun man."

She looked at me and stuck her tongue out at me. "Girl, I may be uncouth, but you, my best friend, know you love me."

"Yes, I do love you, and you keep me…um…let's say entertained. And most of all, you tell me the finer arts of flying your freak flag, because we all know you let it fly high and proud with Derrick." I burst into hysterical laughter.

Jahane huffed in protest. "Well, I still think it would be good for you."

As she got up to grab a book from the shelf, I peeked over the edge of my book and smiled at her.

We had put our books down and had begun a gab fest when I heard the roar of a motorcycle rumbled outside. The door opened and Remi, Derrick, and Gabby strolled in.

"Hey guys, how's the weather?" I asked.

"It's getting worse," Remi replied. "Where's the plywood for the windows, Rosie?"

"In the storeroom." I watched as the two guys walked into the back, joking and laughing.

As the guys started putting up the boards, Gabby regaled us with stories of her biker days. Since I'd met her, she had gotten a few more tattoos.

"Gabby, did it hurt?" I asked, pointing to the one spiraling down her ear.

"No, I have so many I say a little spell before I get them. Rosie, you should think about getting one, maybe to cover your scars; maybe some pretty roses with vines and leaves. No one would ever be able to tell you had scars at all." Her gaze fell to my legs covered in denim. I almost asked how she knew, but remembered the night at the park.

"I don't think so, Gabby, I've never been too fond of needles. Besides, I've become fond of my scars." I stood up from the sofa and walked over to get some tea from the counter.

"Rosie, has anyone heard any more information on Julian?"

Thoughts of Julian swam into my head. The feel of his soft lips and his fingers as he touched and kissed my legs, and how he told me they were beautiful, brought a smile to my face as I mentally traced the lines. I was deep in thought until the sound of Remi's voice brought me out of my daydreams.

"Huh, what?" I asked, and tried to pull myself out of my thoughts.

Remi grinned at what I was sure was a deep crimson on my face. "Rosie, we have all the boards up, and I'm going to head out with these guys. Are you sure you want to stay here alone?"

"Yes, I'm sure, Remi. I'm going to curl up with a good book and Athena. And, I have the generator hooked up, so if I lose lights, I won't be uncomfortable."

He nodded, walked over to where I stood, and hugged me, and I watched over his shoulder as Jahane did a risqué dance move. I pulled away from Remi and busted into a fit of laughter. Remi looked over at Jahane as she was mid gyrate.

"Little Jah, you never cease to amaze me." He turned to Derrick. "Man, you sure have your hands full with her, don't you?"

Derrick pulled her in close and smiled down at her. "Man, I can handle this one, I promise." He laughed and kissed her pouty bottom lip.

"Oh, man, I'm sure you can, Derrick." He winked at Jahane.

I watched the playfulness of my friends and began to pine for Julian even more. "Okay, y'all, I need to finish cleaning up the store and head upstairs to read."

"Hey, guys, I think Rosie is kicking us out." Gabby grabbed Remi as they all headed towards the door.

I pretended to yawn and held up one of the books. "You know me and my books."

Jahane walked over to me and hugged me. "Text me if you need me, Rosie. I love you…be safe."

After my friends left, I curled up on the sofa. Athena stepped up on the sofa and turned around three times. The whole time, she jostled the sofa until she was settled and placed her head on the arm rest opposite me. I opened the book I had been reading and rubbed her ears. She sighed as my hand continuously petted her as I flipped the pages of the book I was so ensconced in.

Later, I listened to the rain, which came down in a torrential downpour. I hurried to move the items I didn't want to get ruined, in case. Afterwards, I poured myself a cup of steaming hot herbal tea. Mug in hand, I sipped as I finished the last chapter. It tasted a tad funny, but I ignored it and kept drinking. Once I had completed it, I closed the book, got up, and placed my cup down on the counter. With the book under my arm, I went to lock the door. The loud rain pelted down on the wood placed over the window. The thunder cracked, and the lightning boomed in the sky.

The tea had actually calmed me. As I walked to the back of the shop, I reached for my phone in my pocket as the sound of a text came through. It was from Jahane, messaging me, she was safe with Derrick and would see me in the morning.

A strange noise echoed from the front of the shop and sent an odd eerie tingle though me. Magic, but not good magic, escalated around in a fury, and a cold breeze passed through me. The soft tinkle of the bell above the door alerted me to someone coming in as the door slammed open.

"We are closed for the night!" I yelled from the back.

Athena growled loudly and ran from my side straight into the disturbance. I followed her, but before I made it all the way, I started to get light headed. I grasped onto the counter and saw my Guardian, her teeth bared at a hooded figure standing in the open doorway. The figure glided inside, and I noticed the door to my shop whip open and closed in the throes of the storm brewing outside. My eyes began to get heavy and I heard a yip and a thud as my dog flew into the wall and slid down. My eyes widened at the sight of the lifeless body of my dog.

"Athenaa, nooo!" My gut wrenching scream bounced off the walls and into the storm outside.

In a last ditch effort to get to my Guardian, I staggered, and when I reached her, I fell to my knees. As I caressed her head, I sensed someone near me, and I pulled my attention from the limp form of my dog to stare at the cloaked figure towering above us. All I could see besides the cloak were its red eyes. I choked back sobs as the tears flowed down my cheeks. Not once did I take my eyes off the creature as I passed a hand over my Guardian's still and lifeless body.

All of a sudden, the figure before me became blurry. I tried hard to focus but couldn't. Fear registered on my face, and I couldn't pull my gaze away from those red eyes.

"Did you do this to me?" I asked as I fumbled in my pocket for my voodoo doll. *Where is it?* I wondered.

"Why, yes I did, dear," the figure said in a sing song voice that rumbled from the back of its throat. "And are you looking for this?" It dangled the little doll from its hand. I watched the doll begin to burn its bony fingers, and when tiny flames danced, the creature tossed it aside and flung curses. With the way the thing threw it, I knew the doll had some power.

"A rag doll will do me no harm, and your mother should have known," he spoke eerily.

I looked up at this person who had invaded the sanctity of my home and hurt my Guardian. "But…why and…how?" I stammered out.

"Ahhh, yes…well, the why is because I could. I killed your mother. We knew you would become stronger with your mother gone, and with her out of the way we were able to get to you easier…though we hadn't thought of you getting a Guardian." The voice dripped with cruelty, and the laugh echoed from the hidden mouth chilled me to the bone. "And the how is…well, simple." The voice sent shivers up my spine, and I knew this was pure evil. The long bony fingers reached deep into its pockets and pulled out a deep purple glass bottle.

The entity smiled at me, or at least looked as if it smiled, and then the voice spoke to me. "This, dear, is bella donna. I slipped it into your tea. You know, in a way, it was genius, and the best way to poison you. I needed better access to you. I hoped it wouldn't take as long with the small doses I used. We had to get to you some way."

At the mention of what had been my poison, I started to drift into unconsciousness. The sights and sounds around me became hazy. I tried to get a hold on my senses and figure out who stood before me. It was like a light bulb went off, and the voice became suddenly recognizable.

"Why? I thought we were..."

Before I could finish my sentence the voice interrupted me. "Because, Rosie, you're too powerful and must not be allowed to live. We have plans for you." With an evil laugh, it raised its hands. As I succumbed to unconsciousness, the sound of distorted laughter echoed through my head.

As my eyesight got hazy, my eyes could no longer stay open. A bright light illuminated the shop, but before everything went dark and I succumbed, I murmured, "Julian, where are you?"

TO BE CONTINUED...

Enjoy a sneak peek of *Bred by Magic!*

BORN

At the reassuring thump, thump of my mother's heartbeat and the warm protection of her body, I stirred. Hunger ravaged my tummy as I wriggled around until I found her milk. I was even more ravenous at each suck, but the moment the warm substance flowed through me, my tummy no longer growled. With my swollen belly full to the brim, I rolled over on my side and stretched, then crawled over to a vacant spot and fell fast asleep.

When I woke, I wore a warm blanket of my siblings. I kicked my back legs and shuffled my body around until I was free of them. Even though my eyes and ears were void of the outside world, I sensed an overpowering mystical magic whirling in the room.

I crawled over to my mother. Mommy, what's that noise?

Oh, dear, that's the voices of Alexander and Karl discussing the future of this litter. You know, if you snuggle closer to me you may be able to make out more of what they are saying.

At her prodding, I nestled closer to her, and the softness of her fur bristled along my body. With my head against her I heard their voices vibrate off her. As I listened to the two men, my brothers and sisters scooted in closer, pushing me further up next to my mother's warm body. Her fur tickled my nose as I leaned in even closer. "Alexander, it looks like we have a good litter this time. We have two females and four males. I think we can find good homes for the males where they can become great warriors for their warlocks. The females will find good homes with witches they will guard. Yes, this litter is made of excellent stock." The man said softly.

"Ja. I agree Karl." Alexander's thick Danish accent was heavier than normal in his excitement. "I see lots of promise in this litter. I hope this one goes better than the last. But, before we get ahead of ourselves, let's see how many make it through the transition. We need to make sure the magic infused into their blood stream works well with the potion we will give them after they are a few weeks old. Oh, and don't forget to get the amulets ready for the tear drops."

"Yes, sire," Karl nodded, and hurried from the room.

After I listened to the two men speak of our future and what a great one it was to be, I closed my eyes and fell asleep.

ACKNOWLEDGEMENTS & THANKS

When I first started writing I was told by Deena Remiel, it takes a village to write a book and trust me no truer words have ever been spoken. In a year I have met so many wonderful people willing to help make a wonderful story come to life.

To my big sister Rhonda Plumhoff, I love you; more than chocolate.

I want to extend a big thank you to everyone who supported me and encouraged me throughout this endeavor, especially my other family who gave me a chance to write and watched me grow in my storytelling. Y'all pushed me to be the writer I knew I could be. You truly are a blessing to me. Especially Stacie Jandik-Stopen who told me to suck it up and write. You are such a talented person in your own right. Thanks to Simi who brought creativity as well to my stories.

Anya Kelleye what more can I say you designed a beautiful cover. You created a second masterpiece with the help of Melissa Deanching and Tionna Petramalo.

My cheerleaders: Tidia McCarney, Morgan Kearns, Deena Remiel, Susan McCray, Carol Hauser, Angel Downing, Lisa Wheeler, Stephanie Kraus and Tammy McCann for encouraging me, I could not have done it without you all.

To Franziska Popp, thank you for believing in my writing. You encouraged me to reach for the stars.

M.K. Hensley: my spell caster, thank goodness you can rhyme. You know you mean the world to me.

Belinda Boring, thanks for listening to me when I heard the voices in my head and informing me I was officially a writer.

James D. Magnussen, who inspired my character, Julian Quibadeaux.

Daphne of The Haunted History Tours of New Orleans; I'm thrilled I met you and thankful for your vast knowledge on voodoo. You are a fantastic storyteller who weaves truth and history into every story you tell.

Finally to my mom, I have no words to express how much I love you.

ABOUT THE AUTHOR

As a young girl, Diana Marie Dubois was an avid reader and was often found in the local public library. Now you find her working in her local library. Hailing from the culture filled state of Louisiana, just outside of New Orleans; her biggest inspiration has always been the infa-mous Anne Rice and her tales of Vampires. It was those very stories that inspired Diana to take hold of her dreams and begin writing. She is now working on her first series, Voodoo Vows.

Amazon: www.amazon.com/-/e/B00O97TWUO

Facebook: www.facebook.com/diana.m.dubois

Goodreads: www.goodreads.com/author/show/7690662.Diana_Marie_DuBois

Instagram: www.instagram.com/dianamariedubois

Pintererst: www.pinterest.com/dianamdubois

Twitter: www.twitter.com/DianaMDuBois

Tumblr: www.dianamariedubois.tumblr.com

Website: www.dianamariedubois.com

Made in the USA
Columbia, SC
16 September 2022

67185726R10150